THE PROPHECY

"You will travel, and far, by water as well as by land," he said to Jamie in his soft, lilting voice. "The water beneath you is gray sometimes, sometimes a blue that hurts my eyes.

"Also, I see a great stone city, with a dark woman there. A dark woman who calls herself friend. Battles—many battles, and many dead, and much blood. Your blood too, but not your death—not from what may be seen. What may not be seen is . . ."

The voice trailed off, and Jamie shifted impatiently. He was not worried about dying. The question was—would he return to the valley, and if so, when?

Gordon R. Dickson
with Roland Green

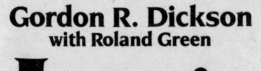

Jamie the Red

ACE FANTASY BOOKS
NEW YORK

JAMIE THE RED

An Ace Fantasy Book/published by arrangement with
the authors

PRINTING HISTORY
Ace Original/April 1984

ISBN: 0-441-38245-2

Ace Fantasy Books are published by
The Berkley Publishing Group,
200 Madison Avenue, New York, New York 10016.
PRINTED IN THE UNITED STATES OF AMERICA

Chapter One

THE FIGHT BEGAN on the stone staircase winding up the wall from the first level of the old keep tower that, standing alone, had been the solitary ancestor of the castle.

The two Jamies—the Red and the Black—rolled locked together down the hard steps to the grateful softness of the earth and bracken and muck that was the floor of the stables on that lowest level. The horses whinnied and reared in their stalls as what seemed like half the rest of the inhabitants of the castle flooded down behind the two struggling bodies to stand about them in a circle and watch—giving them plenty of room, for after all they were princes of the blood and it was a contest between the two that had been expected for some time now.

At first sight, they both seemed to be fairly evenly matched. Jamie the Red was a full head taller than his older half brother and well-muscled, as were all the five sons of Walter, the King—and, for that matter, Moraig, his daughter. But Jamie the Black was built like a mountain oak, with enormous breadth of shoulders and muscle that made his younger brother seem almost slight by comparison. He was also four years the older, for Jamie the Red had just turned nineteen, and Jamie the Black was of a hard, bitter disposition, so that most of the people of the castle watching tended to favor the younger one of the two.

Being related by blood, neither made any move to draw the dirk at his belt or the short knife in his right boot. It was fists, feet, knees, nails, teeth, and—for one moment—in Jamie the Red's hand a stool that had strayed from the pens of the kitchen

1

milk cattle. But the Black knocked it out of our Jamie's grasp and closed with him again.

Indeed that was the usual error of Jamie the Black that, once enraged, he had no thought but to get those long, powerful arms of his around his opponent and crush him into submission. Jamie the Red, on the other hand, was determined to avoid exactly such a happening; and, beyond that, he was looking for a chance to maneuver into a position in which he could have his older half brother at a disadvantage. He had almost been caught at the bottom of the stairs, when Jamie the Black had ended their tumble with a firm grip on him. However, by the good fortune of being the one on top, and therefore in a position to grind the Black's face into the soft floor of the stables, our Jamie managed to escape and get back on his feet. From then on the fight became the next thing to a fencing match, with fist blows being traded instead of sword cuts.

Jamie the Red was an observer by nature. In fact, this had always been the most noticeable thing about him; and sometime since, concluding that he was better fitted than his oldest brothers to follow as King after his father, he had begun a campaign to fight his way up the ladder of his older brothers, so to speak. It had been a literal campaign, with careful plans and study of each of his opponents. He had scouted the weaknesses of each of his older siblings more intensively than ever before in his life; and arranged, when the fights actually came, to take advantage of those weaknesses.

In the case of Jamie the Black, the elder's vulnerability lay in the fact that he was not either as quick or as mobile as his younger brother. Now, seeing his chance, Jamie gave ground, pretended to stumble backward. He dodged, picked up a handful of bracken and shoved it in Jamie the Black's face; then ducked around behind the other to catch him in something halfway between an armlock and a stranglehold; and together they fell to the floor.

The younger Jamie was effectively and happily proceeding to strangle the other into submission when there was a stir among the people ranging around in the stables and up the staircase; and Hamish, the oldest of the King's sons, shoved his way through, followed by Moraig, their one sister, Andrew, the middle brother, and young Simon, after Jamie the youngest of the six.

The common run of people in the castle had, of course, not

dared to interfere until this moment. But it was a different matter with Hamish there.

"Grab them," Hamish snapped sourly to the men closest to him. "Pull them apart!"

Hamish himself helped. Multiple pairs of hard-calloused hands separated the two Jamies and held them apart from each other.

"And that's enough of that," Hamish said. "Bring them along to Father."

He turned and led the way up the stairs. The crowd parted before him; and the family group continued upstairs into the living quarters of the castle, to its newer section, which was a great deal more comfortable than the old, having even some glass in the windows on third and uppermost level. There they found Walter, the King—their father—trying on a new pair of boots as he sat on the edge of his bed.

The common herd, of course, had dropped back out of sight as the royal chambers were approached. The Princes and the Princess came in alone. Walter looked up at them all with disfavor.

"What now?" he demanded harshly.

"Fighting, Father," said Hamish; with a gleam, thought Jamie the Red, of more than slight triumph in the eyes of the oldest brother's saturnine face.

Walter's eyes sought Jamie the Red.

"You again?" he said.

"It was him who started it!" said Jamie the Red, all injured innocence.

Walter's eyes went to Jamie the Black

"Is this true?" he asked his second son.

Jamie the Black had had time to recover from the bull-like fury into which he always fell when actually fighting. He hung his head.

"Yes, Father," he said.

"You sheep-wit!" said Hamish to Jamie the Black. "Do you think our Jamie doesn't know how to get you into a fight anytime he wants it?"

"Aye," said Walter. His eyes fixed on Jamie the Red. "Out. The rest of you, all of you, out! Our Jamie, you stay."

"Shouldn't I stay too, Father?" asked Hamish.

"Out, I said!"

Hamish reluctantly went. Moraig also lingered, until a glare from under her father's gray-thatched eyebrows drove her out of the room.

"And close the door behind you!" shouted Walter.

As the door swung heavily to and latched, the King turned back to stare at his fifth son. Jamie the Red was doing his best to look both penitent and bewildered. Walter glared at him grimly.

"All right, boy," said the King. "There's no curing you; and I warned you. Didn't I say I'd send you off unless you stopped what you were doing?"

"Doing, Father?" said Jamie.

"Don't play the idiot with me!" roared Walter, starting to his feet and wincing as a fold in the top of one of the new boots, the right one, bit him sharply across the toes. "The whole castle doesn't call you 'the clever one' for nothing! You know what you've been doing. I know what you've been doing. You're not going to do it here, do you hear me?"

Jamie did, of course, know very well what he had been doing; but he was more than a little startled that the King, his father, should have divined his purpose—which was simply to win such an ascendancy over his older brothers that he would be able to direct things once Hamish or any of the rest should inherit the throne before him. Or had his father divined it on his own? Walter was a good king, and experienced, but not the brightest mind in the castle. Who, wondered Jamie, could have seen through Jamie's own plan and also had the courage to acquaint his father with it? Certainly not even Hamish, the oldest brother, had suspected—Jamie would swear to that.

. . . But his father was still talking.

"It's the others, Father," muttered Jamie. "They're always picking on me because I'm younger."

"I said stop taking me for an idiot, boy!" Walter's voice dropped to an unhappy growl. He limped across to the window in the round wall of his bedroom and looked out for a minute at the valley surrounding the spur of rock on which the castle stood. "It's not easy on me to send one of your dead mother's sons out of this valley. But it's no case of them picking on you, and you know that as well as I do. It's you who's out to beat them all down—yes, and including Hamish as soon as you've got Jamie the Black tamed. You've got your eye on following after me in authority here, boy; and I tell you it's not going to be while I've anything to say about it. This crown and all that rides with it is going to belong to the oldest son, and that's Hamish.''

"I'd make a better king, Father,'' said Jamie, greatly daring. ''And now you know it.''

"I know nothing of the kind!'' roared Walter, turning back to him. His bushy full beard, its black now beginning to be streaked with white, bristled with his anger. It was a fearsome sight. Jamie was the tallest of the tall sons, but his father overtopped him by some inches. ''I know just the opposite! You think you'd make a better king, but you would not! And I'll tell you why you would not! There's things you've never learned—and I think you never will. One of them is that people make the clan, make the kingdom and the country. But you think only of yourself and what you could do, ruling and owning them all. That's not the sort of king will rule our people long. I don't care how well you can fight, how clever you are; in the end it's not your strength that keeps the kingdom, it's the strength of those who love you. You live only by their help; and that's what you've never learned. It's what you'll never learn; and without it you're a danger to us all. Therefore, you go!''

Jamie the Red had heard this threat from his father before; but he had never really taken it seriously. To him, the world beyond the valley was a fascinating place in which anything could happen; and part of him yearned to go out and adventure in it. At the same time, it was not a real world. Reality was here; and the thought that he could be separated from this castle and this valley, this land where he had grown up, was unthinkable. For the first time now, staring at the hard set of his father's features, hearing a new note in the older man's voice, the thought woke in him that the King might mean exactly what he said.

"You'd not really banish me from home?'' He heard himself saying the words as if it were somebody else speaking.

"Do you think I like doing it?'' snarled Walter.

He limped back to his bed and sat down. Slowly, he started taking off his new boots and pulling on the comfortable shapes of his older ones, fitted to his feet by many days of rain, then sunshine. ''As long as you were small, I could close my eyes to what you were doing. Now you're grown, and I can't. You must go, our Jamie, and that's the end of it! Now—go make yourself ready to leave, tomorrow!''

He stood up. Jamie's head was in a whirl. Disbelief still smothered him like a witch's garment. He turned and stumbled out.

The chamber that Jamie shared with Simon lay in the wall of the keep. With his hands clasped on top of his head he could not stand upright in it, and with his sword in either hand he could stand in the middle and touch all the walls. The window was no more than an arrow slit, shuttered with a board.

It was still no pleasure for Jamie to look upon it in the knowledge that he might never do so again. No, *would not* do so again. His father's decision was made, and there could be no altering of it; not even the attempt, without shedding kin's blood. And to be known as a man so lost to all law and good reason could do nothing to give him back what he was about to lose.

So he sat on the bed with all that he might find useful in the world beyond the valley strewn upon the floor at his feet. He saw none of it at the moment, except the sword laid across his knees, its blade gleaming with fresh oil and the tarnish picked out of the silverwork on the hilt. He was picking up a file to work on the edge when the door opened.

It was his sister Moraig and his youngest brother Simon. Moraig's hair was tangled and her usually sharp blue eyes were red. Simon, who had just this past year seemed to gain knowledge of what to do with his hands and feet, had turned back to being a gawky youth.

"You've been to see Father," Jamie said. Moraig nodded. "And," Jamie went on, "it was wasted breath."

"You owe her more thanks than that," said Simon. "She went on her knees to him."

Jamie's eyebrows rose. Moraig on her knees was something no one had seen outside of church since she had been five years old. It was said that she was still unwed only because Walter did not want to be at feud with the kin of her husband after she broke said husband's head over the first blow he struck her. Certainly she had no lack of any quality useful to draw men to her, at least those who did not mind being overtopped by at least two fingers' breadth and outridden on nearly any horse over any kind of ground.

"Thanks, my sister," said Jamie. "But you might have known there was no good to be done for me, and perhaps some harm to yourself. This is Hamish's hour of triumph. With his place carved in stone for all to see, he'll not be as easy about seeing you unwed as Father's been.''

If Moraig had been a cat, her ears would have been back and her bristling tail lashing from side to side. Before she could say a word, Simon spoke.

"Jamie!'' he blurted out. "If you've got to go, then take me along with you.''

Moraig stared suddenly at the youngster, then turned to stare again at Jamie.

It was on the tip of Jamie's tongue to say yes, if only to see the pain in his father's eyes as the youngest son rode off with the one who had been exiled. Besides, Simon was the one brother Jamie was close to. But a feeling he had never felt before laid its hand upon him, a feeling more for Simon than for himself. He would not insult his brother by asking "Do you mean that?'' nor did he doubt Simon's firmness of intent. His sense, yes, but not Simon's willingness, to ride beside his older brother out through the Pass of the Black Rocks into the world beyond.

Yet, it was tempting. For a moment more, Jamie let himself imagine the two of them riding south, ever south, side by side, guarding each other's backs until they reached the Great City of Constantinople and joined its Guards. They would both rise to command companies, each attract the favor of some rich merchant with a fair daughter, both command more men and wealth than their entire valley held, even for its King. . . .

Jamie sighed.

The thought was folly. Simon had only worn a man's sword for a year, and was far from being able to use it with a man's skill. What purpose did it serve, to have your back guarded by a boy who could barely guard his own? And if he was your kin, and you were bound to let anything done against him draw you into a fight, a fight which might indeed turn out to be a trap set for the both of you . . . And then there was what Hamish would say, and how little their father would do to keep him from saying it.

Slowly, Jamie shook his head.

"It can't be, Simon,'' he said, softly—for him. "I'm sorry. You've something to do here in the valley, and that's to stand by your sister. When I leave, there'll be only the one of us to care for her as you and I've always done, and as a brother should. Andrew hardly looks beyond his lute and his books even if he wasn't too short-sighted to use a bow, and with little more muscle than Moraig herself. Against Hamish, or even against Black Jamie, Andrew's no more than a stalk of grass in a gale. So, it's up to you.''

Simon swallowed. For a moment he looked ready to argue, but years of following Jamie's lead had built a habit of obedience into him. Jamie nodded in approval at his silence.

"Good," he said. "Now you also must swear never to speak of what you offered me. I'll not forget it; but no one else should hear of it. Hamish, if he does, will claim it was Moraig's idea.''

"If he tries to persuade Father of that, he'll overreach himself," Moraig snapped. Her hands were clenched into fists.

"Hamish will try and keep trying," said Jamie. "That, and other things. Father's as tough as an old oak and may outlive us all. But he's also old enough to see forward to the time when he'll have no choice but to pass the kingdom on to his heir.''

For a moment his voice cracked.

"If he wasn't," he added, "do you think we'd all be here as we are?''

Jamie had picked up his sword without thinking. Now he laid it softly back down again on the bed and stood up. "At least I'm leaving the valley. That puts one of us out of Hamish's reach.''

"There is that," said Moraig.

Simon's wide eyes moved from his sister to his brother, clearly lost at being one in such frank discussion of matters usually discussed only when he was not around.

"So you'll swear," said Jamie, turning to him.

Simon reached out and lifted Jamie's sword from the bed.

"On this sword, and on my life, I swear it," he said, his young voice shaking a little. "To never speak, except to Moraig, of what has passed between us now, and here.''

He laid the sword back down. Jamie ran his tongue around a suddenly dry mouth.

"I'm going to call for drinks," he began, then saw Moraig shaking her head.

"Why not?''

"I've already sent word for Hobie Yaro to come and read your future for us, Jamie. He's back down behind the angle of the next lower landing now, waiting for me to call him up here.''

Jamie grinned mirthlessly.

"What can Hobie Yaro tell to help me now?"

"If a spaeman like Hobie sees you returning to the kingdom, and it's known that he's seen it, by both your friends and your enemies . . ." Moraig began.

Jamie cut her short.

"Aye. There's that much to be gained. Something useful might come of it in the long run. Or at least no harm will. And most surely Hobie has the Sight."

Jamie did not mention again calling for drink. Moraig was right. Wine and the Seeing did not go well together.

At Moraig's soft call from the half-opened chamber door, Hobie Yaro came in on feet as silent as any poacher's. Moraig closed the door firmly again behind him, and turned to stand with her shoulder blades bracing it shut. Hobie was smaller even than Simon, dressed no better than a crofter, and looked about forty. No one could remember when he had looked younger. He carried a rolled-up piece of white deer hide under one arm and wore a pouch on his belt.

"Shutter the window," was all he said. Moraig moved to obey. Hobie unrolled the hide on the floor, untied the pouch from his belt, and upended it on the hide. More things came out of it than Jamie thought it could contain, including a brazen bowl, small phials of herbs, and other small things of various colors and shapes.

Out of the lot, Hobie pulled a blackened oat cake and broke it in half. "Choose a piece," he told Jamie. Jamie looked at both pieces. They looked like charcoal and felt as hard to his touch. Finally he tapped one with his forefinger.

"That one."

"So be it."

Hobie popped the other piece into his mouth and chewed while he crumbled the chosen one onto a corner of the hide. Then he swept everything else off the hide, emptied the phials of herbs into the brass bowl, and set them alight with flint and steel.

The smoke which curled up was blue and smelled no worse—but little better—than rotten hay. Jamie stirred a little with uneasiness. But no one had ever accused Hobie Yaro of using unlawful or tainted matters to aid him in the Seeing. Jamie took a measure of consolation from the fact.

It was less easy to be consoled when a wind started to blow, this in a chamber where the window was shuttered and the door closed. The smoke no longer curled but streamed away from the bowl in a long, level plume, which reached almost as far as the door, then vanished—where, Jamie would not have cared to ask, let alone learn. The wind blew on. Moraig slipped her arm through his and was clearly trying not to shiver. But for her, Jamie would not so have tried.

Still silent, the wind rose to a climax. Suddenly, all the crumbs of the oat cake were in the air, dancing like a swarm of midges above the hide. Hobie muttered some of what Jamie assumed were words, and the midges danced faster.

Then the wind died, and so did the midge-dance. The crumbs floated down onto the hide. Hobie knelt on hands and knees, his nose and mustache practically among the crumbs, and stared at them for what seemed several long minutes, breathing in steadily of the smoke as he did. Then he sat down cross-legged and began to speak.

"It is that you will travel, and far, by water as well as by land," he said in his soft, lilting voice. "The water beneath you is gray sometimes, sometimes a blue that hurts my eyes.

"Also, I see cities—and one a great stone city, with a dark woman there. A dark woman who calls herself friend. Battles—many battles, and many dead, and much blood. Your blood too, but not your death—not from what may be seen. What may not be seen is . . ." His voice trailed off, and Jamie shifted impatiently. He was not worried about dying, or at least no more now than ever. The question was—would he return to the valley, and if so, when?

Hobie's head snapped up, as violently as that of a hanged man when the noose goes tight. "Another city. Not great, not stone, all white, with the bright blue sea on one side and bright brown land on the other. That city—the end of the travels I see. The end of your being alone, perhaps. Perhaps not. . . ." Again a voice trailing off into silence which lasted until the herbs in the bowl burned out and the smoke stopped rising.

Hobie sat as if asleep, his head now sunk on his chest. At last Moraig dared break the silence by moving to the window and pulling out the shutter. The night wind blew in, and the chamber was no longer stifling with herb smoke.

The fresh air woke Hobie. He stood up and shook himself like a wet dog, then met Jamie's eyes and saw the question in them.

"I did not see your return. But I did see aught that would stand forever in your path, if you learn what you are called on to learn."

"What is that?"

"I did not see that."

"Will I learn it?"

"That I cannot say, for I did not see it, our Jamie. Nor would I say, even if I had seen. Not to you, in any case. To say to you that you will be learning something would be as good as telling you that you learned it already. That would bring your blood on my hands."

"Your blood will be—" began Jamie, clenching his fists. The words rasped, but Moraig gripped his shoulder so hard her fingers dented his flesh through the wool of his tunic. After a moment, he remembered that Hobie or any other with the Sight was inviolate, unless it could be proved he had been paid to lie while pretending to See. To lay hands on the man now would make more than his father stand ready to punish him, and with more than banishment. His fists unclenched and Moraig's hand fell away.

But for the first time, a spark; it was as if a spark leaped into his mind to set a candle alight in one dark corner. The one man about the castle with the wit to see through what Jamie had been doing would be this little man before him. Hobie Yaro. Why Hobie should tell his father would be another question— but there was none so likely to be able to divine from Jamie's actions alone what his intentions had been. Jamie stared at the little man, and for just a second their eyes met; Jamie could swear that once more a spark jumped—and he was sure that it was Hobie who had told his father.

Long after Hobie and Moraig had gone, right up to the moment he fell asleep, it seemed to Jamie as he lay in bed with Simon sleeping across the chamber from him, that he could still feel the spell-wind on his face.

He felt a wind even colder and stronger at dawn the next morning, as he rode alone and early up the Pass of the Black Rocks. This was a natural wind, though, and familiar, if no more friendly than ever.

He reined in his horse between two gigantic dark boulders which flanked the road and gave the pass its name. He dismounted and went through his saddle bags while the horse drank from the stream which bubbled up at the foot of the boulder to the north.

He'd packed everything he could find in his chamber which he might need on the road—sword and scabbard, knives, clothing and boots fit for the vilest weather, a short bow and a quiver with a score of hunting arrows, even a pewter drinking cup. He did not truly imagine that Walter would send a son of his body into banishment as naked as a worm, but he wished to give no hostages to fortune, either.

It had been in his mind to leave like this, alone and without ceremony, to show his father and Hamish how indeed he welcomed his banishment. But his true reluctance to leave the valley stopped him. Still, he was glad he had reached the pass before the royal party came up.

When they came it was no small group. Hamish and the King's last wife—the mother of Moraig and Simon—rode with him. Following them by a horse-length or two were the other sons and the one daughter, then another small gap and a dozen or so members of the household, with last of all the long-nosed man they call Brethin Geal—Geal, or "white," for the fact that his hair and eyebrows (he was clean-shaven otherwise) had turned white in his early twenties.

Brethin had been his father's personal servant and shield-bearer for twenty years, since he turned seventeen. He was dressed in his full chain armor now and led a laden sumpter horse, a dapple gelding, plus the King's own destrier or war-horse, and the gray palfrey Jamie had never been allowed to ride among all the other horses in the King's stable—which was never ridden except by the one who would bestride it in battle.

The entourage came up to Jamie and stopped. The King dismounted heavily and drew the sword he was wearing.

"Approach, James of Illareth," he said.

A bitter thrill went through Jamie. So, he was son no longer to his father, but must be addressed as any inferior tenant of the King would be. Illareth was a holding of less than two dozen farms, which had been given to Jamie at birth, as each of the royal children had been given land of his or her own, in case some later quarrel with the one who had become king should leave them with no other roof to shelter under.

Jamie walked up to stand before his father. His blue eyes clashed with his father's dark ones.

"Kneel," said the King.

Jamie knelt, on both knees. He hardly knew what to expect. Was his father going to execute him, here and now, instead of carrying through the threat of banishment? In any case, Walter should never hear this son of his beg for mercy.

Jamie felt the flat of the sword strike lightly upon each of his shoulders in turn.

"Rise, Sir James of Illareth, Knight!" said the King; and Jamie heard his father sliding the sword back into its sheath as he slowly rose to his feet. He looked once more into the King's eyes and saw in the face that was as forbidding as ever, that the eyes held a suspicious shine of liquid Jamie had never in his life seen there before.

"Brethin will go with you, to be your man and your shield-bearer," said his father, harshly. "Listen to him if he counsels you, for he's twice your age. I have knighted you; and I send you forth with armor, weapons, horse and baggage. James of Illareth, you are banished from this my realm, in the sight of these witnesses. You shall go forth, never to return except by my grace, or the grace of him who shall be king after me—"

Out of the corner of his eye, Jamie saw Hamish smile sourly.

"—and you shall in no wise set foot once more in this land, under pain of immediate death. You are barred from food and water, fire and shelter, the company of man, woman and beast, with all the lands of this our realm, until such time as the lawful King may grant full pardon."

Jamie rose to his feet.

"If I ever come back, it'll be needing no food, fire or shelter!" he said.

"Boy," answered his father harshly. "I've done what I could for you—all I can do, and more than you deserve. Brethin, attend him! Now go, the both of you!"

Jamie turned and mounted the palfrey that Brethin had led up to stand beside him. Together they rode away down the path from the Pass of the Black Rocks toward the world outside.

"I tell you, Brethin," said Jamie between his teeth, but without turning to look at the other man, "when I come back here, it'll be with money enough to buy this kingdom for my plaything and fame of the sort an emperor might envy!"

Brethin said nothing.

Chapter Two

WHEN THEY REACHED a firmer stretch of ground, Brethin got down on one knee and began to scrape the foul seaside mud from the boots of his lord. In the dead-gray sky above, gulls rode the wind in circles, their shrill cries a prickle to Jamie's irritation as he waited on his man's ministrations. Those who passed by on the harbor ways were usually busy enough to ignore them; a few who might not have been perhaps read something in the large man's demeanor that kept their feet moving.

Jerking to adjust his hose as Brethin scraped with a clam-shell at the ooze that had splashed above the boot-tops, Jamie's glance was a glare that covered the harbor. On this, their first full day in the Port of Winchelsea, Jamie had hurried down to the shore to find the ship that would take him to his destiny, his fortune. And it was only as he reached the nearest vessel and found himself confronting a small, clean, sun-browned fellow that he realized just how ignorant he really was.

The man spoke some foreign tongue that Jamie had never heard before; and it was only after some difficulty that another crewman, who spoke a mutilated Norman English even worse than Jamie's, was brought up. During his long trip south Jamie had assumed that when he reached a harbor his way would be clear to him; but it was now becoming obvious that he really did not know what he needed to do—not even who to talk to, or how he should go, or where.

After a few minutes of fumbling attempts at communication, Jamie had tried to stalk off with his dignity intact. With temper up, he'd found himself unable to ask advice of strangers; and so he'd stomped about the waterfront for some hours, trying to look as if he knew what he was about. Now he muttered yet one more hastening command to Brethin, while his eyes searched for signs of laughter on the faces that his temper said must be sharply aware of the foul-smelling filth that encrusted them both.

"Enough!" he growled—the sound reminded him irritatingly of his father—and immediately began to stride away, stiff-legged and uncomfortable, hot and sticky, without giving his companion time to clean himself. Brethin followed, contenting himself with swiping at his legs between strides.

As they made their way back to the inn they had stayed in last night, Jamie's steps slowed and his mood cooled, becoming more somber. Brethin found it easier to keep up with him. By the time they had settled down in the inn's common room with a bit of food left cold from last night's offerings, and wine, Jamie's mind had begun to work on the problem presented by his own ignorance. Brethin ate placidly and picked drying mud from his person.

Jamie sat in the common room the rest of that day, slowly reverting to his calmer, observer's nature. The polite ways that he, as a member of the noble class, was customarily obliged to show, returned, and he got on well with the serving women who responded to his infrequent calls for a refill—he had switched to ale. Brethin sat quietly in the corner nearby, beginning to mutter at the world now that nothing was happening immediately to take his mind off the possibilities presented by this strange country. He'd been doing it since they left the valley, and Jamie thought it was always the same words, like a short prayer; he dismissed the matter.

A heavier depression than he had ever experienced before had been growing all day in Jamie. He found himself longing for Moraig, or someone equal and familiar with whom he could relieve this unnatural gloom by talking about it to her— or him. He could not do so with Brethin. His responsibility as the man's lord required that he carry such burdens as this by himself. He tried to shake the feeling from him now, telling himself it was only a hangover of fatigue from the long journey south. They had stayed in a number of inns along the way. . . .

Staring across the room into the fire in the center of the floor, Jamie's eyes saw the blurred memories of a month of roads, gray and blue skies, and tiny taverns all the same. It came to him now that he had been moving to no plan, but acting by reflex—so shocked out of his usual thinking habits had he been all this time by his abrupt expulsion from his valley and home. He should have been learning more about the world on his way, but instead he had moved as if deaf and dumb, no more than a vagrant stranger forgotten by all he passed the moment he was gone by.

The door thumped open suddenly against the stone that served it for a stop. A small breeze stirred the smoke inside the inn, and Jamie looked up from the flames that had been engrossing him. The doorway had just been filled by a couple of newcomers.

Newcomers, but not strangers here, Jamie's mind noted automatically. The new arrivals were being welcomed by their friends already there—almost, it seemed, by everyone in the room except Jamie and Brethin. This sort of thing, too, had been part of the pattern he had been in on all that long road south. All along the way, in every inn and tavern, they had been the newcomers, the strangers. Everyone else seemed to belong to a company of friends, but he and Brethin had always been left out, excluded from the camaraderie. It had added to the pocket of silence that seemed to isolate him, moving always to contain Brethin and himself—Northerners, Scots, and strangers not to be trusted.

In that silence he now got heavily to his feet and moved off to sleep in the next room, dogged at his heel as always by Brethin.

But as he broke his fast the next morning, a new clearness woke in Jamie's mind. He had yet a distance to go to reach the fabled Constantinople that he sought. This land was certainly not golden, nor had he yet crossed the two seas legend said he must traverse to find the city. With the sea in his face now, he could ride no further. He would have to make plans for his next actions.

"Lord Jamie—" It was Brethin breaking into his thoughts.

"What is it?" Jamie stifled his irritation at having his revival of optimism interrupted.

"There's a Southern here who begs a word with you."

Brethin's thumb indicated an older man, dressed in what appeared to be cast-off sailor's garb, with little hair, a potbelly, and thin arms and legs. The man bowed low before him and then looked at him, rolling his eyeballs up in his skull in an effort to see Jamie's face, while his face reddened and his breath began to labor with the strain of holding the pose.

"Stand up, man!" Jamie barked, irritated at the man for no reason. "What is it?"

He felt vaguely ashamed of himself for letting his irritation show so readily, conscious of the need to be worthy of his position.

"My lord," the older man began, "it is said, among those who know such things, that my lord is attended only by this single servant here, which is surely a shameful thing, my lord, and therefore I offer my own services—" Jamie frowned, puzzled but listening while the man produced a lengthy list of his qualifications and experience.

The man—Jamie didn't remember hearing a name—was right about one thing, anyway: no man of Jamie's position went about virtually unattended. In fact, now that he thought of it, he realized that this was a factor in the shock that had seemed to numb his thinking all this time—he'd been used, all his life, to having people about him who did things for him— and, he suddenly realized, startled—also to guide him into doing what he should do.

He sat back on his bench, leaning against the wall, and the man before him broke off his presentation, afraid.

"I will consider," Jamie said confidently. The man opened his mouth, swallowed, closed his mouth—and then bowed sketchily and edged away. Jamie stared up into a corner while he thought.

Jamie spent the rest of that day watching the waterfront, trying to become familiar with the many ongoing activities. He also spent some time talking with Brethin about the Great City, the Varangian Guard, or anything involving over-the-sea travel. But Brethin was singularly unhelpful, for he not only knew nothing of such matters, but he did not want to know anything. He became, it seemed to Jamie, sullen and morose, perceiving that Jamie's mind seemed set on a course to take them farther and farther from home. Jamie had never told Brethin of the spaeman's seeing, for no strong reason, other than the fact that things that came close to magic were best kept to oneself. He congratulated himself on that restraint now, as for the first time he began to consider that Brethin might well turn out to be more trouble than help in the long run.

Nonetheless, their talk seemed to have had the effect of

raising Brethin's spirits over the next several days, during which they continued to lounge about the port, listening to conversations and, on Jamie's part at least, hoping for news of a ship headed east. However, what he gleaned was speculation on the upcoming weather and reports on the fishing. Now and then he was rewarded with mentions of the progress of the wars of the Norman king, Geoffrey III, in France, which was gossip more to his taste. But no one in all the Port of Winchelsea ever seemed to talk of the Great City and its heroes.

In the early afternoon of their sixth day in the city, Jamie walked down from the town along the river—whose name, he realized, he had not learned—and out upon a small, grassy promontory that jutted into the shallow sea. Here there was no beach, but only an imperceptible merging of land into mud and marsh, with the small waves beyond them in the distance. Down among the waves he could occasionally discern the lines of submerged walls, the only markers for the watery grave of old Winchelsea. Behind him by a few yards Brethin squatted beside the stone upon which, Jamie had been told, the present English king's great-grandfather and his wizard had been incinerated, when their attempt to hold back the sea from the old town by magic had failed.

Jamie turned suddenly and looked down at the stone; then he walked back around it and inspected its surface—but found no trace of ash on the weathered rock. He looked at it for a moment, and then nodded to himself, unaware of Brethin's gaze until he looked up.

With no word, Jamie stepped up on the rock and turned to look back at the sea. That was next for him, then.

He stepped back down and without a word began moving back towards the city, followed by his man. He paced quickly, eyes unseeing, caught up in the decision he'd finally come to and anxious to carry it through. It was better, he told himself again, as he had at the rock, to take action, even though you fail—than to sit like a priest and wait for God to bring what you need to you. Like the stone, you didn't leave much sign behind, either way. If these people did not know about the Great City, he would have to go elsewhere, to find those who did. He would have to cross the sea.

The next morning he ordered Brethin to settle with the innkeeper and they were on their way, down the coast road toward the bustling port of Pevensey. It was there, he had learned, that one would be more likely to find a ship departing for places beyond Christendom.

"My lord," Brethin spoke up suddenly from where the servant was riding, just behind him, once they were clear of the town.

"Yes, Brethin?"

"My lord, I settled with the innkeeper as you told me," Brethin said, sounding faintly embarrassed.

"Very good," Jamie said. "And did you then distribute the remainder of the purse amongst the servants, as I directed you?"

"Er—no, my lord." Brethin's voice was softer, and fraught with some emotion that caused Jamie to forget his anger for puzzlement.

"No?" Jamie said.

"No, my lord," Brethin said, somewhat stronger of voice. "It is that there was nothing left for them after I settled our host's score."

Jamie turned his face forward and let his horse carry him at an even pace, saying nothing; and Brethin, after a moment, dropped back again in silence.

Money. Of course, thought Jamie in a few moments, once he managed to quiet the sudden racing clamor of thought that had exploded in his head briefly. Once again he had not been thinking clearly enough to realize all aspects of his situation—for the first time in his life he was without the resources of his father and his family, which he had always taken for granted. And the lesson that Brethin had left unspoken was that he must not only care for what money he had, but seek some way of replenishing it as he went.

For a moment shame stirred in him and his breath quickened. For him, a *nobleman,* and a *knight,* to have to entertain such thoughts—he turned his face to the cool breeze that rode down from the inland hills on his left. He made himself breathe more slowly, and in a moment or two the feeling of shame faded from him. What must be, must be.

He considered the possibilities. The only course open to them was for Jamie to find employment as a warrior—Brethin knew that, of course, for no other avenue was to be considered suitable for one of Jamie's position.

In fact, Jamie reminded himself, he had already taken the correct first step, because Pevensey was the main port from which fighters left England for the wars in France and beyond.

Certainly it would be easy for him to find a place in some
company headed toward the wars in France. And in war he
would find the riches he needed for his journey farther east.

Jamie smiled to himself. War would also give him the
chance to perform deeds of valor, and to become a name that
men would fear and gleemen would sing of. And those songs
would spread across the world, perhaps even preceding him to
the Great City.

He chuckled. He would like to be home to see the faces of
his family when the first such songs reached them.

By the afternoon of their fourth day in Pevensey, Jamie's
hopes had once more ebbed to a low level. Now he sat in the
corner he was used to frequenting, of the inn he had chosen,
the Red Boar; and he noticed only absently when Kate, the
server, came by to see if he wanted more ale. Ale was not what
he needed.

From the inn he had sallied forth each morning in all his
finery, wearing some of his armor and attended by Brethin.
The latter carried Jamie's shield, which bore his freshly
painted device-gules: three wolves' heads sable within a bor-
dure argent. It was by now impossible that anyone in the town
should not know that a large and eager young knight was
about—and yet he had not found a place. The only people he
had talked to, a couple of other young knights, had not themselves been able to offer him a place; he knew a captain would
have to do that. But he had seen no captain, and none had sent
for him.

Perhaps, he speculated, he would have to take himself
across the sea, closer to where the fighting was—captains there
might be more eager to find new warriors. Maybe, he mused,
maybe . . . maybe he could drift unnoticed into some great
battle, and perform some great deed. Then the captains, or
perhaps—why not? even the White Prince himself!—might
begin to inquire as to the identity of the valorous young
stranger. . . . He smiled absently and picked up his cup,
warmed by the dream.

"Lord Jamie?" It was Brethin, seeking his attention in that
same tone of voice he always seemed to use when suppliants
came seeking a place in Jamie's service. Jamie had by now
learned that Brethin regarded all these seekers as no better than
vagabonds looking for a free handout and a warm bed.

"Yes, Brethin, what is it?"

"Ah—" Brethin seemed to stumble on what he was about to

say, and in the pause another voice spoke up, loud and strong, resonant in the low registers, and carrying an accent Jamie had not heard before.

"Edward Pennworthy, of Tintagel, Esquire," the voice asserted itself. Jamie found himself looking up at a man almost as tall as himself, and broader, at least in the breadth of a great barrel of a body. The face that had named itself Pennworthy was older than Jamie—perhaps in his mid-twenties—and was ruddy of complexion, with black hair much thinned-out atop. The man's eyes were dark and shiny under bushy dark eyebrows, and he carried a goodly dirk at his side.

"And what do you want with me, Master Pennworthy?" Jamie said into the pause that had followed the man's words.

The dark eyes had not smiled at him at all, and Jamie felt that they were watching him, seeking to weigh him in some balance of which Jamie was totally ignorant. He felt obscurely challenged, and stifled an impulse to bristle a little, knowing the need to preserve his image as superior to supplicant.

"If my lord will forgive me, I have come to inquire as to my lord's situation, in the hope that I might be of some small service to my lord," the man said. The pits around the dark eyes had narrowed a little as the man spoke, as if he did not like the words he was saying.

"Indeed?" said Jamie, injecting a note of coldness in response to this boldness. "And how could you serve me, sir?"

Even as the man's nostrils flared slightly, Jamie realized that he had been pushing at the fellow without waiting to hear what he might have to say—and it might be wise to do that. There was an air of challenge about the man; but that might be nothing against him. Jamie relented a little.

"Come, Master Pennworthy," he said. "Sit here and say what you would."

He waved vaguely in the direction of the next bench, and the other looked down at it, and then relaxed, moved over, and sat.

"I crave my lord's pardon," Pennworthy began, "and I presume too much. But it had come to my attention—as to the attention of any in this town"— he even smiled thinly at this— "that my lord is here to take service in some company on its way into France." It was not a question, but he paused, and Jamie nodded barely.

"While my lord appears a most puissant knight," Pennworthy continued, "it seems my lord doth ride alone." At this

Brethin, still standing to one side, glared, but the other added smoothly, "with the exception of this good fellow, of course. But certainly my lord seems to be without the number of retainers necessary for his lance."

This time the comment was a thinly veiled question in all seriousness, and Jamie knew it. He also knew that the answer to the query could only be agreement.

For it was true: in this age no knight fought alone, except for the occasional tourney single combat. The idea of the errant, lonely knight had vanished—a fact Jamie had long known and regretted—it was a romantic notion whose time had passed with the rise of this more practical, warlike age. Jamie admitted it to himself.

It was true. Nowadays a knight was of only minor value to his leader unless he was accompanied by his retinue—his lance—of retainers, most of whom also fought for the leader. And Jamie, with only Brethin to serve him, could not present any captain with a hireable full unit for service.

He had known this, but had been hoping that he would be employed by some captain who would provide him with the retainers he needed. Now, he admitted to himself, the chance of anyone providing retainers for an untried and unknown warrior was so small as to be insignificant. Suddenly Jamie got an inkling of Pennworthy's purpose here; he looked across at the other man again, and knew that his query was written on his face.

Pennworthy nodded before continuing.

"Yes, my lord," he said. "I offer myself and my three fellows to your service." He paused a moment, and then continued, telling his story obliquely as he laid out for Jamie his experience.

"I'm an experienced squire, my lord," Pennworthy said. "I was three years in the service of Sir Hugh Glasswell, who had fought for the Duke of Wessey against the Burgundians. We saw much fighting. However, Sir Hugh was maimed in a tourney, I brought him home, and remained to serve him for the last two years." Pennworthy paused.

"Go on," said Jamie, "if you already have a lord, why seek me out?" The other man sighed.

"Just three weeks since," he said, "the good Sir Hugh, rest his soul, died of a swelling of the belly; and his family had never had much love for me. It came to me that my best place was back in the wars beyond the water, and the sooner I was there, the better. Friends I had—like the three men I can bring you—but money had I none.''

Jamie leaned back on his bench against the wall and raised his cup, taking another drink while thinking hard, conscious of the gaze of Pennworthy from behind his own cup.

"I'm far from rich myself," he said bluntly. "What exactly is it you wish from me?" He eyed the other.

Pennworthy flushed, and for a moment the air of challenge fell away from him, so that, unexpectedly, he looked younger.

"My lord—" he began; and then paused, taking a breath and obviously collecting himself. "Forgive me, my lord," he went on, "I thought I had made myself clear. I seek to offer myself into your service as your squire, and bring with me these three men to serve as your retainers."

"Yes, that was clear," Jamie said. "But just what is it *you* want from *me?*" His tone now was heavy with a sort of sarcasm, as he sought to indicate to the other that he would not be put off with the sort of vague politenesses nobles were used to hearing from people who wanted things.

Pennworthy looked back at him, meeting his gaze and holding it while no answer came. Then the challenging feeling returned, strong as ever.

"My lord," Pennworthy said after a moment, "we seek to go with you to France, and to fight, and to come away with a just share of the proceeds you take."

There, that was blunt enough, Jamie thought. But the nagging question would not go away, and yet it was an impossible one to ask. Why should Pennworthy seek out an untried fighter like himself? Surely, if the other had the experience he claimed, he could find a post with a wealthier or more experienced leader. Jamie paused to frame his words carefully.

"Surely, Master Pennworthy," Jamie said, "there are many others in your situation. Why, then, should I take you over them?" He looked at the man squarely.

The dark eyes met his gaze without faltering, as if from above crossed blades, and Pennworthy spoke with no sign of discomposure.

"Because," he said, "I am known to Sir John de Guays, who is high in the service of the Captal de Buch. If I ask, he will recommend—a knight—to some worthy captain. And that is what is necessary for a knight to obtain a profitable place, these days."

Jamie found that he had leaned forward slightly and caught a breath in his throat; so now he was careful to relax without making an obvious show of it. This was important indeed, and meant—if true, he reminded himself, but he thought it was—a great deal. And that led him to his next question.

"Well, then, Pennworthy," he said softly, "tell me this. With such a mighty friend at your call, why come to a friendless knight to offer your services?" He leaned back again, one finger toying aimlessly with a puddle on the table before him as he watched the other man react to the question.

The challenge had dropped from Pennworthy as he digested the question, and now he obviously had a struggle to find an answer that he felt he could safely give. His eyes wandered slightly, returning to Jamie only when he spoke, after a few moments' pause.

"My lord—" he said, and then stopped again. Then he drew a breath and continued.

"My lord would not like to be lied to, I am sure," he said, "and so I will say this: my lord may be a most powerful knight—I cannot tell until I see my lord in battle. But as it happens I have little choice, for there are no other lanceless knights nearby whom I have not some cause to mistrust, and I and my men have not the ability to get to France by ourselves."

"I see," Jamie said. "You are short of funds, then?"

Pennworthy bowed his head, and Jamie realized that the man was ashamed of his admissions.

"Sir Squire," Jamie said, "do you then prepare our immediate passage to France."

Chapter Three

HIS BARE, RAPIDLY browning feet slapping on the pine decking of the *Anne*, Jamie leapt down from the tun he had been balancing on. The Biscay sun that warmed the planks to a pleasant sting in his soles was a harbinger of his bright future in the rich, warm south. Already he had forgotten the week of seasickness departure from Pevensey had brought him. Now only the cool salt air, and the warmed, sticky resins that gripped his feet as he moved with the swaying ship, held his attention.

Reveling in all the sensations on his skin, eyes squinting half-closed against sun and sweat, Jamie still noted Pennworthy's first movement in his direction. The fellow had arranged their passage on the vessel of a Master Cotter smartly enough, and Jamie had tucked away a good deal of knowledge gained in the process, providently aware that there was very little which bound the Cornishman to his service, except a sense of honor whose limits were unknown, and a sense of expediency that could vanish with the next breeze.

In the days when Jamie had agonized through the cold sweats, weeping eyes and aching nausea of *mal de mer*, which he had never even heard of before, Pennworthy, true to the experienced sailor's tradition, had been glaringly unsympathetic to his condition. The man had lounged comfortably on a bench while Jamie, lying on his disgustingly soiled pallet between two such benches, had been battered against them as the ship malevolently rolled him about. And even when he succeeded in wedging himself under a bench, to bring a peaceful darkness to aching eyes, and an illusion of stability to his never still frame, Jamie's ears could not shut out the calm, reasonable, maddening—and hellishly ceaseless!—slow stream of the other man's philosophies.

The greasy, gray, dancing seas had not even caused Pennworthy to lose his appetite. But the helpless Scot had heard all as Pennworthy had time to recall the many wisdoms that had been beaten into him by father, brothers, uncles, priests, horses, captains, seas and storms. It was not clear to Jamie whether he resented it all because of his awful illness, or because of the seemingly vast fund of experience it revealed.

It also rankled in Jamie that he had been too sick to really fulfill his duties to Brethin, whose bout with the illness had made Jamie's pale by comparison; indeed, the man had gotten so terribly sick that Pennworthy had begun to worry. No jokes were made in Brethin's case, and the ship's carpenter—by tradition the healer in the crew—had come to help with his various remedies. Those had helped a bit, but the man had put into words a thing experienced sailors knew.

"The sea's an unforgiving enemy to some men, yes; and when that happens there's no help for it—nor shame either."

Even now, as Jamie enjoyed the sensations of a sailor's balancing abilities, Brethin lay in the hold. He was still quite ill, but the carpenter this morning had commented that he seemed to have become aware of the awful stink in that confined space; Pennworthy agreed sagely that this was a sure sign of improvement.

"You've been below, then?" Jamie let his smile of friendly greeting turn to an expression of serious concern.

"Yes," the other answered. "He's kept down the broth we gave him, and the carpenter said it would be well to bring him up into the airs. Will and Tom will be up with him."

Now he smiled. "I think he'll be all right now, unless another storm comes upon us before we reach Bordeaux."

Suddenly Jamie felt a relaxing of muscles he had not known had tensed up, and he smiled at Pennworthy without thinking.

"That's good to hear," he said; and then laughed shortly. "Aye, and what would my father have said were I to lose his parting gift so soon, eh?" He laughed again and turned away; then turned back, clapping Pennworthy lightly with half-curled hand on linen-shirted shoulder.

"And thank you, my friend. You've been of great aid to me in this matter. Now shall we drink some of the ale we shipped and talk of the southern lands, eh?"

Pennworthy paused, and then followed Jamie toward the bow hatch—switching his momentarily bleak gaze from Jamie toward the water streaming beside the ship. Jamie wondered what he was thinking.

A splash attracted his attention and turned his mind from the subject. He watched idly as they moved, for another fish out of the water.

At about that same time the next day Jamie and Pennworthy—Jamie was calling him Edward now—threw themselves down into the scant shade furnished by the starboard railing, panting. They'd begun to exercise themselves lightly an hour before, and found themselves first sparring, then grappling in a wrestling bout that at times impressed onlookers among crew and passengers as a matter of serious intent.

However, the contest had dissolved into snorts of laughter gulped in with gasps of air, tension having been relieved by a loud popping that was the seam of Edward's breeches giving way during a particularly silent moment. Ale became the order of the day.

During all this the normal life of a working ship had proceeded around them. From the sterncastle's deck the master's nephew was being put through his paces, as befitted the newest member of the crew, made to run from place to place about the deck, and always by way of the rigging lines that arched above all the ship.

Now, tired but breathing easier, Jamie looked up as the boy stopped—perhaps to catch a breath himself, or wipe his brow—and so he saw the youngster's gaze moving about the horizon. The lad's eyes returned to settle on an area behind them, as an excited cry burst from him.

"A sail! Behind us!"

The general movement toward the stern of the ship included Jamie, who lined up along the railing with a number of his fellow passengers. This was not wholly comfortable; many of them had been as sick as he, and smelled worse than he did in consequence.

Jamie noted that Pennworthy had joined the crew in ascending the rigging lines for a better viewpoint; and he could be seen swaying near the ship's master, Will Cotter. And so in looking upward at Edward, Jamie saw from the master's face that the man had quickly located and identified the other vessel—before Jamie had even seen it from his own position.

Master Cotter was back on deck and issuing orders to spread

more sail; but even to Jamie's eyes it was soon apparent that the other vessel was gaining. Within an hour the newcomer was close enough that Jamie could also see that she was larger than the *Anne,* and had castles at both bow and stern. In that time the faces of those around him became sober—and he heard the name "Sanscoeur" muttered.

About to ask about this "Sanscoeur," Jamie abruptly realized that Brethin stood before him, patiently awaiting his attention.

"Yes, Brethin, what *is* it?"

His own excitement and the tension he always felt before a fight came through as irritation.

"Lord Jamie, the sailors say it's a sea battle we're in for. D'ye want me to fetch up our gear?" The face before Jamie, though paler than usual, was calm, and the voice quiet. The paleness would be from illness only; Brethin's concept of his duty to Jamie gave him the security of knowing his place at such a time.

As Edward drew near behind Brethin, Jamie realized that he also knew his duty at such a time.

"Yes, Brethin—and Master Pennworthy's, also." Jamie was suddenly very conscious of the sea breeze on his face. "Tell Master Cotter we are at his orders—then bring ale for the three of us, eh?"

He felt a touch on his elbow and turned to see Pennworthy. "That ship's the *Red Moon,*" the other man said. "I was on her once before Jacques took her. Jacques Sanscoeur is what they call her captain, and he's a hard man."

"'Sanscoeur,'" Pennworthy asked, mutilating the French name in fine style, "doesn't that mean—"

"'No heart,'" broke in the ship's carpenter, who had come to the rail beside them for a look at the *Red Moon.* "Aye, and heartless he is. We all fight here on the sea, from time to time. But this one likes to kill slowly the prisoners he takes—and take our own poor ship he will—"

"To your place, now, Tom, there's a good lad." The voice of the *Anne*'s master interrupted him. "I want you with the young ones, to hold them steady as we wait for the close."

"Oh, aye, sir," the carpenter replied, and began to turn toward the waist. "But it'll be no good . . ." His voice trailed behind him as he went.

The master, eyes searching Jamie and Pennworthy sharply, paused beside them.

"If you gentlemen have never fought at sea before, remember to dodge the bolts from the crossbowmen that yon ship will have up in both castles to shoot down on our deck." He immediately began to move off.

"Wait, Master Cotter," Edward halted him. "What can we expect of the Sanscoeur?"

Cotter turned about swiftly, and snapped.

"You can expect to be gutted alive!"

Then he softened his tone. "They must board to take us in the end, and in that lies our only chance, for all they have numbers on us. If we can repel them as they board, we may yet win free to live this day. Otherwise—not."

"Can't you keep away from him so he can't board?" Pennworthy asked as Jamie watched.

"Oh, aye, that's what I'll try," the master replied, by now addressing the covey of passengers that had quickly formed about their conversation. "But it's long 'til dark, and they had the legs and wind of us. So I hope you'll all be ready." He began to walk aft.

But within another hour the two ships were so close that it was plain that the encounter could not be avoided before the sun set. Jamie, having had time to use his ever-active wit to some extent, sought out Will Cotter on the sterncastle.

"Master Cotter," said Jamie, "have you thought of using fire arrows on them?"

"Thought of them? Of course not," the master snarled.

Caught up in enthusiasm for his idea, Jamie plunged ahead without taking note of the man's expression.

"I could put arrows into his sails and rigging easily, and with those afire he'd not catch us; probably he'd give over the chase for the danger of damage," Jamie continued.

"Oh, aye," the master replied snappishly. "But I'll remind ye that we have no fire on board now, and I'll have none while we're moving in this fashion."

"But I could—"

"But you shall not, young sir. You've never seen what fire can do to a ship's timbers, once started. Why do you think we light up our cookbox only in calm weather? This ship is all I own, and I'll not risk burning her down to the waterline while hope remains. I'll remind ye that *I* be master of this vessel!"

Jamie paused during a long moment, then grunted something and climbed down the ladder from the castle. In the waist he paused.

"Brethin!" he said, "string my bow and hold my arrows ready."

Without waiting for an answer, he began to move toward the forward hatch.

"What are you planning?" Pennworthy frowned, hastening after him.

"To start a fire," said Jamie, grimly but quietly. Pennworthy pointed at his heels in silence for a moment. "Can you think of another way to save this ship?"

"But think, Jamie! I heard the master just now. He is right about the danger of lighting up in this wind and at this time. If you fire up the cookbox he can hang you lawfully, and he will—"

Jamie managed to keep his voice low. "There's another way," he said.

Edward was silent, moving forward beside him. Jamie glanced about him, lowering his voice still farther.

"Have you ever met a sorcerer, Edward?"

The Cornishman gaped.

"Jamie—do you mean *you're* . . . ?"

"By the Blood, no!" Jamie sliced a hand sideways in the air in emphasis. "But I've known a spaeman all my life, and there's one on this ship who has the same look—that doctor from Oxford up in the neck of the bow. I'm going to seek his aid; and if he's what I think he is, in that heavy chest of his below he'll have the means of making a fire, magical or otherwise. He may be able to brew a rain of serpents to drop on Sanscoeur, or some such."

"But what if he'll not give them to you?" Pennworthy said, as Jamie turned from the bow toward the forward hatch that led below decks.

"I've no time to ask him," grunted Jamie, "and what if for some reason he should say no? Wait up here for me, Edward, and come to warn me if Master Doctor looks like wanting to go below while I'm still down there."

Without being so directed, Brethin was busy selecting among Jamie's bowstrings for those which had kept driest during the trip. He also examined the arrows to search out the truest, even though they were all cloth-yard shafts bought by Jamie only weeks before. He gave no heed to the rather shocking discussion proceeding only feet away—or at least no sign of heed, Jamie thought. But he was muttering under his breath again.

Pennworthy looked as if he felt that it might be better to have Sanscoeur aboard than a sorcerer; but Jamie continued before the Cornishman could formulate his objections.

"It's the sorcerer or the fire, Edward—that or the master's plan, which you know full well cannot work."

Leaving Pennworthy behind, Jamie strode to the forward hatch, fighting to keep himself from running, and found his way partly blocked by two of the other passengers, merchants from the midlands of England.

"But how can this *be*, Roger?" the younger was asking. "You recall! This Jacques fellow was at anchor in Bordeaux when last we were there, and they treated him not whit else from the other captains."

"Look you, Guy," the older man replied, "the sea is very large and all our ships afloat upon it, mere chips; and there are few at sea at any one time. Obviously there are few witnesses to a piracy if a prince seeks to do justice."

"Your pardon—" said Jamie gruffly, pushing between them, and found himself caught by the sleeve and included in their conversation.

"How say you, my lord," said Roger. "It's true—is it not? There be none to do justice except the princes of Christendom, and they each have their own needs. A Burgundian who preys on English ships may be a pirate to Pevensey—but St. Eloi may see him as a most useful citizen indeed."

As Guy sought a suitable reply to convey his indignation at this state of affairs—it was already obvious on his face— Jamie spoke up. He felt he needed to say something before leaving them, or he'd be noticed.

"The sea is as the roads in wild times," he said, feeling unbearably pompous. "If the rules cannot work, all travelers are in danger—and from many directions—I pray you, let me pass!"

He pulled his sleeve from Roger's grasp and plunged down the ladder. Behind him he could hear Roger seizing his point and discoursing on wolves, bogs, and outlaws. The voices faded as the smell of the hold grew before him, and he was soon stooping his way through the dank, dark, low-ceilinged spaces below the deck of the *Anne*.

It was an unpopular and sometimes dangerous—if tolerated—thing to engage in sorcerous doings. Jamie had no desire to make trouble for the doctor from Oxford, who might or might not be a wizard, but the peril to the *Anne*'s company was too immediate for fine concerns. Jamie hastily proceeded to the area where Septilos slept.

He swiftly located the two leather-bound wooden chests the Oxford resident had brought on board the vessel.

A few heavy blows with his short sword laid open the top of the larger trunk, exposing a colorful variety of clothing, several thick books, and a variety of implements of chirurgy. Jamie's guess had been correct. He rifled through the exposed contents and then attacked the smaller trunk.

He found himself looking down through splinters of wood at wooden racking containing literally scores of small bottles. Reaching down, he brushed aside the splinters of the chest lid and lifted out several racks of these—revealing only more and more bottles and jars. Each was labelled neatly in Latin and in English, and those few names Jamie recognized were of well-known medicinal plants.

He sat back on his heels, staring at the ruins he had made of both trunks. He'd been very sure that he'd find fire-making equipment; but the fact that it might be in some unrecognizable form, or labeled in a language he did not understand, had not occurred to him. He dropped his sword in something almost resembling panic, and began to paw violently among the wreckage of the trunks, still hoping what he wanted would reveal itself.

Suddenly he stopped, frozen in place with hands inside the chest. Slowly he pulled them back out, clenching a cloth-swathed bundle the size of his two fists. Something this carefully packed must be potent, indeed. Perhaps not only potent, but valuable enough to force the doctor to create fire as the price of the object's safe return. . . . Gingerly, he placed the bundle on the deck before him and sat back once more on his heels to study it.

After a second of hesitation, he began to unwind the yellow-brown wrapping from about whatever it shielded; and found himself looking at an empty and corkless bottle made of a nearly clear blue glass. He frowned, because he was sure the bundle had moved in his hands as if there were a thing alive within it, a moment ago.

He picked up the bottle to examine it more closely, and started suddenly. His fingers, he realized, were now feeling a shape that his eyes did not see. He closed his eyes and began to run his hands about the bottle.

The vessel was heart-shaped, and felt rather rough to the

touch, as if the surface were profusely etched with intertwined cabalistic designs; and the neck rose in a narrow stem from a small valley in the top of the bottle. There seemed to be a leaden seal about the neck, and—he opened his eyes briefly— yes, despite appearing corkless, the bottle was sealed by the soft, waxy metal. And his blind fingers could trace the patterns of a shape impressed in the metal. Clearly magic was at work under his fingers.

The bottle in his hand jumped unexpectedly, and he nearly dropped it. But his grip tightened. It must be a prison to some enchanted spirit or demon. The hairs on the back of his neck seemed to move, to stir slightly in a nonexistent breeze; his stomach muscles tightened, and Jamie was suddenly very conscious of the fact that his knees had gotten cramped from his ungainly pose. But in a moment he had forced his breathing to even out.

Clearly, it was some form of bottled magical power; perhaps even power enough to ward off the onrushing pirates, certainly enough to give him fire for flaming arrows. A heroic vision of the forthcoming fight rose before his inner eyes. A moment later he was hurriedly retracing his steps to the ladder and up it, carrying the strange bottle and slowing only to retrieve and sheathe his shortsword.

Back in the bright sun and salt-smelling open air of amidships, he hastily noted that the *Red Moon* was a good deal closer, though still out of bowshot. Jamie strode over to where Edward, Brethin, and the rest of their party still prepared for the upcoming fight; he brandished the bottle at them.

"I was right! Edward, look!"

Pennworthy lifted a glance at the apparently empty bottle, and shrugged.

"How is *that* going to help us? And what were you right about?"

"The doctor—he *is* a sorcerer, Edward! And this proves it—here, feel it—no, never mind, there's no time. I've got to figure out how to use this on yon Jacques Sanscoeur. Have you seen the doctor around?"

Pennworthy shook his head, his face indicating a strong desire to have nothing to do with bottle or doctor—and perhaps not with Jamie, either.

"Here! Young sir! That's my bottle, isn't it?"

The voice, a resonant basso with music in every tone, came from behind them, and they recognized it.

''Doctor Septilos,'' Jamie responded eagerly as he turned, ''I've been looking for you—''

''Ah, the Scottish lord. Well, I'm sure you have, my lord. But here I am, now, and you'll give me that bottle if you please, afterward telling me how you came to have it!''

''Doctor, I beg your forgiveness for my acts belowdecks,'' Jamie said. Obviously the sorcerer was upset, but with a little attention to salve the sores, he would certainly see the matter Jamie's way soon enough. ''We need your aid. Specifically we need fire to save the ship and our lives—''

He was suddenly cut off by the vibrant tones of the somberly dressed figure.

''Fire!'' The doctor's eyes were black and now suddenly they radiated heat like coals at the point of bursting into open flames. ''Are you some amateur of the Arts, young man? If so, you've little notion what you hold so lightly in your hand. I insist! You must give that bottle over into my possession immediately! *Now!*''

Jamie took a step backward, watching the older man cautiously. He was at a loss to understand the other's strange insistence on the matter of his own property when their very lives were in peril. . . .

Suddenly, he became conscious that beside him the bottle he held was suddenly giving off light; and his hand beginning to grow warm. He saw both Edward and Brethin staring at him, and from something Hobie the spaeman had once said, and he now remembered, he suddenly understood what he held. The sorcerer had imprisoned a salamander within the bottle.

But his spirits suddenly leaped upward—a salamander was exactly what he needed for the fire arrows.

He turned to the railing. At his side he could hear the sorcerer still saying something—or perhaps it was a sort of singing—but the sound meant nothing to him, caught up as he was in his vision of action. He looked about for Brethin and saw the servant standing behind him with Jamie's heavy bow and quiver of arrows. Jamie grabbed those and sprinted for the ladder to the sterncastle.

As he mounted it he noted that Master Cotter had tacked the *Anne* so as to present her broadside to the *Red Moon*. This was enabling *Anne*'s archers, few though they were, to get more shooting room, while the Burgundian archers had to crowd about their ship's forecastle.

From behind him, in the waist of the *Anne*, he could hear a commotion beginning; and before he strode forward he caught a brief glimpse of Brethin, who had thrown himself at the mage and was attempting to hold back the doctor from following Jamie. Edward was mounting the ladder toward him; everyone else on deck, strangely, seemed to be trying to get as far away as possible from the magician.

As Pennworthy came up behind him with a full quiver, Jamie picked a spot on the forecastle breastwork and began to prepare for his shooting. He set his arrows out beside him, quickly, and then drew his dagger to pick at the leaden seal and stopper of the now brightly-glowing bottle.

The metal was visible now, he realized in a far-off corner of his mind, not stopping.

Abruptly, he was seized about the left ankle. The grip tightened in an instant, and he looked down to see that the free end of a coil of rope which had been lying nearby was beginning to wrap itself about his leg. Edward looked down and gasped as the rope suddenly leapt into the air, pulling Jamie's leg with it and dumping the remainder of him unceremoniously on the planking of the deck. He managed to shield the back of his head from contact with the hard surface, but lost his grip on the bottle.

The glass container, now almost too bright to look at, arced into the air and down into the hand of Septilos, who had fought free of Brethin, somehow—which was surprising in a man his age—and was now standing by the hatch. Brethin lay still on the deck where they had wrestled, blinking, face red and straining, but obviously unable to move any farther.

The rope which held Jamie's ankle suspended in midair continued to rise, threatening to hang him upside down. He drew his dagger and slashed at the portion of it within his reach. But the razor-sharp edge of his blade seemed to merely bounce off the hemp, as if it were woven of metal.

As he rose slowly into the air, Jamie reached for the bow and arrow that were still within his reach, but before his hand could grasp them the mage gestured and the rope suddenly dropped him in a heap on the deck.

Enraged, he leaped up with another arrow already on the string, but the figure of the sorcerer suddenly loomed directly in front of him, its hand already holding the shaft of the arrow he'd drawn. Suddenly, he could not move a muscle. He gasped.

"Be still now!" The doctor's voice tolled in his ears like a bell. "You may save your strength and arrows for some pirates. Later you'll thank me for this, for you will see that you could not have lived if you'd opened that bottle—nor any of us. To unleash a salamander without restraint is the last act of any man, and it is an unclean death."

"If you can do so much," raged Jamie, furious at the spell or whatever it was holding him helpless, "why not destroy the pirates by yourself?"

"Even the most powerful sorcerer has limitations placed on him, whether by the Laws or by those above him," Septilos replied. His tones had warmed strangely, and now his deep voice seemed almost to sing at Jamie. "Come, young man, spare me questions there is no time to answer. Just listen to me for a moment. If you but swear to do only as I tell you, I will give you the fire arrows you desire. What say you?"

"Is your life then in so much danger that you so freely do a thing you just said was dangerous?" Jamie asked after a long pause. "Surely one with your powers is worth a great ransom."

"I—or any other sorcerer—have more enemies than friends," the mage replied. "If Sanscoeur takes me, and learns what I am, he'll know my head to be worth thrice my life. Come now and decide on my bargain."

Jamie eyed the gaping crewmen and passengers, noting the number of them with bows ready for defense against Sanscoeur. They might well be too awestruck to be able to take advantage of a similar offer from the Oxford man—but why should he not do so first? Surely he was in no greater danger than he had been; and who could say what glory might not come to the one bold enough to seize the opportunity when it presented itself?

He turned to the sorcerer.

"Upon my soul, I will follow your bidding in this matter," he said. At a gesture from the figure before him, whatever force was holding Jamie released him so suddenly that he almost fell. The doctor, still holding the bottle, had turned away from him.

As Pennworthy helped him pick up his arrows, Brethin limped up to them. The sorcerer squatted beside the glowing bottle in the middle of the sterncastle deck, making complicated passes over it with his hands and once dipping his beard down almost to the bottle, all the while singing in a language so complicated that Jamie could not even tell where the words began and ended. A few sounds were vaguely reminiscent of things he'd heard from Hobie Yaro in his work—but somehow they sounded strange, as if they'd crept from one tongue to another in the dark at the behest of some monstrous mind.

With a faint pop the remnants of the disguising spell ceased, and the true bottle could be seen, the glow of the figure within brighter than ever. Jamie's interest was fastened on the magician now, and he forgot the uneasiness that had been his habit in the presence of the eerie.

After a very short time the lead seal that had stoppered the bottle began to vibrate, then revolve slowly about the neck. Before it had completed more than a few revolutions, a faint orange mist could be seen creeping out about it; and by the time three turns had finished a ball of the mist was floating above the planking. In mere seconds it grew to be a yard in diameter, floating at the height of a man's chest. The passing breezes had no effect on it, did not even blur it, although Jamie thought it could be seen to pulsate slowly. He now felt no heat from it at all.

Suddenly the doctor shouted a single two-syllable word that twisted Jamie's insides even though he couldn't say what the syllables had been. There was a shriek from the bottle as the stopper twirled back into place, seating itself firmly; the bottle fell over and the sorcerer casually kicked it to the side and out of the way. It rolled across the deck, being widely avoided by all, until it lodged in the scuppers.

Septilos made three more passes with his hands about the orange haze, and it began to shrink. By the time it reached the size of a baby's head, it was giving off heat like that of a blacksmith's forge.

"Give me an arrow, Pennworthy," said the sorcerer. "And you, my lord, be ready. Such fire does not burn well for more than a few seconds, unless it catch. You must be fast."

By the time Jamie reached the railing with his bow up, Pennworthy was hurrying toward him with an arrow, its head completely lost in a searing ball of bright orange. The hair began to curl on the back of Jamie's hands as he nocked the shaft, and he found it hard to take the time to sight on the masthead of the other ship. He released.

The ball of fire maintained its shape, not trailing with the wind of the arrow's passage. There was an eruption of steam as the shaft plunged—short—into the sea. Already Brethin had reached him with another fire arrow.

This one quivered as it thunked into the sea-wet planks of the *Red Moon*, just above the waterline. Now there were shouts from aboard the other vessel, and a few arrows lofted in the direction of the *Anne*, falling well short. Jamie had a brief moment of fear that the other vessel would shear away until they lost their fire.

Meanwhile, Master Cotter had directed the other archers to open fire on the *Red Moon*. Edward, having arrived with the third burning arrow, muttered darkly about having to get it on target this time, but now Jamie knew the other vessel could not pull off its course in time. His third arrow struck at the base of the mast and his fourth in a furled canvas on the deck nearby.

The other archers had the range now, and harassed the Burgundian crew's fire-fighting and course-changing efforts. Jamie just stood by quietly, gathering the strength from within himself that he'd been taught to look for, channeling it into a steady rhythm and a flowing of motions that made the arrows stream from his bow. He was down into the depths of the actions he was involved with now, and in that trancelike state he hardly noticed the heat of the salamander-fire; nor did he notice that he'd reached the end of his arrows until they stopped coming to him.

Edward was tugging at his sleeve, pulling him from the rail of the ship, which was dipping erratically as the *Anne*'s crew was distracted. But he paused to watch the small fires that dotted the other ship as they reduced sails and rigging to ash before dying out. *Red Moon* was already dropping far behind fast.

The orange haze, shrunken to a ball the size of a thumb, was quickly rebottled by the sorcerer, who then walked over to Jamie and graciously thanked him for his aid. Numb, Jamie could only stare as the figure vanished below.

Cheering passengers and a few crewmen suddenly surrounded him, and he found himself in the midst of a celebration badly needed by men who had counted themselves dead. By nightfall his head was buzzing, and as he crawled onto a pallet out on deck, he was still unable to fathom the man who had actually won the victory for them.

As a child he'd always thought that good sorcerers must be able to have all they desired from life, and he'd fantasized befriending one and having his ready services for his own glory and enrichment. Yet this one appeared unable to even save his own life with his lore, without help.

Obviously, there was a good deal more to this sorcery than he had ever dreamed of. But right now his head was heavy, and it didn't seem a good time to puzzle over it. Also, he felt suddenly weak in the knees. He sat down heavily upon a small upright keg that was nearby and rested his heavy head in his hands.

"I hope," a rich voice boomed in his ears, "that this will be a lesson to you, young man, not to take chances in those areas of which you are sublimely ignorant."

He looked up into the face of Septilos.

"Doctor," he said. "I've already apologized for my acts belowdecks with your belongings. More than this I—"

"It's not your acts below deck that concern me, my lord," said Septilos. "In fact, it's not your acts in general that concern me. It is, as I say, your ignorance. Like most of the uneducated world you seem to assume that *things* are what matter, while actually the only elements of power in life are not things at all. They are those matters immaterial—thought and idea itself."

"I pray you," said Jamie, "lecture me at some other time. My head aches—"

"It is precisely because it is at this time that your head aches—which in itself is a punishment imposed by the continuum of ideas upon you for ignoring the power of ideas—that I choose to lecture you now," said Septilos.

"Doctor," said Jamie in desperation, "I will happily leave to you the world of ideas, since that's where you want to belong, and you, in turn, leave me to the world of things, real things, which is my world and where I belong."

"Is it indeed?" Septilos almost sneered. "What if I told you, my lord, that there is no such world as the one you think you belong to? You, I, everyone, belong to the immaterial, of which all you take for real is but the outer show . . ."

"My head is cracking wide open!" said Jamie. "Leave me in peace! Things are what makes life happen and the world be what it is."

"Whatever makes life and the world be what they appear to be, believe me, are not *things,* young man! *Things*—empires, kingdoms, castles and wealth—these are nothing. Mere forms of more enduring entities, here today and gone or in the hands of another a few years hence. Knowledge, ideas—truths— these are the real materials out of which life is made and measured. The great science of philosophy, from which are derived all the lesser sciences, including that even of magic, which is of the realm of ideas and knowledge—"

"Doctor," Jamie interrupted, "What good are all these ideas of yours if I take my sword right now and cut your head off? Where are your ideas then?"

"Young man," said Septilos with a strange smile, "why don't you try just that and find out? . . . Well? Come, come, what stops you?"

"You know very well what stops me," Jamie growled. "Master Shipman here and his merry men would string me up by the neck if I slew you without reason."

"Ah, and why?" said Septilos. "Would they not do so because it is a belief of theirs that you should not do that? And what is a belief but an idea, and what is an idea but part of a philosophy—for they, like all others, think they live by wind and wave and blade, but actually they live each by a personal philosophy that dictates how they must act and react to these and all other things—"

Jamie got wearily to his feet.

"Doctor," he said, "I will agree with anything you say. I will believe anything you say. Will that satisfy you?"

"No," said Septilos.

"And why not? What more can you want?" Jamie cried in exasperation.

"I would want you to understand what I'm trying to tell you, my lord," said Septilos. "But I see it's no use. I would save you considerable agony and trouble by telling you of things as they are, instead of how they appear to you—a difference that, I need hardly remind you, almost caused your death from the fire inherent in my salamander. But I see that, like all those in your position, you'll be taught only by hard and bitter experience. I leave you to it, then. Let us both pray you learn in time that the value of ideas and philosophy is everything and that of what you call real *things* is nothing. Good afternoon—I leave you happily to your ignorance and your fate!"

And with that he stalked off, going belowdecks.

"Well," said Jamie after a moment, turning to Edward who had appeared beside him, "what was all that about?"

"I don't know," answered Edward. But the Cornishman shivered suddenly. "But best to steer clear of such a man. Mark my words, those like him mean the end of matters as we know them. I can feel that much in my bones—for all his salamander helped save our lives this day!"

Chapter Four

AS JAMIE WATCHED idly from under the archway of the gallery outside the room he and Brethin shared, another rat stole from the dark crevices at the base of the house facing them, to join those already nosing at and in the nearest heap of offal in the street. When there were no dangerous feet near, the street seemed to fairly quiver as the vermin foraged among the refuse left in the wake of men and beasts. It was like this in most streets of the city, Jamie now knew, except that in the main avenues where traffic was heavy the rats left the pickings to the city's dogs and St. Anthony's pigs, those specially favored animals belonging to the Hospital of St. Anthony who, alone among the rest of their tribe, had the exclusive right to prospect among the garbage of Bordeaux. But Jamie had now and again noticed tattered human figures too, poking at the noisome piles.

Abruptly uneasy, Jamie sought another subject for his restless mind to engage, swinging his gaze back to his companion as he did so. Brethin was squatting comfortably in the shade of the arch's opposite corner, facing his lord and with eyes open, but seeming nevertheless to have his gaze focused somewhere in the interior of France. Jamie caught himself beginning to frown with thought, and carefully kept his expression more quiet—he was not, after all, angry with Brethin, and did not want to give him cause to think otherwise.

Jamie shifted his gaze slightly and stared through the stone uprights to face Brethin across the narrow archway. Since their debarkation from the *Anne*, Brethin had been recovering his strength at a steady pace, although even now, after two weeks in Bordeaux, he was not yet as strong or as steady as usual. Even more disturbing, though, was the man's lack of response to the new environment his master had led him to. In truth, Jamie could not say he had really noticed how Brethin had reacted to the strange country they'd crossed since leaving the Pass of the Black Rocks. He had, he realized suddenly now, not been watching Brethin at all, having his mind on more pressing matters, like his own problems. Now, however, Jamie found himself examining his retainer more carefully. Stupid of him not to have noticed it before, but the feeling of wrongness in Brethin was like an itch that could not be located exactly. Jamie's agile mind began to consider ways of finding out what was bothering his liege man—to whom he owed a responsibility, even as Brethin owed a responsibility to him.

The sound of a door to their rooms creaking open reached his ears; and Jamie was automatically on his feet. Edward Pennworthy seemed to suddenly jump into the sunlight from the shadows of the corridor outside. His round, expressive face told Jamie all he needed to know of the interview from which he had just come and which must have just ended. Jamie followed him out of the room; but Edward neither paused nor spoke as they strode off down the street toward a set of tables outside the tavern.

"Well?" demanded Jamie when they were seated.

Pennworthy shook his head, signaling for wine. "I'm sorry, Jamie," he said. "But it seems times are bad."

The wine came and he went on to explain.

It was not that there was no one in Bordeaux hiring fighters. At least eight captains Pennworthy knew personally were either in the city or had agents there; and he had learned the names of several more. Nor was he himself totally unknown to good soldiers among those of the English side in the French Wars, generally. But all the captains, whether English or other, seemed to be primarily in the market for the sort of rabble that were becoming more and more common—"rabble" was certainly the correct word, Jamie thought to himself—in modern warfare. They only wanted bodies to stand on the field filling it up, and, if necessary, to fall there.

Of course, there were yet many leaders who wanted the lance, headed by its armored horsemen; the nobility still held their traditional place in the front of the battle. But here in the peaceful sea town of Bordeaux, far from the fields and the encampments of the leaders, those places open for horsemen had become valuable in themselves, pieces in the speculations of men who bet their lives on surviving and growing rich with loot and awards—and here such places were to be had only through the favoritism of blood or money. Since Jamie's supply of coin had been shrinking rapidly, thanks to the cost of living in a war-economy city, he and Edward had determined to find places simply on their merits.

But it seemed as if no captain could even be talked to unless palms along the way were made heavy; and so far they had not been able to even get in for Edward's short word with Sir John de Guays. The doors would not open for them. Jamie looked up at the bright blue sky that pulled the eye away from the dirty gray stone and worn wood of the city's buildings; then he returned his attention to the muddy streets.

"Ah, he was no worse than all the rest, of course!" Pennworthy had not remained in low spirits long; and now, as they admired the wider, sunnier, and crowded Avenue of St. John's Church, he actually chuckled. "He knew me, and he'd have liked to have been able to present me to his captain like a well-trained war-horse. But when I showed Raymond no silver for himself, and let him know that all I wanted was a word with Sir John . . . well, he knew there'd be none for him to hand to Hubert van Ghent for the privilege of joining his company, and so . . ."

His right hand flipped into the air, fingers spread wide. He seemed, Jamie reflected absently, to have taken to using gestures more since they had landed and he had begun to talk to all sorts of outlanders.

They finished their drinks and headed back toward the inn. Jamie dodged around a cart from which a one-legged man was hawking bread. He was trying to frame a question in terms that wouldn't offend Edward, who could yet be quite useful to him—although so far little had gone as he had planned.

"Is this Thomas then not so much a friend as you had thought?"

"This is no true test of that," Edward said. "One makes a friend at war, but one loses them as quickly--he may even be the enemy next time. One must take even friendship as it comes. And certainly Thomas is no more able to control the ways of the men around him than are we."

Jamie was frowning to begin a reply when a sudden clatter of hooves, mixed with a chorus of shouts, heralded the rapid approach of a party of horsemen from a sidestreet into the avenue. Jamie could not yet understand the French words being trumpeted by the party's outriders, but he had already learned enough to get out of their way. He leaped almost six feet sideways, landing, still on his feet, beside Edward in the gutter.

Jamie's landing had the softness and grace of the trained athlete or warrior, and he was quite used to the filth that now submerged his feet. Edward came down more heavily and splashed everyone in the vicinity, but none took offense. It was, unfortunately, Brethin who landed himself in trouble.

Still not back to his full strength after the rigors of the sea voyage, and rushed by the fact that he was several feet closer to the horsemen, he blundered as he landed off-balance, into a large blond man wearing livery of green and orange and carrying a pike, who had also just jumped. The man tumbled on his side into the muck, losing his weapon, while Brethin recovered himself on one knee. Both froze in that position while the horsemen passed their heads in a blur of legs and colored trappings.

After they had passed, Brethin moved to help the pikeman up, once more at his by now habitual muttering. But the blond man, on his back in the mud, gaped up at the Scot and then kicked him in the stomach. Winded, Brethin doubled over, mouth open and gasping, while the stranger sprang to his feet, smashing his head into the other's jaw as he did so. Brethin catapulted backward, arms now wide, and narrowly missed having a hand crushed under a cart wheel as he fell on his back in the street.

The blond man stood above Brethin and yelled "Witch!" as he raised a foot to stave in the Scot's ribs. "He tried to spell me!" The driving foot slid sideways as Jamie, from behind, clubbed him in the side with two joined fists.

The blond man staggered several steps to the side while recovering his balance, which he did with the aid of a wall. Jamie had followed his movements, though, and swung a fist into the man's gut as he came to rest. It was now the pikeman's turn to double over, breathless, and as he did so Jamie met his descending nose with a bony knee.

Grunting, the other straightened up somewhat, and Jamie smashed into his ribs with the side of his right fist. His opponent was turned sideways by the blow, but lashed out wildly with a heavily calloused fist. Jamie easily evaded the looping swing, and heard the other shriek as his fist smashed into a corner of the stone building. Jamie stepped in closer and slammed into the man's jaw with his leather-shielded elbow; and the other dropped back into the gutters.

The fight was over in mere seconds. Few common foot soldiers could hope to stand up to a trained warrior—particularly one who had so often practiced on large brothers. Jamie had wanted to end the matter quickly, before steel could be drawn, which might have turned a mere brawl into a bloody melee that the watch would have had to notice.

Three other similarly dressed men were approaching quickly even as Jamie looked up; but they halted abruptly as Edward stepped forward, hands on the hilts of sword and dagger. He continued to watch them as they watched Jamie pull Brethin to his feet; and the others waited until they had moved away before tending to the blond man. Jamie's party moved off toward their inn, the *Cygne D'Or*.

They had stayed in that rather large inn near the waterfront since they had left the *Anne* two weeks earlier. Jamie knew he could have had a free passage with Master Cotter; but the *Anne* was bound for the Flemish ports, and there was nothing there now for Jamie's hopes. Besides, who could have dreamed it would be so hard to find an employer in war-ravaged France?

When it came to that, Brethin might well not be able to endure another voyage so quickly—for that matter, Jamie thought he would prefer to wait before taking to the sea again, also.

Brethin had been sorely battered, so at first their progress toward their inn was painfully slow; but in a while the man proved able to straighten up a bit and move faster. As they moved to the inn, Edward waved for the local barber-surgeon to come from his stall and tend Brethin with them, inside, as they drank.

After the man had investigated Brethin's person, opined that there were no broken bones, and suggested a few viands that he stay away from for some days, he joined them with an ale as his fee, and listened as Edward described the short fight to Will and Tom, who had been left to watch their gear.

"A good man with his hands or feet, our Lord Jamie!" Edward finished up, and turned to look sideways at the younger man. "This may all work out well for us still."

"But what did Brethin *do?*" Tom broke in; he was the youngest of the party, an inexperienced bowman but good enough in the butts, at least. He was the cousin of Will, who, a good deal older, was now trying to shush him.

"And that's the lesson to be learned by the young, Tom," Edward boomed over Will's quiet remonstrances. "In this world trouble will come whether you send for it or no. So it's best to be ready for it at all times."

"Did you say something to him, Brethin?" Jamie asked the other Scot, who now lounged rather stiffly on his pallet near them, nursing a very watered wine over bruised lips.

"No, Lord Jamie," the other replied softly, very earnest. "I was going to help him up but I'd said no word to him yet."

"I believe you," Jamie nodded. "But it seemed he thought not." He paused a moment, pursing his lips.

"Was there anything else you did that he might have seen?" Jamie leaned forward a little, discovered himself doing it even as he did so, and tried to return to his former stance unnoticed.

Brethin looked blank. But now his lips began to move, although the words were so soft as to be beyond understanding.

"What?" Jamie said.

Brethin's eyes focused on his.

"What is it, Lord Jamie?"

"You said something just now, did you not?"

"No, Lord Jamie—oh, unless you mean the little chant Hobie Yaro gave me. . . ." His voice trailed off.

After a moment he spoke again, very quietly.

"D'ye mean I was saying magic words—that I really was spelling him?" Now Brethin looked both aghast and angry, as if he felt he had been made a pawn in some game that even now he did not understand. But Jamie waved a hand before him that got his attention and quieted him down.

"No, I don't think that could be it," he said. "Hobie never used curses for his magic, and wouldn't do that to one of our people simply to strike some total stranger." He paused to think for a moment, conscious that the eyes of those about him were large and fearful. For a moment he savored the feeling of power, knowing he could use the fear and incredulity he sensed to his own purposes.

For that matter, he realized, he couldn't really envision how that would help his situation. He sighed and looked down idly at the tabletop. Hobie, though . . . Perhaps the valley had not been left so far behind as he had thought.

"Brethin," Jamie intoned carefully, trying to speak slowly

and calmly, "please try to say for me exactly what Hobie said to you, and exactly the words he gave you. Can you do that?"

"Aye, Lord Jamie . . . I think I can," Brethin said, looking puzzled but reassured by Jamie's demeanor. He looked down at the floor between his upraised knees as if the sight steadied his memory, and paused for a long moment.

"It was after my mother had asked him to read the signs for me," Brethin began. He stopped and shook his head lightly a moment, then continued. "He said he could na' do so, for he'd already breathed the smoke once that day."

Jamie nodded. For him, that had been.

"My mother was sore disappointed," Brethin went on, "but he could say nothing to help her, and so he left us. But in the morning as I went to the stables of your father the King, he—Hobie, I mean—met me there. And he told me he had for me a small charm—like a prayer—he said it was, and that I must say it often, as long as I am with you, Lord Jamie."

He stopped abruptly, as if he'd just noticed himself walking to the edge of a cliff. After a moment's silence Jamie nodded again and crooked a finger at him.

"And what are these words, Brethin?"

The man started, licked his lips, and then mumbled something Jamie didn't catch. To the side Edward squinted in Brethin's direction, cocking his head from over his cup and grimacing. The barber leaned forward.

"Speak a bit louder, Brethin, I didn't catch that," Jamie said. The other nodded and the soft, unintelligible sounds came again.

"By the Ox, man!" Jamie snarled, suddenly leaning forward, "can you speak no louder? Give me that first word again, loudly." This was ridiculous, he thought to himself. What could the man be afraid of? Could this be some elaborate game such as the archers played on each other from time to time?

He shook his head, instantly regretting that he did so because the watchers couldn't know what it referred to. But the idea made no sense. Brethin was not of that sort, and this was no topic for humor. The man had always had good sense for that sort of propriety. He looked up.

Brethin was gulping and stammering, voice not clear and loud. And behind him the barber had also risen, moving up behind the Scot to look over his shoulder at Jamie.

"My lord," the man said, "if I may be so bold as to speak in this affair . . ." The voice trailed off with the tone of a question. Jamie looked at him, curious, and then nodded.

"My lord, I believe this young man is unable to make clear to you the words he speaks because of the effect of the sorcery in them," the man continued. "In my healing trade I have a few small arts myself, and good enough to know magic words when I hear them."

"We knew they were magic words, surgeon," Edward threw in; but he subsided as Jamie threw a cold look in his direction.

"You mean that these words are something more than a small charm to protect the speaker, don't you?" Jamie asked the barber. Something in his tone caused the barber's eyes to widen and his hands to clasp before him.

"Yes, yes, I think so, my lord," he said hurriedly, and then hastened on, "that is, I can't be sure, my lord—" He paused, but as Jamie frowned resumed quickly.

"What I mean, my lord, is that the words themselves seem to be spelled, to protect them from the hearing of any except those intended to hear them. Your man cannot say them more loudly; the spell prevents him."

"You are suggesting," Jamie said, "that the words themselves are a secret, as if some sort of hidden message?"

"Err—aye, that might be," the man brightened, then frowned and shook his head. "No, that cannot be; there seems no way to ensure delivery to the correct ears."

"True, true." Jamie stopped to consider, but noticed Brethin still standing before him, stricken of face.

"Sit down, Brethin, and drink some of your wine. You have done no wrong here, and I believe little or none has been done to you." The man returned stiffly to the floor, his bruises showing again in his movements.

"Barber," Jamie said, "if I mistake not, you can hear the words more clearly than we, can you not?" He eyed the man sternly, trying for effect.

"Ah—yes, my lord, that may be." The man stumbled a bit over the words. "That is, I cannot be sure, but it seems so to these unpracticed ears . . ."

"So, can *you* tell me what the words say?"

"Err—no, my lord, I'm afraid not."

"And why not?"

"It appears the spell works almost as well upon me as upon

your man, here," the barber answered. "I know I can hear the words well, but I can take no meaning from them. And if I simply try to repeat for you the sounds, they slip from my mind before my tongue can grasp them." He shrugged.

"What do you think might be the purpose of these words?" Jamie asked.

The man shrugged again.

"Do you think them dangerous?" Jamie pressed.

"Who can say? The work of the great sorcerers is beyond the knowing of ordinary men," the barber replied.

Jamie nodded, hiding a certain bemusement. It was not his way to think of Hobie Yaro, so familiar and so knowing, as a "great sorcerer." The concept was unfamiliar, but he had already been learning that much of the life in his home valley had gone unseen by his supposedly sharp eyes.

"So, then." He looked up at the barber. "Who is the best sorcerer in this city, do you think?" He raised an eyebrow as the man crossed himself, hiding a smile.

"Without a doubt that would be the witch Brunewarts," he said, with no hint of a smile at the unwieldy name. "She can be found living in the stables behind the inn by the Eastern Gate—the inn whose sign has fallen." He crossed himself again. "She is said to be a most powerful person, and fiercely unforgiving of those who bother her without good reason."

Jamie nodded. "We will see her tomorrow, then," he added. He felt some pleasure in noting that Tom looked properly impressed and awed by his assertion; but the looks on the faces of Edward and Will made him less comfortable. The barber stole quietly away.

Morning dawned gray and wet, filled with a cold light rain that presaged the coming winter—or so Edward said. It was more certain that the rain was turning the customary mud into a sort of thin, dark soup, which made walking both harder and more dangerous for pedestrians—Jamie had decided not to risk the horses in such ground. And so it was mid-morning before they found themselves standing before the unnamed inn to which they had been directed.

The customary sign above the door was missing, it was true, but otherwise the place seemed to be in rather good shape. The inn itself seemed clean, solid, and well-made, a two-story stone structure that extended back some distance under a well-maintained thatched roof. Smoke curled into the mists from its several chimneys.

The ground before the building was of course muddy, but a series of flat stones was cleverly placed for easy footing in just these conditions, leading to the front door; another series of stones curved around the corner of the building, through a particularly deep puddle and out of sight.

Looking back at Edward and Brethin, who huddled together dourly behind him, Jamie got no response that he could make use of. He shrugged and started forward, following the stones that led to the door, then switching to the other path. He heard shuffling behind him, and the low drone of Brethin's incantation. Certainly, he thought, it didn't seem to be an incantation directed at getting the recipients dry ground to fight from, something warriors could always use.

Through an archway in the stone wall they came to the stable yard, a wide space that stretched between the inn itself and its stables. This area, too, was well-maintained and clean; apparently it was also little trafficked, for the ground, though wet, was still relatively unmarked by recent human feet, and therefore not yet churned into mud. It even seemed to support frequent clumps of vegetation.

He stopped. He was in the middle of someone's garden, he realized, and the stones had ended some steps back. He looked around him. There was neither human or animal figure visible, only the blank wall of the inn, with windows small and shuttered; and the wall of the stable, long and low, with low wooden doors, three of them, all closed.

"I wonder where they keep the horses," Jamie said conversationally as he heard the other two squelch up behind him.

"D'ye think an inn with a witch gets many customers?" Edward asked. He still looked sour, but the words were in an amused tone, and his eyes rested on the well-kept inn with meaning Jamie took quickly—someone certainly kept this inn in customers, or at least in money.

Brethin sneezed, and then grimaced and held his ribs on the left side in reaction.

Jamie grinned and then stepped forward to rap at the central of the three doors in the stables building. As his fingers approached the wood, he seemed to hear a faint popping sound; and he found himself sinking, quite rapidly, in a liquid mud that had suddenly appeared under his feet.

In a matter of short seconds he was sunk into the liquid to above his boot-tops—his boots being ankle high in the fashion of the day. And just as quickly, at that point, he stopped sinking. A curse from behind suggested that the same thing had befallen Edward and Brethin, but Jamie found he could not turn to look at them—the material around his feet now seemed to have rehardened; and he was locked into his own footsteps, quite literally.

"Lord Jamie," Brethin's voice came from behind him, "are you all right?"

"Aye, Brethin, that I am," he replied. Now he managed to look back over his shoulder at them both. "It seems we've sprung a trap set for uninvited guests. It seems to me a sensible precaution which we should have been expecting. But it is not going to be dangerous to us, unless we cannot account for ourselves satisfactorily when the witch returns to examine her trap."

"We hope," Edward muttered caustically under his breath. Jamie chose to ignore it.

"After all, Brethin, is it not the motto of my mother's family, that we 'Stand Our Ground'?" Jamie hid his smile until he had turned back to face the door in front of him. He reached out and rapped sharply on it, three times.

There was no response.

They stood in the stable yard for almost three hours before someone came.

When the door finally opened before him, Jamie was more than a little startled to see in front of him a small, blonde woman. Jamie's imagination, having had plenty of time to work with the name "Brunewarts," was not prepared to deal with someone who looked to be a petite, motherly forty-year-old. Jamie's mind, though, did notice that the slate-gray eyes were most cool and calm as they regarded him. He had no illusions as to whom he might be facing.

"What is it you gentlemen wish?" the woman enquired quietly.

"We crave your pardon, lady." Jamie had to smile at the absurd courtliness of the conversation; but he appreciated fully that the smile added to the charm with which he made his bow, awkward though it was with frozen feet. "We find ourselves with a problem that demands the attention of the greatest of mages," he went on. "We were informed that in this area you were the most puissant about; and so we came to beg your indulgence."

He bowed again, trying to remember more of the great lines he had heard from various wandering troubadours.

"Indeed," the woman murmured; and Jamie found himself telling her of the words Hobie Yaro had given to Brethin and his curiosity concerning them. Later Jamie pondered whether he had actually told the story of his own free will. If not, it had been a most subtle spell that had been used on him. In any case, he concluded, it mattered little, for he had not planned to hide the story anyway.

"Come in, then," the woman said. She turned, and vanished into the darkness behind the doorway. For a moment Jamie stared after her; then he found that his feet were once more free. He stirred them in their sockets in the now solid ground, and then pulled them loose and up, one at a time. The dry soil caked, then broke off and powdered as it fell from about his short boots. A fine dust remained, no doubt sifted into his clothing; but one was used to living with more dirt than that in any case. He looked down at the holes his feet had left, with their mounds of upheaved earth about them; then he stretched some of the kinks from his weary legs. He could hear Edward and Brethin also moving about, behind him, but he did not look back. It came to him that Edward had been thoroughly silent since the witch appeared on the scene; but a grin would not be appreciated by Squire Pennworthy at this time. Over an ale this evening, perhaps.

He stepped into the doorway where the witch had vanished, and stopped, more than a little surprised by what he saw. The interior of the vast stable seemed to contain no more than a single, moderate-sized room. The ceiling was high and airy, and a plentitude of windows let in the light to stream cheerily down upon a polished wooden floor and a hearth that was currently without a fire. Here the rain was banished.

"Sit down," the witch's voice came from behind him, "and bring your men in too."

She stepped into his view from behind an iron construction that seemed to have been built over a fire, upon which water was boiling in a round pot. She moved over toward the largest window, and he turned to wave Edward and Brethin forward.

Seated at one end of a bench in front of the window the witch was facing, Jamie bade Brethin, who squatted on the floor to his left side, repeat the words he'd gotten from Hobie Yaro. Again, Jamie found them an unintelligible murmuring; but the blonde woman nodded thoughtfully without comment, merely taking another sip from the brew she had infused in the boiling water. There was a dead silence in the room.

Jamie's attention wandered, and his eyes began to rove idly about the room, picking out the details of the wooden beams, of the whited stones, of the cloth-work scattered all about on floors and tables and hanging from walls. Cooking implements and a variety of dried foods hung from the beams across the space about their heads, and a fly droned in the sunlight from the many windows. A sense of peace settled about him, and he felt himself relaxing, even getting sleepy. . . .

Into the pool of light on the floor before him the witch stepped, gown glowing, white with a pale blue design, in the sun. Her blonde hair shone like the best of spun flax, looking at once soft and strong enough to take the caresses of sword-worn hands—and she stepped closer to him, eyes widening before him, no longer slate-gray, but warmly violet. Her hands reached for his, and he stood.

It seemed to take forever to stir his body into motion, and to rise; and at the same time he seemed to be looking down at her face so abruptly that it made him dizzy with the transition. Now, this close to her, he saw that she was much younger than she had seemed, her skin creamy and white as if untouched by sun's rays. Her scent, some rich and musky fragrance he had never encountered before, rose to his nostrils as her lips rose toward his. . . .

As their lips pressed, trading subtle pressures in response to unknown signals, he could hear her soft breathing; with eyes closed he listened to it, hearing it quicken, as did his own, as the kiss went on. And suddenly he realized that he was hearing a third sound, the respirations of another person in the silent room. And even as he listened, that sound slowed, slowed—and stopped.

His eyes opened, looking down on the witch; her own eyes were now coming open. He looked around, seeing no one else except Edward and Brethin. Edward was down at the far end of the bench, too far away for his breath to be heard. He seemed to be asleep. But still on the floor nearby was Brethin, also apparently asleep—but he was not breathing at all!

With a yell aimed at rousing Edward, Jamie reached down to shake Brethin's shoulder. Edward did not move, but Brethin fell over sideways, to lie curled on the wood. Jamie shook him, and then reached angrily for his sword.

"Wait." It was the voice of the witch, of the blonde woman, who still stood before him, close and fragrant. Her head was tilted back as she looked up at him, and his arm

slowed as he pulled at his weapon. But he got it out of its
sheath, and awkwardly held it to the side at her neck's level—
she was really too close for this, he thought confusedly.

"They are not hurt," she said now, "and you will not be.
Be at ease, for the spell is broken now and they will awaken
soon." She backed away from him a step, then another. Then
she turned and walked around behind an arras that hung on
what appeared to be an outer wall, and she was gone.

Behind and below him he heard a sneeze from Brethin; and
to the side Edward yawned noisily and grumbled something
about a drink. Feeling foolish, as if there were people watching
him somewhere he could not see, Jamie returned his sword to
its scabbard and sat down. Silence reigned in the room while
his mind grappled with the memories it carried. His body still
carried a reminder of the reality it had seen; he wondered what
might not have happened.

Presently the door through which they had entered swung
open almost noiselessly, and a serving maid, probably from the
inn, appeared. She carried a tray with a large pitcher, three cups,
and both meat and cheese. She deposited them on the table near
the hearth and left without a word, though she smiled shyly
when Edward asked her name.

All of them found themselves to be famished, and they fell
to with speed. When the first edge of appetite was sated, the
witch appeared again; but she seated herself on a bolster beside
a window nearby—odd, thought Jamie; the sun seemed to be
coming in on all sides!—and quietly did a little needlework as
they finished eating.

"What Hobie Yaro did to your companion," she began
without preamble as Jamie finished his last bit of cheese, "was
of no danger to him, and may turn out to be of great benefit to
you all." She now rose and paced forward a few steps, the
stones of two rings on her right hand flashing in the last sun as
she moved into the shadow. Jamie averted his head and his
gaze from the glistening, a chill spreading down his back.
Probably it was no danger, but those old tales. . . .

The woman looked at him a moment longer, and then turned
away, her face unreadable.

"The words are a message," she went on after a moment,
"and can only be understood by certain ears. I have understood
them, but I will not say to you what message is passed. But
you need not fear them." She paused, and her eyes settled

once more on Jamie; they were again slate-gray and unreadable. In another moment she went on.

"Go to the inn outside the keep at the town called Pont l'Archveque," she said. "One there will take you to the Captal de Buch; you may make of the opportunity what you will."

Jamie flushed at the words.

When he looked up the woman was waving them toward the door by which they had entered. There seemed nothing for it but to leave.

Outside the stable yard, it was raining again.

Chapter Five

W‌HEN J‌AMIE A‌WOKE in the gray predawn the wind, which seemed an eternal feature of the landscape of the plain here beside the Aisne, had turned chill. It was not cold enough to cause him to shiver—a man from the highlands was used to far worse—but he suspected he would hear grumbling among the thin-blooded southerners who made up over half of his wing.

As he stumbled through the dying night toward the river, he heard the whip-crack sound of one of the siege engines, followed closely by the whoosh that was its cargo being delivered. Probably the engine called *Robin Hood*, he thought, grinning; its crewmen from the west of England were always eager to add to their reputations.

He was almost at the river when another engine sounded, this at almost the moment he stumbled on something in his path. That was unusual, and caused him to curse faintly; most loose stones had long ago been removed from this, a long-used encampment.

Then again, it might be something the besieged Burgundians had thrown out overnight by one of their own casting engines. It might even be the head of one of those sappers who had been captured yesterday when the rain had collapsed the mine Buckingham had ordered them to drive under the city wall.

At the river's edge he doffed his cloak and knelt to the water, first checking upriver to see if anyone else might be fouling his water. Between the mist and the darkness it was hard to see whether anyone was close; but then, he couldn't hear anyone either. He had a drink and then began to wash a little, thinking about today's work.

The chill certainly meant that winter was well on its way; and so the plans for today's attack would almost certainly go forward unchanged. To delay further was to risk attacking over the snow, and that was anathema for horsemen.

What would this be, his eighth or ninth fight since joining the army of the kingdom of France and England? And, truth to tell, none of them had been the sort of battle he'd heard of, grand heroic melees between the steel-jacketed pillars of chivalry.

He'd been given a place, with his lance, in the free company led by the Chevalier de Bennault—Raoul. And he thought he'd acquitted himself well, learned his trade and what was expected of him. But he had never had an opportunity to become a hero, nor an opportunity to become rich. It was only a dirty, hot—sometimes cold—and usually very boring sort of work. Gods, it was almost a trade!

Wrapping himself in the dark blue cloak, he trudged back toward the camp. The eastern sky was lighter now, and more sound could be heard from the area of the tents. There were the sounds of horses, and of metal being prepared for use; and under it came the sound of a mass being quickly sung. There seemed no talking yet, but soon there would be, with the subliminal bass grumble that came before every fight, unless it was a surprise. He found that his steps had quickened, and that his blood, moving faster as a consequence, had warmed and loosened him.

He slung the edge of the cloak back over his right shoulder, freeing his sword arm and his stride. Maybe this would be the day. . . .

"Lord Jamie," Brethin greeted him as he reached the tent they all shared, "I'm afraid you'll have to break your fast while riding this day. Sir Henry has sent word that he wishes to talk to each knight and squire before the sun parts with the horizon. Master Pennworthy has already gone to his quarters, so as to have time to discuss the strategy of the day's plans."

"Very good, Brethin," Jamie responded, unable to resist a grin that broke out on his face now. "Have you and the others made all your preparations?"

"Aye, that we have."

"Very well, then, give me something to chew as we go and we'll leave right now. Have Tom bring my armor and I'll put it on when I have an idea what's needed." He moved off with a portion of fowl and a wineskin, toward the tent that served as headquarters of Sir Henry Bowler, his wing commander. Behind him he could hear Will loading the metal upon young Tom, while cursing him fondly for some probably imagined sin.

Sir Henry stepped out as Jamie threw his scraps to the hounds that were everywhere in the camp. The man was short but very broad, with a barrel chest that turned the thoughts of the irreverent to corpulence. His face was habitually flushed and greasy, and long luxuriant mustaches curled down from the sides of his mouth. He affected the most colorful of clothing and the richest of furs, and his voice was a jovial roar that could be heard for half the camp in simple conversation. For all that, though, he was known as a hard man to bring down in a fight, and Jamie was pretty sure that the little pig-like eyes missed very little indeed.

"Jamie," the deep voice roared in his very ear. "I was about to look for you. Come sit with me and break your fast once more, eh? At least a little wine?" He had already virtually pulled Jamie by the shoulder into the great tent.

It was smoky inside, a sign that Sir Henry had been up and about for some hours, using the light. They perched on little camp stools while Sir Henry roared for wine, which appeared very swiftly. There was a relative silence for a moment or two—relative, because Sir Henry tended to be a noisy eater and drinker. In a moment he put aside his cup, belched lightly, and smiled at the younger man.

"Jamie, my lad, you are a picture that makes the heart of a commander swell with pride. Young, strong, and smart too—with an army of men like you, any king would be well served." Jamie cocked an eye over his cup of watered wine, but said nothing. He thought about wiping smoke from his right eye, but decided not to, since his fingers were still greasy. He took a moment to wipe those fingers on his tunic and then rub them gently in his wine. Sir Henry had continued speaking.

"Do you know what day this is, Jamie?" Sir Henry seldom waited for the answers to his questions, even if Jamie had known them.

"Today is the Feast Day of St. Martin of Tours," the jovial man continued, and paused to beam at the young Scot. "Ah, but a bold warrior, and a young one, like yourself, may well not recognize that name; so I'll tell you why it's important, Jamie." He leaned forward on his stool.

"St. Martin of Tours was a chevalier, a horseman, Jamie—yes, just as we are! And he was in the Roman army here in

France—perhaps he sat once on this very spot, who can tell?"
He waggled a fat finger before Jamie's face.

"This is a day for the horsemen, Jamie, mark my words!
The saint himself will be with us. Mark my words well, for
you'll see—well, listen to this." And he proceeded to outline
the plan for the day's actions.

Since the mine had failed yesterday, today would see an
attempt to take the city before them by a frontal assault. That
would be done by other forces and was no concern of theirs, of
course. But they would be standing by, ready to intervene in
the event of a sortie from the city against the flank of the
assaulting party.

"This will require discipline, Jamie, for we'll have to sit for
hours on our steeds, ready to charge but perhaps never charging at all—d'ye think ye can do that, lad?"

Jamie looked at him coolly, knowing why he was being
teased but playing the game.

"And have I ever failed you, Sir Henry?" he pretended
offense and was swiftly met by the other man's posture of
mortification—Sir Henry was a dramatist at heart.

"Young Jamie," he pleaded, "how can you forgive my
foolish words? It is that my poor mind fails to instruct the
tongue in what it should say." He beat his breast, a favorite
gesture.

"Here I be," he moaned, "lost in a foreign land, friendless,
and I grievously insult the most dependable and courageous
friend I have!" He moaned again, and then paused to take
another drink.

"It is only, Jamie," he continued, now on one knee and
looking up, "that I need your level head and firm control so
very much. These hot-blooded southern knights of ours may be
the most gallant of fighters"—he looked about cautiously—
"but they tend to get carried away and forget their orders, and
so they end up piled in heaps on the field." He shuddered and
suddenly turned very serious.

"That is, in fact, what I need from you, Jamie. I know that
you're young, and you'd like a chance to charge off and do
brave deeds—and I'll wager you'd *do* them, too!" He paused,
and then sat back on his stool, watching Jamie's face all the
while.

"Anyway," he said in a half-sigh after another moment,
"there's no help for it. Those of us who don't lose our heads in
our mad desire to go charging into the arrows and pikes—we

have to try to keep the rest of our idiot fellows alive, in case they might be needed.'' He stopped, and there was silence in the dim, smoky space.

Jamie stood and walked toward the entrance. He knew no answer would be needed. But as he went, for the first time Sir Henry did something uncharacteristic.

''Do you know,'' he said, ''that St. Martin of Tours tried to retire from the army, and they accused him of cowardice? So he offered to go into the front line with no armor at all, and only peace prevented that. My brother, the abbot, told me all about that, once.'' He stopped and sighed again. ''And all the rest of his life people kept asking him to do things, like be a bishop, and they wouldn't let him refuse.''

Sir Henry was yelling for his page as Jamie left the tent.

Outside, the sun had been rapidly heating up the day, and Jamie doffed his cloak and threw it across the outstretched arms of Brethin, who had to function as both page and valet. Brethin folded it and gave it to Tom, who turned to the sumpter and tucked it into one of her saddlebags.

When Brethin turned his gaze back to his lord, he saw that Jamie had paced off a little distance.

In the open space to the side of Sir Henry's tent, Jamie stood and watched the town they had been besieging all these weeks. The place was tiny and perched uneasily atop a small knoll above the river. Its brown stone walls rose from foundations that had been placed directly above a moat. It looked strong and hard to get at, the way a tortoise must look to the hungriest of dogs. . . .

From this position he could watch the figures that were men at arms, straggling across the plain toward the walls. He envisioned riding across the open area to charge the wall with his lance, or to ride up to it and smite mightily with his sword. . . . Sir Henry was right, of course; there was no place in this kind of war for the men in iron on horses.

''My armor, Brethin,'' he said in the direction of the town; and turned to see that his companion had it all laid out and ready for him.

It was a long process, getting into his armor. He had one of the better equipments in the army, it seemed, if a wee bit old-fashioned. But it was slow and tedious work to put it on. Once the hauberk—the leather tunic bearing interlocking mail circles—was draped about him, much time had to be spent in locking about him the various plaques—the steel sheaths that independently covered much of his trunk and limbs. In fact, he could not have done it all by himself without considerable strain and much expenditure of time.

As Jamie pulled on his right gauntlet, Edward rode up leading Jamie's palfrey. He already had Jamie's helm, shield, and lance with him about his saddle, as was his duty. Brethin moved off to see to his own courser, as well as return with Jamie's destrier, or war-horse.

"Good morning, my lord," Edward intoned cheerfully. He always, Jamie had noticed, sounded depressingly like a priest intoning a joyful mass, as they prepared for any battle.

"Good morn, Edward," Jamie said, preserving the courtesies. "Have you learned anything of use this day?"

"Possibly," the other said. He moved forward a bit to a position from which they could both see the wall of the town and the plain below them. Brethin came up with the massive destrier, tall and heavy-boned for the job of carrying a man in full armor and meeting the shock of head-on contact with other, equally heavy horses. Jamie mounted his palfrey and joined Edward as the other pointed out relevant features of the place.

"Our forces will move across that plain—in fact, they already are," he said. "The siege engines are moving forward, too, although that's much harder to see as yet. But the moat has been filled and part of the wall on this side has been undermined. The men will be trying to bring up the engines at the same time the sappers try to bring down part of the wall. It should work at least well enough to frighten the Burgundians into coming out from their walls, which is where we come in." He pointed out a party of horsemen that was even now circling wide around the town.

"That party, led by the banner of the Chevalier himself, will let itself be seen far out of position. Our own group, obviously considerably smaller in numbers, will station itself as a covering force to the assault." He paused and glanced at Jamie, who had grasped the idea and knew what must follow.

"And the Burgundians can count, of course," he said. "They'll know how far they outnumber us locally, and they will come out to deal us, as well as the men on foot, a strong blow." He looked back at Edward, beginning to be excited, and found his look met by the familiar grin.

"I take it," Jamie went on, forcing his voice lower and

ducking his head into his shoulders, "that the party of the Chevalier is not as strong as it appears?"

"That's right," Edward said, nodding. "Your head is strong as ever, my lord. The Chevalier's page leads his master's destrier there, accompanied by a host of valets and, just for protection, a number of the other knights." He grinned again. "I think they haven't been told the plan."

"And so the Burgundians will come out, and those of us in the known party will have to try and delay them until the hidden party may come up," Jamie carried on with his surmises. He looked up at the pale blue sky with its thin wispy cloud cover, and realized that he was smiling eagerly. His face once more felt hot and flushed, and his breath came in short, rapid pulses. This would not do, he told himself, forcing his head down and closing his eyes.

From behind the cooler darkness of his lids, while he watched the odd patches of color he spoke to Edward once again.

"That is what Sir Henry meant, then, when he spoke to me. Our role will provide much opportunity for each knight to show an individual heroism, challenging the Burgundian knights to single combats." He paused and sighed.

"And if we do that, the few of us will be overwhelmed and the day lost before the Chevalier can arrive. Is that it?" He opened his eyes and looked into Edward's. "Is that it?"

"Yes," the other nodded, more somber now. "Our party must stand together, like arrows in a quiver."

"No heroes. And no ransoms for us," Jamie said. "Noise and danger and death. Glory exists not."

"Yet this is the road to victory," Edward said, "and on that road bannerless knights may become bannerets—and the favor of the victorious king is assuredly worth more . . ."

Brethin rode up, leading the fresh war-horse that Jamie would switch to as battle neared. He was followed by Will and Tom, each also mounted and armed, on light, fast horses, though only lightly armored in boiled leather and iron caps.

Together they rode, slowly and carefully, through the camp and down to the plain, joining in a defile at its near edge the remainder of the party led by Sir Henry. When they had formed, he led them across the rolling terrain to a small hillock from which they would be able to command a view of both the city's gates and much of the assaulting party. This was about where they would be expected to place themselves. On arrival

there the archers separated themselves, dismounted, and set up
their anti-cavalry stakes, behind which they aligned themselves
ready for their work. Brethin had found them a spot of shade
under some beech trees; and he, with Edward, stayed by Jamie
on his flanks. They all waited, knowing that the Burgundians
would let their attackers bake in the hot sun for some time
before offering action.

Down before them the town stood like a toy that had been
made for a small prince. The great wooden engines crept toward it, pushed by the drably clad figures that were engineers
or villeins. Other small figures, more colorfully garbed and
with bits of steel armor that glinted the sun off their persons,
moved ahead of and around the great machines. They herded
other drab figures that carried large bundles of sticks towards
the moat, which itself could now be seen only as a rough,
uneven scar in the sere earth.

From the walls stones and arrows could be seen pelting
down toward the figures that were so exposed on the plain, and
many of them dropped. Others simply dropped whatever they
were carrying and turned back from the town. It could not be
seen what had happened to these latter, for they vanished into
the folds of ground around the edge of the plain. But it could
be noted that mounted figures patrolled those areas, with
swords out.

The figures on the plain seemed as numerous as ever,
though; and now they seemed to be concentrating themselves
behind the shields formed by the great engines, or behind the
large wicker shields borne by some of their number. They were
closer to the wall.

Now for the first time Jamie noticed that more figures were
busy at the visible ends of the long, plank-roofed trenches that
had been cut across the plain toward the town. Most of them
were, of course, flush with the earth and thus hard to see, but
now it seemed that the men in the besieged town had begun to
concentrate their fire upon them, raining down rocks and hot
pitch. But at the farther end the trenches had reached the moat,
and shielded activity probed at the foot of the wall to Jamie's
right.

Ladders were near the wall now, he saw; and he was
abruptly aware that several hours had passed while he sat
watching the spectacle before him. He knew this because
Brethin had reached forward to pluck at his arm and suggest
that he have a drink from the waterskin. Jamie did so and

passed it back to Edward, never removing his eyes from the
scene before him.

Wagons had rolled onto the ramp that led to the gate itself;
one had been hit by a large stone and now hung over one edge,
but the other was waiting at the lip as engineers tried to complete a substitute for the drawbridge that was now raised into
the castle wall. A giant grapple mounted on the ramparts was
reaching down in an effort to disrupt the activity below. And in
that instant the drawbridge slammed down into the makeshift
structure below.

Sir Henry bellowed something unintelligible, but no one
needed to be told what to do. Like the other knights, Jamie
dismounted from his palfrey and strode heavily in his armor,
trying to be calm, toward the destrier, the great gray horse that
Brethin now held by the bit. Edward handed Jamie up, and he
settled himself into the massive high saddle that held him in
place like a vast socket. Brethin moved about after handing
him up the reins, taking care to plant Jamie's feet firmly in
their stirrups, and after that checking the harness and rearrang-
ing the folds of cloth that, in Jamie's colors of red and black,
draped the great beast almost to ground level.

"Sir Henry wants you two men over from him, on his
right." Jamie looked down at the voice, to see Edward there,
preparing to hand up his helm. Jamie nodded without saying
anything and took the helm that was handed up to him. It
slipped on over his hauberk, its long tail, in the German style,
protecting his neck. For the moment he kept the visor up,
while he transferred the reins to his right hand and reached
with his left hand for a grip on his shield, which was now
handed up to him.

That settled firmly in place, he finally took the great lance
that was handed up to him. The powerful horse he now rode
was impatient and eager to be off and running; he could not
fault the animal for that—he felt much the same. And, looking
about, he was sure the same reckless desire for action rode the
pulses of those knights about him. But he noted that Sir Henry
was moving about, having quiet words with several of the
mounted men. And the more experienced squires, in some
cases older and more experienced than their knights, seemed to
be exerting a restraining influence where they could as well.

Jamie looked back for Edward and saw that he had moved
off a few paces, sitting patiently in the saddle of his own
horse while Brethin attended to some small detail of his ar-

mor—yes, he was trying to fasten the breteche, the movable nose-covering of his basinet, his conical helmet. Edward, Jamie had noted, had had some trouble with the latch of that piece of equipment before. Edward's armor was of an older style than Jamie's, mostly leather reinforced with metal at strategic spots, except for the hauberk itself, which covered his head and shoulders like a hood down to chest level.

There, they had it. Edward gathered the reins of his horse and took his position on Jamie's right flank as the latter wheeled his charger into the line that was now forming up from the guide of Sir Henry's shoulders. Jamie could hear Brethin cursing his own animal in the rear; the beast was nervous and not yet properly responsive to knee signals—which probably could not be expected from a newly trained animal. Brethin's previous mount had been killed several months before by an arrow.

The dust raised by their movements was obscuring their view of the field, when Jamie returned his attention to the area ahead of them. But it settled, and he was soon able to see that the gates of the city had opened. A melee appeared to be taking place around the great wagon that blocked the ramp from the gate to the level of the plain; details could not be seen, but abruptly the wagon moved several feet backward, even as Sir Henry rode out in front of the line of men he commanded, stopped several paces in front of them and turned to address them. He was certainly the one with the voice to do it, Jamie thought irreverently.

Sir Henry did not use that voice this time, though; he only sat his horse and stared at the line of knights before him, eyes buried in the pool of shadow under the raised visor of his basinet. A preternatural silence seemed to descend upon their part of the field, and Jamie abruptly shivered.

The phenomenon disturbed him in a way he could not understand, and he felt his eyes shy away when Sir Henry's swept down the line of knights toward him. He fingered a strap of the armor on his left arm, then realized what he was doing and looked up. Sir Henry had swung his horse around again and was watching the Burgundians, who had now succeeded in pushing the wagon off the ramp and were rushing down it, almost to its bottom. Jamie felt his face flush and cursed. For a brief moment he despised himself totally.

Then Sir Henry raised his sword and looked back at the line of knights behind him.

"Hold your place," he roared at them; and began to move forward toward the town.

He kept his horse at a walk for the first hundred yards, and the line of knights, followed by their squires and other auxiliaries, held its formation while slowly drifting forward on their leader to enclose him again within their ranks.

A line of the Burgundians—all horsemen—had peeled off from their main body, to act as a screening force while the main body itself slaughtered the attackers on foot around the angle of the wall. Those men had been warned and could be seen from this position dropping into protective formation—some ran—or gathering in clumps, raising hedges of spear points. Farther back, a small group of archers placed themselves.

"When I give the word," Sir Henry yelled, as their pace began to pick up speed, "cut through these men and turn for the gate. Form on me there."

Jamie understood the intent—they were hoping to raise a wall with their own bodies to prevent the Burgundians from returning to the shelter of their town's walls when the Chevalier's men appeared from wherever they were hidden.

They were at a canter now, and the man on Jamie's right was edging forward, as if hoping to be the first to make contact with the enemy—stoneheads who had swallowed too many of the tales of the troubadours always seemed to believe that heroism lay first and foremost in that. Jamie leaned forward and placed the flat of his sword across the other's chest. The man seemed not to notice, so Jamie tried it again, but with a good deal more vigor. The hound-skulled helm turned toward him, and the sword in the off-hand was raised into the air. But then the head nodded, and the sword came back down. In a few moments the man was back in the line.

Their movement was still picking up speed, and now Jamie swept his visor down across his face. He was the last in the line to do so. That was his habit, for he always hated to cut off his visibility with the protecting metal. He could see the Burgundians spreading out across their path now, only fifty yards away, colorful in their trappings, metal gleaming in the sun. He admired the sight of them; they shone like the purest knights of the stories.

His attention was riveted totally on them now, and his eyes picked out every detail of the scene before him. Even at this distance he seemed to know which man would front him. He

watched that man and did not notice, except off in a far corner
of his mind that he was not listening to, that he was no longer
hearing the thundering of the great hooves that carried the iron
men together.

Eyes always forward, he settled himself in his saddle, seeking to plant himself firmly in it. He drove his feet down and
back into the stirrups, locking his knees so as to make himself
lean forward slightly; and even as he did so his lance came
down, its pennon whipping, and its butt settled under his right
arm. The man before him had done the same, like an image in
some great mirror; and he seemed to be virtually leaping,
a-horseback, across the field toward the young Scot. The wind
whipped among the folds of the blue—a bright, shocking
blue—trappings that covered the man's destrier, and the eyes
of the horse could be seen flashing from within them. Behind
the horse's head the man's shield was planted, well-settled,
covering almost all the target; and the lance aimed out from
behind like a knife reaching for Jamie's throat. In that same
instant Jamie saw the great round helm of the man in front of
him lean forward, and the whole machine that was his enemy
seemed to leap at him.

Jamie saw that and leaned sideways without taking the time
to think about it, twisting his shield slightly so that it took the
man's lance-point and deflected it to the left without damage.
Jamie did not watch it. His eyes were on his own point, which
seemed to go where he willed it without having to trouble with
the intermediaries of arm or hand or haft. And that point
lowered in the instant after the other ducked his head, striking
the bottom of the man's shield and smashing it back and up,
allowing the point to glance off the saddle and smash the blue-
tunicked man in the left hip.

Possibly the man screamed; Jamie never knew, for the shock
of the collision rocked him back in his saddle, and for an
instant his view from the inside of his helm was cut off. He
almost lost his grip on his lance as it caught in something,
dipped and twisted like a large, heavy live thing; but then it
slipped from and recoiled upward, and he could see again, and
was by his enemy among the Burgundian second rank. He slid
under the badly aimed lance of a young squire; and his destrier,
a fierce and well-trained fighter himself, charged into the
other's horse, its greater weight setting the other animal back
on its heels. The squire bounced forward in his saddle, and
Jamie reached forward to grab him by the shoulder and pull

him from his perch. The lad hit the ground and curled up, trying to cover himself as much as possible from the hooves striking the ground about him.

Jamie had already shifted his attention back to his right side, but Edward seemed to have come through the front rank just behind him and was trading blows with a lightly armored older man on a brown horse. Jamie drew his sword and moved back to his left, guiding his war-horse with virtually unconscious knee movements while his eyes sought targets and his hands busied themselves with sword and shield.

Farther to his left he could see that Sir Henry had also succeeded in breaking into the rear ranks of the Burgundians; but apparently both of the men who had been between them had failed to do so. However, he recognized near him the figure of Etienne le Roux, an older man who was squire to the young Provençal knight Gilbert de Valery. Le Roux was possibly the most experienced man in their party, except perhaps for Sir Henry himself; and with him there Sir Henry was well-sided. Jamie supposed his presence there meant that young de Valery was down.

Jamie checked the impulse to rein his horse around and charge back into the affray from which he had just emerged. That was just the sort of error that Sir Henry had many times warned them not to do. Jamie threw a glance over his shoulder to see how his back side was, and saw that Brethin too had made it through the press of bodies safely. Brethin now circled his horse, which seemed to have left its nervous disposition behind, directly behind his master, the coustille of his headgear raised while his eyes searched for approaching danger. Jamie noted also that the slim, daggerlike sword Brethin held was bloody, and that under the kettle hat the slim dour face seemed to be grinning.

Jamie looked back to his front. Edward's opponent had fallen from his horse. While the animal blocked others of the foe from reaching him, Edward tilted his head to right and left, plainly peering through his visor, and Jamie knew that the other would be looking for his knight. Jamie waved his sword and kneed his horse forward to his squire's side.

The men before them seemed to melt away, and as they swept past the rearmost ranks of the Burgundians, Jamie led those about him in a left oblique turn. Together they rounded behind their enemy, who, very conscious of strange swords to their rear, began to peel away from the front of their enemy.

The way now cleared for most of Sir Henry's party to move forward and to the side, and this they did, Jamie in the lead and Sir Henry close behind.

Well before their party reached the foot of the ramp that was the only access to the gates, missiles from within had begun to fall about them. Behind them a pursuit was forming, and the seventeen of them who had come to the ramp seemed in deadly peril indeed.

"Up!" Sir Henry bellowed. "Ride up the ramp—hold, there! Squires and others first, then the knights!"

Jamie checked his first reaction of disbelief at this command, which not only seemed to denigrate the status of the knights, but seemed to be moving them all into even greater danger from the town's missiles, the arrows and rocks that fell constantly about them now. He saw about him that the other knights were shocked and angered by the orders, too. He edged his horse near to the closest of them, got his attention, and raised his visor. The other man did the same, revealing brown eyes in a tanned face that was set in an angry expression.

"Brother, now we will be heroes!" Jamie cried loudly; and the other man, startled, paused before venting his anger. From nearby others turned their heads, and Jamie spoke quickly before he could lose his audience.

"Sir Henry," Jamie yelled then, "tell them your plan and how we fit in!" The heads turned from him in the direction of the portly knight, who at that moment turned from saying something to the squire Etienne le Roux. He looked at them, at Jamie, and then back down the ramp a few paces. But he halted his excited charger at a level that still kept him well above their heads, for the knights had all stayed on the level ground. They were now forced to look up at him and listen.

"The others will go up first," he boomed out, "and when halfway up the ramp will stop and turn. The knights—you—will follow behind them, and then turn. And so we shall all face the enemy from a position above them, and have a running start at them as they come to us."

He paused, looking down at them and smoothing his mustaches, then smiled roguishly.

"The Burgundians will be coming for us," he said, and every one of them could hear him. "We must hold here, and then our fellows can take them—in fact, there appears the Chevalier now!" He gestured with his head only, and they all turned to see the cloud of dust that mushroomed above the nearer swale.

"The Burgundians will see, too," he yelled, recapturing their attention, "and it may well be that none of us will live in this. Greet the Lord God and prepare to die!"

Amid the cheers that several of the knights insisted on venting, Sir Henry and Jamie managed to get everyone up into his place. Above, Jamie saw even as he wrestled to turn his great horse on the small ramp, the wall of the town was being lined by onlookers, and the showers of arrows and rock had ended abruptly.

Is it that they prefer to watch a more colorful show? Jamie wondered; *or is it that they admire our chivalry and wish to be fair?* He shook his head, trying to dislodge a bead of perspiration that had crept into his left eye, stinging there. As he did so he saw that a small party of the squires, led by le Roux, had gone up the ramp to wrestle the great wagon back into its position blocking the route. And now they were piling within it a variety of the detritus that lay in the area—yes, and they were setting it afire! *O clever man!* Jamie thought, *whoever it was who thought of that!*

He shook his head again. He hoped it was chivalry that kept the arrows from them, and that it lasted.

A call from Sir Henry alerted him, and he just had time to bring his head back around, take a quick view of the field below them, and lower his visor; then with Sir Henry's shout of "St. Martin and France!" they pushed off down the ramp.

With the hard, dirt-crusted stone under them, their ride seemed unusually hard and thunderous. Jamie felt crowded, penned in on both sides by the close ranks of the knights about him; and ahead of him he could see the group of Burgundian knights that would reach them first. They had formed a line wider than the width of the ramp, and now had to slow and jockey for position as they neared its floor, lest some of them fall from it, or even not be able to ascend at all.

Jamie settled his lance under his arm once more—he didn't even remember anyone handing it to him, but someone, perhaps Brethin, must have done so. He picked a figure from the mass that seemed to be leaping up toward him and settled himself for the shock of collision; and *now* they hit!

Two closely packed masses of flesh and metal collided, all at virtually the same instant, and the shock of each encounter was transmitted through the closely packed bodies to every other one. The din was enormous, a great roar that Jamie, this time, remained fully conscious of, even as his opponent's lance glanced from his shield and into his helm.

Jamie did not feel his own lance twisting sideways as it hit, which he supposed meant a solid, piercing hit. But it was ripped from his grasp immediately thereafter. He, however, did not see that, for the point of his enemy's lance had caught in some crevice of his helm briefly before disengaging, twisting both helm and head and leaving his helm turned from its proper position. He was left blind.

Unable to locate his viewing slot, he ducked his head and tried to hide himself behind the cover of his shield, while his right arm, still numb from the shock it had taken when the lance was ripped away, rose and pawed at the helm, trying to right it. In that position he found himself violently swayed this way and that, and the closely packed bodies about him fell and fought, screamed and died, each jostling for the room it needed to do so.

There was a fierce shock transmitted through his shield, and then a blow that clanged at the top of his head, which probably projected from the top of the shield. But now his eyes caught a glimpse of light, and he located his visor again. He shoved at it, trying to raise it so that he could see, while his horse screamed and reared, probably attacking someone in front of him. He pushed savagely with his right hand, ineffective in its gauntlet; then raised his head and lowered it sharply again, banging it fiercely into the rim of his shield.

Ah! And now he could see again. He raised his head to look about him even as his right hand fell to the hilt of his sword and began to draw it. He seemed to be packed in the midst of a jam of bodies, a swaying pack of men and horses who probably were having a great deal of trouble dealing effective blows.

At that moment the whole mass swayed to the pressure of another tremendous blow; he assumed it was the result of the next group of Burgundians arriving, as they smashed into the mass. It seemed to make little difference to the struggling adversaries already on the ground.

Jamie saw an unfamiliar design painted on the shield nearest him on his right front, and smote an overhand blow that the man caught on the shield.

They traded blows for a few moments before the press about them pulled them apart; Jamie found himself whaling away at yet another foeman, until that one, too, moved away. For some time thereafter that was the way of the battle for him, as the eddies that moved men and horses about in the jam of flesh brought enemies near, then moved them elsewhere, replacing them.

Once Jamie caught his man with a strong blow in the shoulder, and the foeman slumped in his saddle; he seemed to be slowly falling backward from it as his horse moved off. At another time Jamie's war-horse savaged the horse of a foe, ripping at its throat with large, strong teeth. The horse collapsed, dumping its rider beneath the press of hooves. At almost the same moment Jamie took a solid blow from the rear, on his right side.

He could not tell how badly he was injured, but he felt himself reeling in his saddle. It was impossible to move his shield into that quarter, so he concentrated on retaining his hold on his sword, and tried to turn with it in front of him. What he saw when he turned was a thickset Burgundian figure, wearing a maroon tunic over its armor, and with its back turned to him as it fought off an attack on the other side from Edward. Without thinking, Jamie swung his sword, and the figure near him took it in the back of the neck, falling forward and out of his saddle.

Edward pushed his horse forward past the now riderless animal of the Burgundian, to Jamie's side; but the din remained too loud for any effective communication. Jamie turned back, finding himself still slightly dizzy, to defend his other side.

Figures came and went; and several times he heard within himself some instinct that warned him not to strike at one shape or another. He always obeyed that instinct, but as the minutes passed the occasion came about less and less. Sweat was in his eyes, and his arm was weary; there was pain in his back. Perhaps it was stiffening up on him—or just numbing. He swung again. . . .

Chapter Six

THE HOT, HIGH sky above this country called Italy made Jamie's head spin slightly whenever he looked up into the eye-searing blueness. Almost six months had gone by since the siege at St. Marcel. It was hard to believe no more time had passed to bring him to this moment in which he was lying on his back, watching a hawk that spun in large, slow circles above the copse of trees that lapped like a green tongue at the hillside across the way. Jamie was waiting for the hunter to stoop upon some prey, but it had not done so yet, and gave no indication that it ever would.

Perhaps there was no prey for the bird to seize, Jamie speculated; the hawk might do better to move onward, to some other grove.

His eyes were dazzled by the glare, which seemed to shine punishingly off the sweat on his nose and cheekbones. He closed them for a moment, while bringing his head back down to ease the strain on his neck. His head danced for a moment, caught in the whirling of the multicolored spots that grew and moved and died behind his lids. But after a moment the sensations faded somewhat, and he felt himself steady, returning back to control of his body.

He was not sure if such a sensation was something new to him, or not. The old sorcerer had warned him that his head would buzz occasionally for a while, until he got used to the pentecost spell he had bought after the taking of St. Marcel, and it had, too; but this did not seem to be the same thing at all. Perhaps it was just the heat.

He opened his eyes again, finding that his face remained

directed at the hillside—two hillsides, rather—between which the green wave of trees seemed to pour like frozen water down the yellow land. That green was so dark and cool—shadowy, and almost black. *It would be most pleasant under their boughs,* he thought.

The hawk still floated at his post above them, waiting patiently for his appointment with destiny. Probably, Jamie thought, he would not have liked it under the branches anyway—he needed more room to be himself. He turned his head to look down the road ahead.

Beside him Edward dozed in his saddle, his palfrey plodding along at a relaxed gait that left them both reasonably comfortable. The Cornishman looked thinner to Jamie's eye. No doubt he was, for the wound taken before Carcasonne last autumn had been quite severe, and had left him bedridden for quite a time. The scar on the man's left side, among the ribs, was most unsightly even yet, he knew; and the surgeons had undeniably been astounded that the man had lived even two days. Edward was a tough one, though, no doubt of that.

Jamie and Brethin, who had gotten through the latest battle unscathed, had had a job on their hands nursing the big man. But they had done the job, remembering all the while that Edward had done the same for both of them after the melee before the wall of St. Marcel, now six months gone. In the meantime early spring had turned to autumn, and the oncoming winter had moved them—veterans all now—to warmer country.

Jamie's thoughts evaporated as his attention was caught by the first visible movement on the road ahead, where it bent into sight around the bottom of the hill. Brethin had obviously noticed it too, for he swung out from behind Jamie, without waiting to be ordered, and galloped down the road toward the cart that now revealed itself. Young Tom paused only to untie the lead rope his animal carried, handing it to Armand; then he followed Brethin, moving more slowly while he backed up the Scot.

Not that trouble was really expected, but one never knew. At the same time, it was a good job for a knight's page to find out ahead of time who they were encountering; and besides, he'd paid a hefty sum to that same old magician for the spell that taught both Brethin and Edward their Italian—he might as well get some value out of it.

His thoughts wandered again. He had paid a large sum—

nearly a third of his gains from the taking and looting of St. Marcel, to buy the spell of tongues—the pentecostal spell—from that strange old wizard who had wandered among the tents of the conquerors after the city had been taken and celebration was in process.

If Jamie had not been wounded, Brethin would never have brought the wizard to Jamie to see if he could be of help in healing the wound. And if Jamie had not been half-drunk—for all his Scot's head for alcohol—from the wine they had poured into him to ease the pain, he might never have agreed to pay so much wealth for such a spell.

It was not the sort of spell he might have picked first to buy had he been sober—but the wizard, with Brethin's backing (although now Brethin swore he remembered no such presumptuous interference) had made it seem so attractive a purchase. But it was not even a spell that allowed Jamie to speak any language he encountered; it was only one that gave him the gift of learning such a language very swiftly. It was strange how the wizard, small and cramped as he was, had reminded Jamie of Doctor Septilos from Oxford, though the two were nothing alike physically. Come to think of it, the witch, Brunewarts, had also somehow reminded him of the doctor, although there could be no reason for that at all.

Jamie jerked his thoughts back to the present.

As Brethin swung by, Edward had roused himself enough to view the scene ahead; evidently he thought it harmless, but nevertheless he stopped his horse in place. So did Jamie; and when Edward signaled behind him for the wineskin, Jamie was ready and got to it first, as Antoine, the most trusted of the new men, handed it forward. Edward grinned at this, but Jamie, after the show, took only a tiny swallow and handed it over.

The wine was warm—Jamie made a face—which in the case of this local product meant it simulated a most unpleasant weak acid. He much preferred water while traveling these days, but he'd been told that the water in Italy was bad for one, causing all sorts of grievous bowel inflictions. He wondered if they would have ale in Milan.

Brethin had reined in beside the cart ahead, from the top of which a dirty, ragged fellow peered shortsightedly down at him. Jamie could not hear the conversation, but he watched and drew conclusions—mainly that Brethin had done all the talking, receiving only monosyllables for answers. Peasants generally were not of any value, he had found, being uniformly suspicious and ignorant.

Brethin turned his horse and came back toward Jamie at a slower pace; as he drew near he shrugged, not saying anything. Jamie grinned at him, reflecting inwardly that although Brethin had changed a great deal since they had left the valley, this one thing remained—he was still spare with words. Except for that damned mumbling.

The thought of the pentecostal spell returned to him and he felt his mood suddenly altered, as the memory of that occult device Hobie Yaro had planted in Brethin arose again. Occasionally, Brethin would make his mumble before men who paused suddenly to look at him curiously—and then at Jamie, with a certain speculative glance that made the latter abruptly uneasy. Nothing had come of it, of course, but Jamie still had the feeling that he might be sitting next to one of those timed spells that the tales occasionally spoke of, the sort that hid in quiet for years before suddenly acting. . . .

Jamie cursed under his breath at the thought, forcing it all from his mind, spurring his palfrey forward unexpectedly. Brethin pulled hurriedly out of his way, moving briefly into the road in front of the oncoming cart, before taking his place behind Edward as that worthy, also caught by surprise, spurred to catch up with his leader. The six men who now followed them with the pack animals were of a more phlegmatic nature and simply waited their turn to move as the short column slowly jerked into its train of motion again. The cart passed to the right without a word being exchanged. Antoine swung up into the saddle of his own horse as one of the other men held it for him, and followed the rest.

They rode on through the hot noon hour, Jamie having decided that Milan must be close enough now so that its walls must be in sight soon. They passed several armed parties like their own, lounging in the occasional bits of shade along the route, groups who responded when spoken to in the bastard form of Norman French that was the lingua franca of soldiers in western Europe generally; they agreed that Milan was only a few hours away. Privately, Jamie suspected, they also agreed that these northerners were mad to be traveling in this hottest part of the day.

Still, Jamie felt the effort had been worth it when the smoke that hung above the city showed on the horizon, some hours later. The spirits of the rest of the party rose too, and as they rounded a bend between two low hills to see walls, at last, small in the distance though they were, their pace began to pick up noticeably.

They made it to the gate well before curfew sounded, but then were almost refused admittance to the city. Although it was peacetime, the guard was suspicious, and new faces, above strange foreign dress, called for many questions. Jamie was able to mention the name of the leader who had taken over when Sir Henry had been badly wounded, as Ned had, at Carcassone. The name of Pietro Claveggio had the effect of passing them eventually through the thickly walled gateway into the stench of the city streets.

Evening was close upon them, and they moved out of the thin remaining sunlight into shadowy darkness. Each of the party had put his hand on the hilt of his blade instinctively, untrusting of the sudden deprivation of vision. The guardsmen they passed made no protest—perhaps knowing the reputation of their city as well as any—or perhaps making a note not to trifle with these northmen.

Here, just by the gate, the streets were slimy and their progress necessarily careful and slow. But Jamie had good directions from Pietro, and they found their way to the recommended inn in decent time, settling in for the night. There was no ale, Jamie found—what sort of barbarian drink might that be? But he found the wine here to be better than that Antoine had appropriated on the road.

In the morning Jamie made his way to the ducal palace, presenting himself to the guards there and requesting the attention of Pietro Claveggio.

Jamie and his men had come into the service of Claveggio after Sir Henry's grievous wounds at the battle of Carcassone, and all had been prepared to resent the lean, dark, foppish Italian knight. But he had turned out to be as wise and experienced a battle leader as Sir Henry had been—if totally different in all other ways. With the pentecostal spell helping him, Jamie had picked up Tuscan Italian swiftly, and perhaps that was why Pietro seemed to take a liking to this towering northerner who spoke to him in the accents of home.

Perhaps also it was why, when Pietro had left the service of Philip the Glorious to return to the court of Sigismundo Bablingero, Duke of Milan, he had suggested that Jamie might profit by following him.

At any rate Jamie and his small personal band were now here, in one of the largest and most powerful cities of Europe, knocking—in effect—on the Duke's door. It was not yet mid-morning. Edward and Brethin had accompanied Jamie, trying not to stare at the vast buildings, but showing their awareness that people stared at *them* more than a little condescendingly. It was their clothing again, Jamie suspected; they stood out like priests on a battlefield; and possibly—though it was too late to do anything about this now—smelled a good deal worse. They should have paused along the way to buy enough perfumes to help hide their stink. The attitudes of the Duke's servants hinted as much. They were shown into a small unfurnished room with an armed man standing outside its doors, clearly some sort of guardroom, and told to wait. It was some hours before Claveggio appeared, but Jamie was not insulted by this. The man himself had warned him, before they last parted, that things were run that way in Italy. He had also warned Jamie about the dangers of taking offense, for any reason. Not swords, but politics, were the weapons of the court. Jamie and his men should go carefully until they knew to whom it was safe to answer back.

Nonetheless, Jamie felt uncomfortable. Edward and Brethin had had no qualms at simply locating a shady wall in the room and settling to squat in coolness; but Jamie was not sure if his own lineage and rank would allow such indignity before these foreigners. He stood somewhat defiantly in the middle of the room for a half hour or so before coming to his senses and hunkering down like the rest.

Claveggio, he thought as he squatted, had tried to tell him that this would be a very different country from that he had grown up in, or the France he had become a veteran soldier in. But he suspected now that he really had not been fully prepared for the transition.

At last a servant in green livery arrived, an imperious-seeming, dark-visaged young fellow, who said something low to the guard outside the door that Jamie did not manage to catch—he did not want to listen too obviously and be noticed doing so. The guard turned and waved in Jamie's direction; and the servant—Jamie supposed he was a servant, for he wore the same style and green color of clothing the other servant wore—approached the three of them.

"Ser Jamie?" he said. His voice was high-pitched but not loud, and he did not wait for an answer before continuing.

"Ser Pietro Claveggio requests that you all come with me."
He turned and walked back toward the gateway that the guards
manned, not looking back to see if he was followed. Feeling
challenged, Jamie moved after him, and managed to affect a
languid, nonchalant air that he thought would suggest to the
guards that he was firmly in control. Behind him, Edward and
Brethin jumped up and trotted after him, swords clanking on
some bit of metal and footsteps loud in the silence. Jamie
winced internally.

They passed down a corridor, out through a door other than
the building's entrance, and crossed a large courtyard that was
bordered on the other side by more of the building. The wall
glowed white in the sunlight, except where green stains
seemed to be painted in odd swatches near the roof, which was
also green. The servant they were following seemed to be
moving very fast, although his gait remained a walk; he
plunged from the gate out into the middle of the inner courtyard, across the bright green grass and passed without speaking
the small groups that dotted the lawn here and there—groups
generally composed of one lady and two or three unarmed,
richly dressed men, all of whom stared at Jamie and his men as
they sped by.

They moved from the grass onto what looked like nothing so
much as a moat that circled about a vast inner palace, a moat
that had been filled in levelly with large chips of white rock
that glinted in tiny spots here and there as they moved across it.
It crunched faintly under their feet.

Then they were rapidly mounting a flight of stairs that rose
toward huge doors, beside which more guards were stationed.
But no, they turned away before reaching the doors, and
moved to the left along a sort of portico that extended for much
of the long length of the building. Finally they came to a
smaller doorway with only one guard outside it; that man only
looked at them, saying nothing, as the servant opened the door
and proceeded inside, leaving Jamie and his men to follow if
they would. They did.

By a variety of shadowy passages and small rooms they
came eventually to a larger room, stone-walled and windowless. At a table sat a man Jamie recognized as Giovanni Colombo, Pietro's squire. Jamie could not prevent himself from
breaking into a smile, which the other man matched.

"Ser Jamie," Colombo said, getting up to clasp hands with

Jamie. "It's good to see you in health, by God's good will. How was your trip?"

"Most enjoyable, Master Giovanni," Jamie replied, in an Italian as smooth as the other's. Pietro's squire nodded.

"It's good to hear you speak our tongue as well as ever," Colombo said. "Will you have some wine—you and your men? I'll wager they made you wait."

"No matter, now we've found you," Jamie said. He took the stool the other was offering him, and Pennworthy and the others seated themselves on a bench which ran along one wall and faced the table at which Colombo had been sitting.

As all were seating themselves—the servant who had conducted them there had vanished somewhere—wine and some food arrived; and they all had a bite or two in the midst of companionable chatter that recalled their days before Carcasonne. Finally Giovanni stretched his long, thin frame and grimaced, indicating with his head a further door of the room.

"You'll have more waiting to do," he said. "There is little help for it. Edward and Brethin can wait here while my man takes you to another anteroom. And there, Jamie, you must wait alone, until they call you to attend Ser Pietro. He will present you to the Duke, and that is what will decide your fate here." He flushed briefly.

"That sounds too ominous," he said. "Say rather that the mood of the Duke during this interview will determine somewhat the ability of Ser Pietro to employ you."

He shrugged. "You know the ways of the court, in any country. The Archduke"—he paused and looked at the doors closely—"leads a coalition of tiny city-states, only because he is a close relative of the Emperor. It is no secret that the Duke is not a popular leader, and while we are not now at war, we might as well be, with all the money that is being spent on arms and men."

He laughed. "And so of course we have now to persuade him to spend more to hire you."

"Am I needed, then?" Jamie asked soberly. It did not sound like a place that would be happy to see him and his men.

"By us, yes," Giovanni said, craning his neck upward as he rubbed it at the back with his left hand, elbow raised into the air. "War is coming, and the only question might be whether from within or without. The Duke is far weaker than he himself realizes, and since we are now his men, we must try to persuade him to do what can be done to strengthen his position. You will be a part—a small part, but valuable—of that strength.'' He yawned and stretched.

''It is time for you to go. Follow my man, and say little at any time.'' He rose and crossed to the door, opening it to reveal a waiting man who looked like a warrior although no arms showed. ''You'll have to leave your arms here.''

Jamie stopped in place and opened his mouth; then closed it again. At home that would be an insult, but he had known he would have to learn new ways. . . .

''All of them?'' Brethin asked, saving Jamie the trouble.

''It would be best,'' Giovanni said. ''The Duke has reason to fear assassination.''

Jamie nodded and began the process of divesting himself of his weapons. He did not have to tell Brethin to keep an eye on them.

Some hours later, Pietro Claveggio strode through another doorway, into yet another of the verdant gardens that seemed to surround the palace on all sides. The man carried his slim figure well, never doubting that the supercilious servants who swarmed everywhere about the palace would take care to please him. Four paces behind him, Jamie had quit trying to match the other's gait and carriage, knowing after a brief struggle that his body was made to do things differently.

The afternoon sun was welcome to Jamie, although he had been neither cold nor in the dark. Somehow it seemed to freshen his spirit, and the sense of his own ignorance and, yes, barbarity, dwindled away. He grinned at the feel of the wind on his limbs again, and found his arms swinging more freely as he moved. He lengthened his stride and moved up beside Claveggio, noticing that his eyes looked slightly down upon the other figure.

''Did the Duke even *see* me, Pietro?'' he asked, with a slight laugh in his voice. The other looked sideways and up at him.

''No doubt,'' the man said. He was sober at first, and now he laughed in his turn, the same rich, rolling chuckle that seemed so incongruous coming from that slim, smooth face. ''How could he not? With that height and that hair, you stand out in any crowd in Italy, I'll wager.'' He sobered a bit, leaning in toward Jamie as he walked and talking in a lower tone, face turned sideways toward the bigger man, hands moving always.

''You must understand,'' he went on, ''that it would never

do for him to make a great deal of any man whose aid he needed. He suspects that would be beneath his dignity." He stopped a moment, then continued. "And it serves me well, at that: for the Archduke to favor any man publicly is to make the man too noticeable a target for the intrigues and plots that surround this palace—and permeate it, too."

They were now across the courtyard and moving through another archway into a shadowed, smaller space whose farther wall was apparently made of high bushes, thick and seemingly impenetrable. Claveggio said nothing as they moved down a narrow path that wound through those bushes; until after a time they found themselves entering a small building that stood under huge old trees of some species Jamie did not know.

Three men lounging inside the doorway nodded but did not arise as Claveggio passed; Jamie noted that their eyes were on him rather than on the other man. And as they passed into the next room he heard a faint click of metal on metal. He kept walking and did not look back.

In the next room were Edward and Brethin, as well as Jamie's weapons; Pietro greeted the other two men, and Colombo, who was with them. He waved a hand at Jamie's gear and then moved on to yet another room. Jamie paused to rearm himself and then followed.

Over wine, Pietro explained what he wanted Jamie to do for him.

"Training!" Jamie almost yelped; and then stared at the man across from him, who merely nodded back at him, simultaneously getting the last scrap of meat from a chicken bone. Jamie pushed himself back on his chair, keeping his mouth shut and telling himself that he had lessons to learn. He wrapped a hand around his cup and cocked an eye at the other, knowing that it was an expression many men interpreted, somehow, in a fashion that made them want to talk more.

"Is it important?" Jamie asked. It must be, he thought; he couldn't envision how Claveggio could so insult him otherwise.

"Yes," Pietro said, and looked directly across at the Scot. "It is important. War is coming, and that soon. And the one thing we absolutely must have is a supply of good troops."

He paused and looked down at the tabletop, suddenly seeming reluctant. Jamie watched him, silently and still, knowing he had the moral advantage now in this conversation. The other could not stop now, unless Jamie gave him an excuse.

"The levies will all balance out, when war comes," Claveggio went on at last. "That is how it has always been. No one really wins by a large margin in these wars; or loses badly, either. There is a certain evenness in these affairs." He stopped again, and Jamie found himself following the train of thought out to its conclusion.

"You're going to overthrow the balance!" he exclaimed, excited in spite of his intentions to be cool and quiet.

"Yes," Claveggio said. "We have mercenaries, as does every lord in the area. But ours will be no leaderless, motley rabble, half of whom vanish on their way to the battlefield—we are training them in small units, and equipping them well. And I want you and your men to take one of the worst of those units and make effective warriors of them." When Jamie nodded he smiled.

"It won't be easy. And never forget that they are mercenaries—you will have to find a new way to lead them, if they are to be effective. They won't give a damn about your golden spurs."

Jamie nodded and looked thoughtful, finding himself intrigued by the idea in spite of its vaguely scandalous air—using the dregs of society as effective fighters, instead of the nobility. It should not work at all—and if it did, it might be the ruination of the order of society . . . but if it worked, it could indeed change the outcome of the upcoming war.

"What methods do your other captains use?" he asked Claveggio as they were leaving the building.

"It doesn't matter," the other said. "These will be the men those methods failed with." He walked away. Edward, mystified, looked as if he were about to ask a question; and Jamie, irritated, scowled at him and walked away.

So began a new and entirely unlooked-for episode in Jamie's quest for fame and fortune. He went to work at it grimly, however, on the principle that if this was how his career at the court of the Duke was to start, at least he could make sure that the start was a good one.

The situation did not look any more attractive when he saw the human material he had been given to shape. The half of a hundred men he had been assigned were one and all individuals who had obviously failed to find a useful place in the world. Still, all of them claimed to have sworn allegiance to the Duke, and they were all Jamie had to work with.

To make the situation even less attractive, the pay for the

men, assigned to Jamie for distribution, was low. Jamie learned that the deficiency was made up in part by the fact that the unit he was training had the use of a small farm that was owned by His Grace, a few miles outside of Milan. At least they ate and slept well enough.

On the morning of the third day, Jamie stood in the center of the area enclosed by the farm living-quarters, the barn, and a few outhouses. Opposite him in a ragged line were the fifty-odd recruits. Between him and them, standing on the dirt and straw of the open yard, was a topless barrel almost full of not-too-clean water, and just on the other side of that were Tom and Armand, two of his own men, holding upright a recruit, a thick-bellied fellow in his mid-thirties with thinning black hair, who stared stupidly about him and who seemed disposed to fall asleep, given half a chance. At Jamie's feet rolled a man named Arno, clutching his head with both hands.

"Oh God it hurts!" Arno was writhing on the ground, doubled up and clutching his head between his forearms. Jamie stood above him and to one side.

"Of course it hurts," he said. "You didn't duck."

"Gods, you've killed me," the man wailed.

"I see," Jamie said; and turned to Brethin. "Bury him."

The shallow hole had already been dug, and when they threw Arno in and the dirt began to fall on him, he arose.

"You see," Jamie told him in a roar that all the others heard, "you're not dead after all. It hurt, but you lived through it. Always try not to be hurt. But if you *do* get hurt, then you should know that pain alone won't kill you. You can still do your job." He smiled. "Guido, here!"

"And I'll take Guido for my side," Edward said with a sly grin. Jamie raised an eyebrow and crooked the corner of his mouth.

"Guido?" he said. "Is there something I don't know?"

"Call it a gamble," Edward said. "He's not strong, but he's fast."

"Well, I've noticed that too," Jamie said. "But can he do anything with that speed?"

"We'll see," Edward said; then grinned and added: "And watch yourself. I've been working him with the sackbut, and he'd like to pull a horseman down with that hook."

"You were right," Jamie said later. "The best thing to do

for them was to dry them out and get them back into good
shape. But they'll still run as they near a battle."

"No," Edward said, "I think not. Or rather, yes, but not as
many, and not as quickly. Most of them don't know how good
they've begun to feel about themselves."

"You're good at this, Edward. You know men."

"So do you," the Cornishman said. "You just don't think
to do it often."

A few screams crossed the farmyard to where Jamie had just
reined in his palfrey beside Brethin, and they sat in silence for
a moment watching the melee that had begun as a mock skir-
mish with wooden weapons. Jamie was not riding his destrier,
for that fierce animal would quite possibly have killed one or
more of the men.

"They took a few blows and then just started swinging
wildly," Brethin said. He spat to the side. "They forgot all we
told 'em."

Jamie nodded without speaking, still watching. A number of
the figures he saw in the dust were still now.

"Shall we stop 'em?" Brethin asked.

"No," he said. "Let them have it out. They need the fight
taken out of them. And perhaps they'll learn by it." He turned
away; Brethin nodded and stayed where he was, watching.

"There's little hope of turning them into fighters in six
weeks," said Brethin harshly.

"Hope or not," said Jamie, "six weeks from now they'll
have no choice but to fight."

Six weeks later, low on the horizon, the swollen August sun
seemed to be broken into three or four horizontal slabs of
blood-red marble by thin bands of sick-looking purple clouds.
Around it the sky was an unhealthy yellow, a color which
darkened imperceptibly as one looked across the sky in any
direction away from the sun itself—darkened to some un-
nameable neutral color that made a man feel there was no sky
there at all.

Jamie sat his horse on the seared crest of a desolate hill just
outside the city wall of Milan. He and Claveggio were looking
down a long valley at a road along which moved a cart piled
high with soldiers' corpses.

"How many have you lost now?" Pietro Claveggio asked.
He kept his gaze aimed down the valley, not looking at his

companion. Jamie wondered, as he often did with this man, whether that was for the creation of some effect or not.

"Thirty-six of the forty-nine," he answered.

"Not much of a unit left."

"It was never much of a unit anyway," Jamie said. "You always knew that." He stopped a moment. "But they would have had some value, perhaps, if used rightly."

"Never mind. They served their purpose."

Jamie frowned and looked at the other enquiringly, trying hard to look a question that he did not want to say out loud.

"They were only a way to hire you without letting others know your importance to me," Claveggio said. "You worked with the dregs of the army, out here, out of sight. You were forgotten, but close enough that I could use you if I needed to. And now you are known and accepted as a mere trainer of mercenaries. Few will comment on what you do or where you go for some time." He laughed dryly. "That makes you priceless to me. I suppose I must pay you more."

Jamie laughed himself. As they rode back to the villa that was Pietro's headquarters away from the plague-stricken city, he maintained his mask of eager cupidity and naive pleasantness; inside he worked hard to keep his eyes from narrowing suspiciously as he watched his companion. For the first time, he was really aware of his erstwhile friend as a manipulator of men.

He realized full well that he was being cynical about the motives of a man who had befriended him, done well by him. His confessor, Jamie thought, probably would have counseled him to feel shame for his ingratitude. But then, Father Dunstan was not here; and that was just as well for him.

Chapter Seven

SUMMER HAD TURNED to winter, the roads had become rivers of mud, then been covered with snow in the mountains; and, as normally happened in consequence here in Italy, all military action was abandoned pending the good weather of spring. Jamie found himself back out of the field and back in Milan— this time with a duty inside the walls of the archducal palace.

It was a cold November morning and he was headed for the quarters of his noble nine-year-old charge, the Archduke's second son, Carlo. Watching his breath puff out before him as he strode across the courtyard and up the stairway on the inside of the wall, Jamie wondered if he would someday get as soft about the weather as these southerners; certainly there was no end of complaining among the members of the guard unit he had been given to command. He laughed and made a note to himself: when you go back to the valley, don't be leading an army of Italians . . .

Atop the wall he turned left, following the structure around a corner and then, quickly, left again to the tower in which Edward had been giving young Carlo some casual instruction in shieldwork—*always a good way,* he thought, *to keep an eager lad out of sight. And also out of energy,* he added with a grin.

As he reached the tower's entrance, though, he encountered Tom, who was leaning against the wall by the door, laughing quietly to himself. Jamie stopped before him and waited amiably, knowing it had to involve something that had embarrassed Ned—that was what he had taken to calling Edward, these late days, as they had become better friends.

Tom just looked back at him and waved rather weakly in the direction of the interior of the tower; so Jamie slipped past him and inside.

No one was there, so he proceeded up the stairs to the building's top surface, pausing just before he reached it to keep out of sight, and to quiet his approach. He listened as he tried to slip further upwards, stealthily.

"Please, Master Carlo," he heard Ned say, somewhat despairingly—there was a strong suggestion in his voice that he had said these words before. "Please come down from there. It's very easy to fall, and that would be my head, as you well know."

"Oh, don't be an old stick, Squire Edward," he heard a youthful voice pipe up. "I won't fall. I've climbed these fortifications before, and I never fell once—"

"It only takes one," Ned suggested feebly.

"—and besides, as my father's son I have to get to know all about such things as fortifications, don't I?" The brightness of that final phrase told Jamie that the young noble was getting a bit cocky; Ned had proved too easy a challenge for him. Perhaps Tom should have stayed here, he thought; that one generally seemed to have no trouble with the lad. Jamie turned and slipped quietly back down the stairs into the tower's interior room, moving to the arrow slit that seemed nearest to where Carlo's voice had been coming from. It was much too small for him to stick his head through, but—he stopped and looked about him; then bent to pick up a battered old practice helm that had been left lying in a corner. He maneuvered it through the slit quietly, not scraping the stone; and then released it to fall straight down into the moat, striking the wall twice on the way.

He heard a roar that had to be from Ned, as well as a small shriek from the younger voice; he grinned, and by the time he got up to the top of the tower again, both Ned and Carlo were there, well away from the edge and rather silent.

"Your Grace," Jamie said, "Ned. I had some difficulty finding you both until I heard your call." He managed to stifle a grin. "How goes the instruction?"

Ned had managed only a few slow words before the young noble launched into an exciting account of the things he had been shown. In another moment he had fetched his own equipment and was butting up against Jamie's legs, demonstrating his points.

". . . and then up under his chin—I can't reach your chin, Sir Jamie. . . ."

"Not if I can help it," Jamie replied half-seriously. "But you couldn't have reached Ned's chin, either. What did you do with him?"

"This!" the lad shrieked, kicking Jamie in the shin. Jamie yelped, and the lesson quickly became a scuffle. And by the time they ceased rolling about the floor, Ned seemed to have regained his composure and was regarding them both with amusement.

"Yes," he said. "That's how the last lesson ended, too."

"And so must this one end," Jamie answered. "Master Carlo must be present for the feast in his father's palace this night. We must all prepare ourselves."

"Another one?" Ned grumbled. "I never thought to find myself feeling so about a dinner, but I could happily look at the end of the last of these. Gods, but it's hard to enjoy one's food when watching everyone in the place!"

"True," Jamie added, with a frown meant to caution Ned's tongue on further impolitic grousing. "Yet we are there only to safeguard the Archduke's son—so consider that you would not be eating at all if not for him."

Carlo crowed in glee at that shaft, and then ducked behind Jamie to avoid Ned's pretended cuff on the ear. As they gathered up the gear that had been strewn about, Jamie speculated that this young fellow was going to be a popular man one day—he seemed to know instinctively how to get into the hearts of those about him.

Jamie found himself back near the edge of the wall, looking down through one of the embrasures into the twilit countryside. The sky was darkening rapidly, and had already reached a deep lavender hue that seemed a fitting backdrop for some dark bird to circle menacingly above them. He scanned the sky before him, but saw no such bird, only the skeletal outline of bare branches dancing against the purple evening. He watched them, but no great bird arose from among them.

Consciously he shook himself, feeling that he had, for a brief moment, been frozen in place like some grim hero in an ancient saga, awaiting the kiss of a goddess to spring back to life. He looked across at Ned and Carlo, and forced a grin—no goddess up here! Anyway, he was no grim old hero doomed to tragedy. . . .

"Hurry it up, you two!" he called, turning suddenly and

moving quickly toward the stair that now lurked in a pool of shadow despite the flambeau on the wall at its foot. "We must not keep His Grace waiting!"

Pietro Claveggio strode toward the archway that led into another of the torchlit gardens of the ducal palace, carrying his slim figure as if he had absolutely no doubt that no obstacles would be placed in his way. No one was at his back and he was apparently unarmed, but he seemed to brandish in the air about him a warning of great power.

Jamie was across the width of the eastern garden as Claveggio vanished; and he did not try too hard to hide his eyes and their movements about the area—that, after all, was part of his job as bodyguard commander to the second surviving son of the Archduke himself. The thought of having to do such a job in all earnestness—the thought of a nine-year-old being in deadly danger of assassination at all—still twisted something in his guts. But he was learning a lot about how these southerners ran their lives and their politics now, and he was sure he was needed.

Claveggio had explained to him that it was a deadly serious job that he was being assigned, indeed; and though he had fought against the indignity of it, Pietro could not be gainsaid. After his post as a trainer of mercenaries, the Italian had said, Jamie was a political nonentity; and so he could be nominated and appointed to this post before opposition had time to align for battle against him. It was important, Pietro said, because the Archduke himself had not yet realized just how many enemies he had within his own establishment.

There is going to be a very dirty war soon, Jamie had thought then; and now, in the garden, he knew that the only way his mind had changed was in its appreciation of just how dirty that war would come to be.

In the meantime, as Claveggio had suggested, he was being a good bodyguard, and keeping himself out of politics and away from the political people. In fact, he'd been trying to cultivate an image as an honest but somewhat stupid foreign sword-carrier—it could not hurt to have possible opponents underestimate him; and besides, that meant he could get out of the almost unavoidable games of jest and repartee that these intriguers seemed so fond of.

Ah—now a couple of servants had come from the passage next to the garden—the south one, Jamie supposed. They were

the ones who always appeared to summon Carlo to his audience with his father. Jamie swept his eyes quickly around the
large area they now occupied, spotting his men all at their
posts and alert: Ned on the great steps, with Armand; Brethin
near him—and six others spotted about. None were allowed to
be armed, of course, but—well, why speculate?

The others collapsed into a loose formation about the boy as
they moved to the archway, several paces behind the court
officers who had carried the summons to them. Ned moved up
to slip in front of Carlo through the arch and Jamie followed
directly behind the lad. But there was no danger beyond the
archway except for the out-of-tune trumpet that blasted near his
ear to announce the herald's presentation of the boy to the
assembled company.

This garden was even larger than the one they had just left,
and was in fact the usual site of the Archduke's entertainments,
in good weather. It was large and lush with exotic vegetation,
beyond which he could hear music. Torches lit most of the
great expanse, although there were a few pools of darkness
here and there; and the smell of their smoke mingled with the
aroma of the roasting meats and fowl to completely mask the
normally rich smell of the vegetation.

He could see the Duke's party now, a large group of richly
dressed people—some were foreigners, he could tell—spread
out in a rough circle amid a larger circle of marble benches
near a large cluster of ferns and trees that provided a dark
background for their showy colors. Jamie slowed his pace as
their party neared the circle, noting that his own men had
dropped off to vanish into the anonymity of the people who
hung about the outer edges of the great garden. Probably they
were finding and identifying themselves to the other body-
guards that would be there—probably in large numbers by
now, he suspected.

Ned, too, had vanished—no doubt to the other side of the
group before him. Jamie halted.

Carlo had now been taken forward into the center of the
circle of the mighty before him, his small form vanishing in the
crowd that centered about his father. He could not follow
there, and so he was left to his own devices until the boy
should be released back into his care. For a moment he found
himself pitying the youngster, wondering how he felt about
having to live in the midst of those people.

Somewhat later he found that his feet had taken him around

the mass of vegetation that dominated the center of the garden;
he was standing at the center of a small, arched marble bridge
that spanned the narrow wasp-waist of a tiny pond. He'd been
looking down at the still surface of the water, watching the not-
quite-real reflections of the torches across the way. And he
became aware that a group of people had stepped onto the
bridge from his left, moving slowly toward him as they talked.

He turned to go, and as he did so he found his eyes first
drawn, and then fastened on, the woman about whom the
group obviously centered. If his feet had not already been
moving to take him from the bridge—and if they had not
continued to do so—he might very well have remained frozen
in his place until she came up to him.

That woman—she was hardly larger than a child, but it was
clear she was anything but that—dominated the group of
courtiers about her with no apparent effort. She wore a clinging
crimson gown that exposed her neck and shoulders, and her
black hair was coiled up within jeweled bands. The red of her
gown seemed wildly at war with every color worn by everyone
in the area; and yet somehow it seemed to suit her well, picking out her lips and contrasting with the dark mass of her hair.
Her clothes were of finer silk than Jamie had ever seen before.
The sheen of the fabric seemed to match that of her hair, he
thought. For an instant he fantasized that he could even see the
torches about them reflected in that mirror. But his reverie was
broken as she raised a hand to brush at a lock of stray hair,
bejeweled fingers caressing bejeweled hair.

Her eyes had brushed his as she passed, he realized. He
watched the group move past him, watched her back—and
then watched the backs of those who followed her along the
path, backs that obscured her from his sight, then hid her. He
watched them anyway—backs of old men, of a slightly built
younger man, of two women.

The last woman to pass turned, even as he watched, looking
back at him over her shoulder as he watched them all. Blue
eyes under blonde hair looked at him, but he dismissed them,
determinedly looking over her shoulder. In a moment she
turned away again, and the party continued away from him.
And he watched, until at last he forced himself away from the
bridge and in the direction of the ducal party.

The dark woman, Jamie learned, was Irene Paleologina,
sister to the Marquess di Montferrat—a minor noble of the
Archduchy, but a distant relative of the Byzantine imperial

family. And even though he had long ago written off his dream of the Great City, Constantinople, as the maundering of an ignorant boy, Jamie's heart quickened a little when he learned that Irene had been raised in Constantinople. She had only recently been returned to Italy, presumably to play her part in the politics of the day by attracting and marrying some good match.

"My lord."

"Uh—yes, what is it, Brethin?"

"My lord, it is past the third hour, and you were to meet Master Colombo on the training ground—"

"Gods, yes! I almost forgot," Jamie exclaimed, and jumped up from the bench he'd been sitting on. "Run ahead and tell him I send my apologies and will follow most directly." He turned back toward his quarters while yelling for Tom to fetch his practice gear.

The weather was quite cool, but within a short time the exertions of their warming exercises chased that consideration from both their minds. He paused to watch Giovanni working out with his new weapon, a French-made flail that he had only recently acquired. He was swinging it rapidly and swiftly in a graduated series of blows at a man-shaped wooden target—and his accuracy was noticeably improving as he worked. The tiny spikes on the weighted head of the macelike weapon were chewing up the wood of the target at a rate that made the onlookers comment nervously; but Jamie was more impressed by the solid sound with which the instrument met its goal. And the flexible chain which attached it to its staff suggested that it would be a deadly thing to any knight who counted on his shield too much for protection.

Jamie shuddered a little. The armorers and weapon-makers might be getting too good at their work, perhaps; it did not seem right to question new things that were being done to try to kill men better and faster—and yet, somehow, he worried. Weapons were getting better faster than the men using them could get better; did that mean that one day the weapon would count for more than the man wielding it? And if armor got so impregnable that no man wearing it could be hurt—what price courage then? What would happen to chivalry?

Giovanni had finished his exercises and was approaching him now, no doubt ready for their normal combat match. He laughed as the sturdy bearded face got near enough to peer up at him out of its shadowed cave.

"Ah, Giovanni!" Jamie laughed. "Have you tired yourself enough on the targets now?"

"Ah, no, Sir Jamie," the other replied. "I just thought to give you time to study my flail. You are good with weapons, and you'll be one who can simply look at it and tell what to do to negate its use."

"Perhaps," said Jamie. "But if I do, how does that help you, who are after all the one using the weapon?"

"But don't you see, Sir Jamie," the Italian went on, "that if you can meet this tactic successfully, then I will have time to find a way to counter your tactics—instead of having to do so in the midst of some battle when I first encounter one who knows how to meet the weapon."

"I see," said Jamie, rubbing his chin and then beginning to put on his own helm. He covered up thereby the racing of his thoughts.

Lord in heaven, this Italy! he thought. Surely there was a word to describe the incredible intricacy of their planning—the detailed plots and subplots, plots within plots . . . all of them seemed to do it, as if they'd all been taught young. Perhaps it was something in the warm air?

It was less than a week after that that Jamie received an invitation to a banquet hosted by the dark lady's brother, Marquess di Montferrat, in the Archduke's very palace, where Jamie had first seen the lady. He regarded that as an unimportant coincidence. But he obtained new finery, and he went—to find himself, ignored and seemingly forgotten, wandering alone in the same large garden he had first seen the lady in.

Darkness had fallen once more; and it was colder now, but not so cold that it bothered Jamie. In fact, he noticed it only as a factor that caused the servants who moved across his field of vision to scurry—when they could do so without injury to dignity.

He looked down into the water, having gravitated to that same marble-arched bridge; and once more he stared into the dark, serene water, watching the bright reflections of the torches that lit the distance.

He had made a mistake coming here, he knew; he did not belong among these people and their court ways. He should take his leave. Why did he not?

"Messer Jamie," a voice came from the foot of the bridge.

He recognized it as belonging to Antonio Belloconte, who seemed to serve some function as Lady Irene's majordomo—or something. It was a polite, smooth voice that emanated as if by no effort from the old potbellied body that carried it about. Jamie had found that he disliked the man from the very beginning of the evening, when the fellow had greeted him upon his arrival; and the feeling had intensified as they ended up seated together at table. Jamie, having been civilly greeted and then obviously dismissed by his host, had been ignored by the Lady Irene altogether—and the forced company of this fellow was just too much more to take.

Antonio stepped up to Jamie—a step closer than the latter found altogether comfortable. Jamie had noted that many of these southerners seemed to like to stand very close to a person they were addressing, much closer than the northerners Jamie had grown up with liked. Antonio stood even closer than most.

Jamie took a small step away again.

Unquestionably, Antonio noted the movement; but he made no sign of reaction and remained where his last step had taken him. One hand, pale and bony, reached out to grasp lightly at Jamie's upper arm, and he spoke again, his voice dropping to a sibilant whisper. Jamie was thankful once more that the man seemed to have little problem with foul odors upon his breath.

"Messer Jamie," the man breathed at him, "we have been wondering where you vanished to. It had made you a true figure of mystery."

He laughed quietly—a laugh much deeper and more powerful than Jamie would have expected to hear from that scrawny, though paunched frame. He bowed his head slightly to keep any reaction from showing on his face.

"I am sorry," Jamie intoned, trying to keep his voice low like that of a German banneret he had once known; he also tried to talk slowly—between them, those two affectations often caused people to think of the speaker as dull of wit.

"Oh, no offense taken, my lad," the Italian went on, back into his whispering tone. "I know you meant no harm by it. But there are people—important people—who desire to meet you. Could you not spare us your company?"

"I just wanted to look into the water," Jamie said in his same tones. "I did that last time I was here."

This is ridiculous! he told himself. Surely he was overdoing it!

"Yes," said Antonio. "I do remember seeing you here that

day.'' He smiled; and said no more but turned back to the palace, leading Jamie by a light grasp on the upper sleeve of his tunic.

As they advanced out of the doorway into the lighted arena of the grand ballroom, Jamie did not fail to notice that a large number of eyes had turned in his direction. He did not know just what that might mean, but he knew something was in the wind. So he kept his expression bland, and said very little; and he found that most of the courtiers he was introduced to were quite eager to fill in any voids in the conversation that he might have left.

It was as well, Jamie thought after a while, that he was saying little—for those about him seemed to be engaged in a particularly virulent form of that game—or war—of words that he had noted before in and about the palace. Indeed, they were beginning to submerge him in a welter of names and references that he could not take in. He stayed in one place, hoping they would swarm off in their buzzing energy and leave him alone.

Suddenly, before him appeared a blue-eyed face that seemed familiar—though of course, most of these faces did, since he had been about the court quite a bit in the last few months. But—yes, that was it: she had been following along behind Lady Irene when he had seen her party on the bridge that night. The memory made him smile slightly; and he saw that she noticed it and smiled back. Obscurely, that made him somehow angry.

"I am Maria," she said; and the smile slid from her face as if she had sensed his anger. Collecting himself, he smiled again.

"Yes," he said. "I have seen you before. With the Lady Irene."

Her face remained bland and expressionless.

"I am of the lady's household," she said. "My brother has given me over into her care."

"And who is your brother?" Jamie asked.

"Andreas Matteleone, the banker of Genoa," she said.

"Ah," said Jamie—and then stopped, finding himself stuck for words. The pause lengthened, and she seemed to be staring up at him with eyes larger and larger; and at length he hurried on.

"In the north heads of families sometimes give their relatives as hostages for good behavior," he said—and then stopped again, realizing by a sudden wince in her eyes that he had struck a sore spot. And in the following silence, Lady Irene was suddenly there in front of him.

Someone was introducing her, or him—he was not sure which—and his eyes seemed to be riveted upon her. He was drinking in the sight of her, but he could not tell what she was wearing. He watched her, and found himself bowing as deeply as he could.

"So this at last is that strange man, the one from the far, frozen north!"—she wrinkled her nose, staring boldly at him—"who commands the guard of our beloved Carlo. There's been much talk of your size and bearing, of your manner and—your dress, northman." Her voice was raised more than seemed necessary, so that nearby all turned and Jamie felt their eyes upon him. Irene laughed a little, looking him up and down.

Jamie had given some thought to wearing his boiled leather armor under his tunic tonight, as he had on most occasions about the palace. Now he was glad he had not done so. He realized now that he had not seen a single armored man in the garden—aside from the guards, of course. In spite of his good intentions to play the back country wantwit, the temptation to reply in kind tricked words from his mouth before he thought to check them.

"For this I am called strange?" he said. "My lady, even the wisest falconer will admit not knowing all the ways of the eagle."

"You exalt yourself greatly, do you not?" she answered, with a wicked little smile—and those listening, laughed.

Jamie made himself smile bewilderedly, but there was a deep sense of relief in him. This woman was brilliant, and dangerous. From now on he would remember his original resolve to stay out of conversation as much as possible. And with *her*, above all other people.

Beside them, Antonio stiffened so pronouncedly that they could not miss it. Then he gave a little gasp; and even as Jamie began to move towards him, there came a clatter of metal from behind them. Jamie whirled.

Several yards away a man Jamie did not know—a thin, brown-haired man not quite in his middle years—had apparently dropped a plate of sweetmeats onto the marble floor. He was standing crouched above it, face contorted as if in a scream that no one could hear, while the cords in his neck rose and fell back into the flesh. His hands began to shake violently, and he dropped the metal cup from which he had been drinking.

The man was obviously in trouble, but it looked like nothing natural that Jamie had ever heard of. The man gurgled loudly, then seemed to be released from the hold of whatever demon had possessed him; and with a loud howl he snatched up a short wooden bench that had been on the floor nearby, and ran toward the group of people Jamie was a part of.

The man was plainly beyond reason. Jamie sidestepped, and managed to fell him with a simple blow of the fist to the ear as the madman rushed past. The man, though stunned, still writhed like someone unconscious but in a fit as he lay on the stone floor, near the cracked bench leg that had broken off when he dropped the piece of furniture. Jamie debated whether he should begin to truss the man up or leave him for the guards already arriving on the scene. But before any such action could be taken, the fellow shuddered all over and went limp. Jamie could see that his lips and fingernails had taken on a blue tint.

"My lady," he began; but she was no longer there. He looked about and discovered her at some little distance, kneeling beside Antonio, who appeared to have fainted. As he watched, she lifted her head momentarily to give instructions to the guards that the fallen man be carried off.

No one seemed interested in Jamie's part in the affair, and he edged his way out through the crowd that was quickly surrounding the body. But near the wall he came face to face once more with Irene, who had evidently abandoned Antonio and was slipping away herself. She appeared, as best as he could judge, to be a little pale but strong and composed for all that. He considered her closely, feeling, to his own surprise, a faint concern for her.

"May I aid you in anything, my lady?"

"No."

"I am sorry if what I did somehow made Master Antonio ill," Jamie said. "And yet it seemed necessary."

"It seemed also pleasurable to you, I thought," she replied.

"Pleasurable?" He was puzzled. Did she believe him one of those who took pleasure in the pain of others? "There was nothing pleasurable about doing my duty to protect my lady— and others."

He realized suddenly that he was about to become angry, which would do him no good with her, and might well do him harm with the rest of the court.

"I bid you good night, my lady," he said; and bowed, ready to turn away.

"Perhaps I misunderstood you, after all." Her voice was suddenly as soft as thistle down. "I have my mind on poor Messer Antonio, after all. He's by no means as strong as he seems to think he is, and sometimes he takes too much upon himself."

She smiled; and in spite of himself, Jamie felt himself warmed by that smile. "But perhaps later there will come a time when neither of us has to see duty warring with pleasure."

She put out her right hand and touched the tips of the two longest fingers lightly on Jamie's left wrist, looking up into his eyes. Then she turned away, and he bowed again after her, as she moved regally toward a nearby door.

Chapter Eight

MARIA MET HIM in the front passage, and stared at him in his new, bright red cloak and jaunty matching hat. Jamie grinned at her, caught up in the dream of the figure he was cutting. But there was that in her face that made his eager good feeling sour, and he felt the grin twist slightly on his face. He made a deep, low bow that made his cloak flare behind him like the explosion of some sorcerer's most fiery concoction, and swept his cap off with one hand while keeping his head down. It was a move he had been practicing since the invitation to dine with the Lady Irene had arrived some days before.

When he looked up, Maria had turned her back and was moving down the hall, apparently to conduct him to the presence of her mistress. Jamie hastily—but with due concern for his dignity, of course—made to follow her, and was only a couple of paces behind as she swept through a door of finely carved brown wood and into a spacious but dark room. Jamie forgot the blonde woman as he looked over her shoulder and saw, far down the room near the end wall, a large table that sat in a pool of bright light—light made all the more real by the cavernous feeling that the darkness of the rest of the vast room gave off.

Maria had continued moving while Jamie stopped and stared, and so once more he had to hasten to follow her. No one else seemed to be about, but it was obvious that someone had been here recently, since the table was richly laid with bright silver dishes and fantastically patterned cloths. In the center of the table a small pastry castle steamed as he watched; and wine had been poured into two jeweled silver goblets.

Jamie managed a grin before Maria turned about and stopped at the head of the table.

"The Lady Irene will attend you directly," she said. "Please be seated there and be comfortable. If there is anything you desire, simply pull this cord and a servant will appear." And she had turned and vanished before Jamie could get a word out.

Even as he watched her vanish into the darkness about the pool of light in which the table sat, soft music began to play, filling the air about his head but not seeming to emanate from any one particular place. Of course, with the echoes in such a large room . . . and with the darkness . . . Jamie carefully reached for the cup of wine before him, striving to appear unconcerned. As the music continued and the level of the wine in his cup lowered, he found that he was listening for flaws in the threads of sound that surrounded him—flaws that could indicate a human origin to the airs. But he heard none, and the irrational certainty that had sprung up full-blown in him remained unshaken.

The melody ended, and with only the barest of pauses a new tune began—Jamie contained himself from raising his head. This one he recognized; it was a song that Moraig had sung sometimes at night in their father's hall. He smiled a little at the memories. He had not really thought of his sister for some time—what had happened to her by now? Had she been married off?

He frowned. Somehow, he had never thought that while he was making a success of himself in the wide world, life would be continuing in the valley he had left behind. He might go back only to find his sister married and gone, his father dead, Simon—who knew? He suddenly felt very desolate, and now stared unseeing into the blackness that surrounded him.

Now the phrase of music brought its words back to him, and he hummed it lightly between his teeth, still staring ahead of him. . . .

> ". . . make for him unhealthy wine
> grape that's tampered on the vine . . .

He could not stop himself from sitting up straight in his chair now. At first frightened, he quickly felt that emotion pass into anger—anger directed almost solely at himself. For one who had considered himself a very clever, cautious man, he had been very quick to pick up the cup of wine that had been placed before him—and here in poisonous Italy, of all places. Anything could have been put into that cup!

He looked down at the goblet he held, swirling it lightly as if searching its bottom for a pearl. He caught and recognized the reference to the old sovereign for poison in a cup, and smiled. He did not happen to have a pearl on him anyway—and besides, what would he do with it, swallow the damned thing? He found himself laughing quietly.

"Is there some jest written in the wine, then, Sir Jamie?" The soft, thrilling voice came from behind him, although he had not heard any sort of movement. He turned to face Irene, finding no difficulty at all in summoning a smile.

"My lady," he said, and rose to his feet in what he hoped was a smooth, fluid movement—it felt rather awkward.

She curtsied to him, not deeply but with extraordinary grace; and perforce, he essayed the same deep, sweeping bow that he had tried out on Maria as he entered. She was smiling at him, and he was sure it had gone over well. He grinned even more deeply.

"You honor my rooms with your presence, Sir Jamie," she said sweetly and almost innocently as she straightened. "I pray you can forgive my presumption in asking of your time, for it is known that you are a busy man and conscientious of your duties."

"It is I who am honored, my lady," he said. "I am but a humble warrior, only, and new to this land. I may be a poor companion for so refined a lady as yourself."

She smiled, dimpling, and he felt his grin become a smile to match hers. There was silence for a moment as they both stood, smiling and watching each other. After a second, she reached over to the cord that summoned servants.

"Be seated, Sir Jamie," she said. For the first time he noticed that she seemed to be pronouncing his name correctly, rather than slurring the initial syllable as most in this city did. He was inordinately pleased by that.

Servants appeared, bringing with them the early courses of the meal that the table's setting had promised. The first of them took away with him the pastry that had steamed on the table as Jamie had entered. They had never touched it; evidently it had been there only to be seen as it cooled, and to be smelled.

Thankfully, the meal was relatively light, and although there were many courses, Jamie never really found himself ap-

proaching the bursting point. But then, he was not really noticing what he was eating, anyway. In a similar fashion, he could
not really recall the substance of any of the conversation that
they had made during the meal, when later he passed the
evening through his memory.

What he remembered first and most was the pause that came
some hours later. It seemed as if he had awakened from a
dream, to see about him with a new clarity—except that it also
felt as if he were still dreaming, as if a different Jamie were
watching a dream-Jamie wake from a dream within a dream.
The darkness that limned the area of the table seemed to have
become a velvet curtain, black and shiny in the places where
the folds caught the light of the torches and candles. The
darkness was scented and rich, musky and resinous; and it
seemed to Jamie that the rich air must certainly cause the
candles to burn more fiercely. Certainly he felt as if he were
doing so.

Irene was silent, near his right hand—she had not sat across
the table from him, but near at hand around the near corner of
it. Now she was silent, still sitting straight in her chair—no, on
her couch—which was it? No matter.

She sat quietly, watching him, eyes dark and bright before
him, face soft and pale, with shadows that emphasized the
round curve of the cheeks. Jamie stilled the movement that his
hand had begun to his wine, and he watched her, beginning to
feel entranced. Had she done that to him? Was this what it felt
like to be captured in a spell?

With a separate part of his mind he reviewed that possibility
and decided that whether it was so or not really did not matter.
He was here because he wanted to be, and she would have
needed no magic to capture him. He had never seen a woman
so beautiful, let alone one who could use her voice, her
hands—in fact, every movement of her body—to such effect.
He could not imagine what she might want of someone like
him, but that too did not matter.

He felt a smile of pure pleasure starting to curve his lips, and
decided that it might be the wrong thing to do unless he dressed
it up a bit. With an effort he made the smile come out more
languid and less direct than it had started, and spoke more
softly:

"My lady, it is as if I have had a vision from God Himself,
to be here in this wonderful place with you."

She spoke no word, but got up gracefully from her place. He

rose hastily to his feet as she came around the corner of the
table to him, reaching out a hand to take his, which had lifted
automatically in response. He felt himself staring at her, down
into her face; but now he did not care what he might look like.
For it seemed as if there were a light—no, a flame—burning
behind her body somewhere, a flame that outlined her in fire,
that made her presence before him seem warm, even hot. Her
gaze was intense on him, and he thought she was demanding
something from him but he could not think what that might
be. . . . He watched her.

He watched her, and she came up to him, walking or gliding
in her smooth fashion directly to him, below him, to where she
could rest her forearms on his chest and look up into his eyes;
and still neither of them spoke. And without thinking, and still
with his eyes fixed on—or in—hers, he bent down and put his
lips on hers.

It was a strangely awkward kiss, as first kisses can be, yet it
seemed to electrify both of them. She responded swiftly, mold-
ing her body against his, even as his arms moved about her and
he pressed her head back farther for a second kiss.

Shortly she led him away from the table, through darkness to
another room—and other things.

"What is it, Brethin?"

"Lord?"

"You've been standing there staring at me since the sun
went down," Jamie said. "Yet you do not say what it is that
you want. Therefore something must be troubling you. What is
it?"

Silence. Exasperated, Jamie looked away from the new
dress sword he had been polishing, and across the room at the
other Scot.

"Call for my palfrey, then. I shall be found at the palace of
Lady Irene, if needed."

Brethin bowed low and turned out of the room.

"Good eve, Master Antonio," Jamie said, bowing as he
encountered the old man. "Will you tell me what entertainments we may find this night, here in this wonderful palace of
delights?"

"Not I, Sir Jamie—never I," the man replied, with a mea-
ger smile on his thin lips. "My lady would never permit it that
we know her intentions too much in advance. You should
know that by now."

"True enough," Jamie observed, his own smile feeling slightly weaker on his lips. He left the other man in the hall and proceeded onward toward the interior of the small palace, with which he was fast becoming intimate. And presently he passed through a large set of dark brown doors, intricately carved, and into the large chamber that dominated the interior of the Palazzo Visconti, as the house was generally styled, after the extinct family that had once built it.

Perhaps fifteen people were in the large room, not including in the count the four musicians discreetly out of the way in a corner, partially behind a screen, nor the servants moving gracefully about with trays and ewers. The fifteen were all known to him, at least by sight, by now; for he had attended a number of these functions in the last three weeks, since the first dinner with the lady. A dozen of them were male, the other three female; and most were quite young. But all were well-placed in the court of the Archduke, and prominent in the social and political talk of the city.

"Sir Jamie—it is good to see you again!" The speaker was an older man, a Greek named Michael—Jamie had not been able to pronounce his last name, and so he did not remember it.

"It's most pleasant to see you all again," Jamie bowed before them, and many, though not all, sketched shallow responses. Jamie did not fail to notice that one, a dark, slender Magyar named Lukas Morhacs, had not only failed to return the salutation, but had turned his back to the Scot. But Jamie had encountered the man's hostility at previous functions, and had determined not to let the man goad him into some rash act.

"Sir Jamie!" a soft hand on his arm claimed his attention at that moment, and he turned and looked down into the brown eyes of one of the few women present, a somewhat plain German lady who was said to be a relative of both the Archduke and the Emperor himself. She was here in Italy without her husband, a Palatine count who was said to be kept busy on the Estonian march at the express order of the Emperor. The lady, it was known, managed to amuse herself in select company.

"My lady," Jamie said, grasping the tips of her fingers as she raised her hand, holding them softly and then bowing slightly while brushing the back of her hand with his lips. "It's a pleasure to see you. Is your health holding up to this terrible cold spell?"

Thank God for Maria, Jamie thought to himself. The blonde

girl had noticed his discomfort at the unending pursuit the German was displaying last week; and, finally taking pity on him, had advised him that one subject alone could displace romance from the lady's thought—her health.

"I feared I would *die* during the High Mass yesterday," the woman began. "Do you know there was actually a skin of ice on the horse trough as we entered St. Ambrose's? It was nearly too much for me, for I knew I had a tender constitution but I had not taken the preparation my old nurse used to fix for me. . . ."

On the other hand, Jamie thought to himself, *is this necessarily any better?* He signaled a servant silently for a cup of wine—Lady Irene always served the best, and tonight saw her providing a fiery, warmed, golden wine that seared the back of the throat but definitely warmed up the coldest of new arrivals. He motioned for the servant to refill the German woman's cup—to the rim.

A few more guests arrived, and Jamie was spared some medical tales by the duty to make them welcome. One of them he knew reasonably well and actually liked a good deal—a slim young Provençal knight named Giles de Haut Sauverne. The blond, handsome man at times seemed quite congenial, happy to talk war and weapons with Jamie in the midst of gossip on the court; at other times, though, he seemed to become clouded by the shadow of some unhappy event; and when that happened, he sulked. It seemed to happen when he had had too much to drink, though what he might be sulking about was a mystery to Jamie.

That was when Irene appeared. Jamie sensed her entrance immediately, even though he happened not to be looking in the direction she came from. Perhaps, he thought, it was only that he saw the reactions of the others who had seen her first; at any rate, it seemed to him as if the atmosphere in the room had livened considerably. But he restrained himself from rushing to greet her, knowing now that she preferred to be left to make her own approaches to each person she had invited. And so he waited; but he did not notice who he was talking to, or on what subject.

After an endless wait she appeared by his side, one hand resting lightly on his left forearm, which was cocked in front of him to hold his cup. The touch seemed to burn through the sleeve of his tunic, and he looked down into her eyes again, as he had been fortunate enough to do so often in these last weeks.

"Jamie," she said. Her voice was bright and hostesslike; but somehow, he thought, she managed to put a touch of extra emotion into the name. "It pleases me you could get away from your duties to join us. How is our dear young Carlo? You must bring him to see me one day."

To those last words no response was really necessary. Jamie bowed low over her hand, brushing it with his lips. He tried to catch her eyes, but she had already moved on to someone else. Still he continued to watch her, and was rewarded shortly by the flash of her dark eyes over Michael's shoulder—just a short signal of her attention, but it warmed him. He stifled a smile and turned away to move across the room and get a refill for his cup. Then he stepped from the close, hot air of the great room into the coolness of the interior garden court of her small palace.

"Sir Jamie?" a soft female voice greeted him from the darkness while he was still somewhat blinded by his movement from light into dimness. But he recognized the voice.

"Maria," he said.

He had been about to say more, but somehow it seemed as if everything he thought of to say would be the wrong thing. This was how it always was when he encountered the blonde woman these days—she was the most uncomfortable person he knew in the city to talk with. Her contrast in this with Irene came forcibly to his mind.

"It's cool out here, at least," she said. "I don't wonder that you wanted to move out of that overheated hall."

She had been moving toward him out of the darkness, and now he picked up her silhouette against the lighter gray of the far wall as his eyes began to adjust to the dark.

"Ah—yes," he answered. "And it's not only hot but noisy inside."

The remark sounded dull, almost like that of some raw young squire, in his own ears.

"Perhaps so," she said. "One wouldn't think a mere fifteen or so could fill such a large room."

An uncomfortable pause intruded on the conversation.

"Though it's true enough," she went on, "that many of them are accounted accomplished talkers. Perhaps they practice on each other."

She laughed at that, and Jamie found himself laughing with her, although he thought the remark only an obvious truth and was not sure just why it might be funny.

"Good night, Sir Jamie," she said again; and was by him and on her way through the door into the palace before he quite realized that she had had no intention at all of stopping longer to talk with him. He stared after her, feeling anger stirring within him—but the unsatisfying kind of anger that has no real target to aim at. It was the sort of situation he had run into sometimes with Moraig.

"Sir Jamie, is that you out there?" The voice was a man's this time. The palace door had reopened, and a figure was peering out.

"Yes, Master Michael," Jamie said, once more recognizing a voice in the darkness.

"Oh, it *is* cooler out here." The door closed and the dark figure moved towards him—Jamie noticed that the Greek made almost no sound at all as he moved.

"Yes," Jamie said. His practice of taciturnity had become almost a habit with him.

"Of course I should have realized that a northerner like yourself would like cool airs rather more than we southerners," the man went on. "Or is it our company that you tire of?"

"I'm afraid I don't understand," Jamie said.

It worried him that Michael often seemed to be probing him. But what could the other want to find out? Jamie was not really privy to any valuable court secrets.

"Ah—I know!" the man exclaimed. "You have an assignation!"

He laughed loudly and heartily. It was the sort of strong male laughter that Jamie heard too seldom in these Italian court circles; and he thought he would have warmed to it if the man had not ended it with a kind of unnaturally swallowed gurgle—it sounded as if Michael had used the opportunity of humor to clear his sinuses surreptitiously.

"But as you can see," Jamie responded after a moment, "there is no one out here but myself."

"Oh, you poor fellow!" Michael slapped Jamie on the shoulder solidly. "You've been misled and betrayed. Come in with me, then. Have a drink and drown your sorrows."

"I *have* a drink," Jamie said. "Nor was I waiting for anyone; I came out only—"

"Yes, yes, I know," the other broke in. "But come along anyway, and let us take care of you."

He wrapped a large hand around Jamie's forearm and began to drag the Scot toward the door.

Fighting an instinct that prompted him to fight the other's pull and knock loose the hand that held him, Jamie reluctantly let himself be taken inside. By the time they stepped once more into the light, he had managed to empty most of his drink into some bushes, leaving only a small swallow which he ostentatiously drained as they entered.

Once again Jamie found himself swarmed about by a mixed group of guests as he entered. And he noted that as soon as Jamie seemed to be thoroughly engaged by them, Michael disappeared somewhere.

Where is Irene? he wondered at that moment; then saw her across the room. For a moment he was ashamed at himself, for his suspicion seemed unworthy of him—and of her. But one disturbing thought led to others in his mind: who was Michael, and why had he become so interested in Jamie? Whoever he might be, Jamie knew now, he was more than a mere courtier; he had betrayed himself—at least to the extent of letting Jamie see that he was a warrior, or had once been one.

The conversations continued to ebb and flow like surf about Jamie as he stood thinking, a fresh glass of red wine now in his hand. A small part of his mind was paying enough attention to the talk to be able to deal with questions aimed in his own direction. But his responses were short and prosaic, in keeping with his role of being no great wit, and, as always, the people about him soon turned their attention away from such a cipher in the game of conversation.

Shortly a stir went through the crowd, and Jamie looked up to see that Master Antonio had appeared in the room for the first time that evening. The magician was dressed in the peculiar looking long satin cloak that Jamie had seen often enough to recognize that its presence meant Antonio was going to present some sort of entertainment for Irene's guests. He was noted for being able to perform showy feats that awed and amused the guests; and these had made Irene's parties even more well-known than they might have been otherwise. At times Antonio had confounded the guests by merely introducing entertainers of a more conventional sort, and then retiring to some corner. But at others he had worked actual wonders himself. Jamie wondered idly which it was to be this evening.

Jamie found himself standing beside the German woman once more—for a moment he struggled to remember her name, but then gave up the effort as unnecessary, since "my lady," could always serve the need of politeness. Fortunately, he saw immediately, her attention seemed directed at Sir Giles, who was standing slightly askew on her far side. From the look on his face, Jamie suspected that the blond man had already taken a good deal to drink, and was about to become his morose other self.

About to move off quietly, Jamie checked himself as he caught a few of the words the German lady was saying to Sir Giles—although the latter was probably not taking them in well.

". . . but then, she was raised in the Imperial court—in Constantinople, I mean," the woman said. "I'd have thought you'd know that . . ." They were talking about Irene, of course.

". . . so it was only good sense that young Carlo stayed safe, here, where they were both born, of course," the German continued. "Are you paying attention?" Sir Giles mumbled something.

"What?" she demanded.

"All too much attention, my dear." The blond knight seemed abruptly to pull himself together, and the glaze departed from his eyes. His posture straightened, and he glared down at her for a brief moment.

Fascinated, and at the same time a little embarrassed, it came suddenly to Jamie that he had just seen some deep wound in the soul of the French knight being salted. But the moment passed, and when the startled German woman made no immediate response, the Frenchman seemed to waver, and turn his gaze inward again. There was silence a brief time, Jamie again thought of moving away, but did not. At the front of the room Master Antonio produced an exotic large green bird from the space between the breast-plate and the chest of one of the guardsmen—to the latter's evident astonishment.

"And the bird will speak!" Antonio proclaimed. "Listen!"

Jamie turned his attention back to the German woman as she once more spoke to Giles.

"She was returned here from Constantinople, of course, to attract a good match, one that will be of some advantage to the Imperial family—and to her own family, of course." The older woman smiled. "And—now you must keep this to your-

self—but, there are those who say that already, in just two
years, she's become the real power here at the archducal
court—and that that Savoyard cow the Archduke married will
soon find herself off in that farmyard she merits. . . .'' The
tone of those last words was low and savage, and Jamie understood that they were not really being said for the benefit of Sir
Giles. He thought again about moving away when an entirely
different matter suddenly claimed his attention.

All the light in the room—torches and candles both—had
abruptly turned green, producing an eerie effect that seemed
without warning to transform all the spectators into gawking,
dirty-faced peasants with blackened lips and smudged cheeks.
Master Antonio was still at work up at the front of the room.
Everyone was staring about at the change in those nearby; then
Michael made some remark that produced a burst of laughter
about him, on the other knight's side of the room. But it drew
everyone's attention back to Antonio.

In that moment a hand touched Jamie softly on his upper
right arm—the side away from the German woman; and he
turned to see a servant, one of the older men on the palace
staff, with a soft, pudgy look. The man said no word as Jamie
turned, but merely beckoned and moved softly to a small re-
cessed doorway in an alcove of the wall. He opened it and
stood inside, holding it open. Jamie followed. As he reached
the alcove, all light vanished from the room for a brief moment—another of Antonio's effects; and in the brief burst of
ohs and ahs, the door opened and Jamie passed through it.

He knew his way from here, and the servant had closed the
door behind him without following. As Jamie walked down the
passageway, his step became eager and he became aware that
he was smiling. Irene would be ahead, waiting for him—or
rather, this candelit passage he now followed would bring him
to a room where he would wait for her. But that she would
come to him there, he knew now beyond doubt, and the stir
that anticipation of her coming produced throughout his body
shocked him.

In his past beddings of occasional whores and peasant
girls—and once the daughter of a minor Burgundian noble—
he had never encountered anyone like the dark-haired, exotic
Greek-Italian woman. Her very appearance could cause his
tightest stomach muscles to quiver lightly, a shiver that ran
down his stomach and onto his thighs—and how she could
follow him up!

"Jamie." Her voice from a tiny side-passage checked him even before he reached the passage he was used to waiting for her in. He turned as she moved forward to confront him, close to him, fragrant. He reached for her, but she put up an arm to hold him back.

"Not yet," she said. "I came to tell you that you must wait for me a longer time." She looked up at him with eyes that were luminous, soft and large.

"Wait?" he asked. "Why? How long?"

The questions tumbled out as hollow sounds from his chest. He felt breathless, sweat cooling on his forehead.

"Just a few hours, my sweet," the low voice hummed in his head. Somewhere within him an old, familiar voice was crying "caution!" but he ignored it. She reached up to brush her fingertips over his lips.

"A few hours?" he echoed.

"Make yourself comfortable in the salon." She pointed ahead of him down the passageway. "Andrea will keep you well-supplied . . . with whatever you like. And then—" her smile tantalized him, "and then I shall return to you."

She turned and was past him before he could say anything more. She was looking back over her shoulder as she vanished into the darkness of the smaller passageway. After a moment Jamie turned and went forward as she had directed.

When at last she returned, Jamie was perhaps more than half-drunk. He had started well on his way to being completely so by drowning his disappointment and impatience in several hastily swallowed cups of the strong sweet wine filling a large pitcher in the salon where he had been told to wait. As for Andrea, the supple dark-haired maid Irene had left to take the edge off any over-powering other appetites he might have—he hardly looked at the girl. A prince, he told himself alcoholically, did not settle for second best.

Gradually, however, his native caution returned to him. *If anyone attacks you now*, he told himself, *you'll play hell defending yourself when halfway to snoring in a gutter*. He forced himself to eat, and to switch to filling his cup with the melt of the ice used to keep the fruits chilled. And by the time the dark woman returned, while he was still pleasantly warm from the wine, most of his wits had returned to him.

"Irene?" The word came out involuntarily, however, when at last a movement appeared in the shadowed doorway he had been eyeing for some hours.

"Yes, it's me," she said, stepping in and smiling at him. He stood hastily, and managed to knock over his chair in the process. At this she smiled a bit more widely, moving sedately forward to take his hand in hers.

"My poor Jamie!" her voice cooed in his ear. "Has it been so long a wait, then?"

"It—yes!" Jamie blurted out. He put out his right arm and wrapped it about her shoulder, pulling her roughly to him.

"Yes!" he said again, growling the word as he bent to kiss her neck and bury his head in her hair. She laughed, throwing her head back to expose the golden marble of her throat, and let him pull her on into the bedroom he had discovered just beyond, some hours since.

Over the course of the next month, the waiting—and sometimes the scene that had followed their first encounter—were repeated more and more often. Once he was even sent home for the night without getting to see her at all; and he found himself for the first time jealously beginning to notice the whereabouts of other men he knew frequented her palace.

Sometimes he woke in the night to look down at her, sleeping, in the light of the candles she never put out. And at those times he found himself filled with a great tenderness that made him want to hold her and protect her forever. But then he would go back to sleep, and in the morning she would rouse him and send him on his way with no more than a kiss and a murmured word—as if the night just passed between them had been no more than a moment's play.

Meanwhile, during all this time, Jamie was seeing a great deal more of court life than he had suspected to exist; and having become an intimate of the lady which gossip said was to be the upcoming power of the court, he found himself receiving many more invitations than he was used to, many from women and not a few from men. At first he did not bother to take them up, feeling that such events would be of no consequence if Irene was not there. But in time he found that during those nights when he was not to see her, time weighed heavily on him; and so he began to go out ever more often.

However, shortly before the Feast of the Nativity, when a sharp frost had crisped the mud and mire in the Milanese streets, he received a shock that sobered him in an instant. He had once again led the escort that took young Carlo to an Archducal entertainment in the great palace—Carlo and his teachers were in residence in the old castle, which had been abandoned when the Archduke's father had completed the new palace some years before. This older castle was located on the north side of the city, near the great circular wall itself—gossip had it that the boy was out of favor in response to the vile temper his mother was displaying toward the Archduke these days.

"Look, Sir Jamie!" the boy exclaimed. "Is that not the great sorcerer, Master Antonio, himself?" He pointed across the great room to the man with whom Jamie had now come to be not only more familiar, but even friendly, bowing to the Archduke's guest of the evening, an ambassador of some sort from one of the Moorish courts in north Africa.

A little amused at the boy's description of Master Antonio, Jamie confirmed that it was indeed he; and noted out loud that since he was wearing the black satin cloak, he was perhaps about to provide entertainment for the guests. At this Carlo crowed and clapped his hands twice before grabbing Jamie's hand in his own and pulling him hastily across the floor to gain a better viewing position.

Settled near the outer wall on a bench behind the boy, Jamie scanned the crowd automatically, checking on the placements of his men. Then he leaned back to watch the show, easily able to see over the lad's head; on impulse he reached forward and tousled the boy's hair briefly. Carlo looked back at him and grinned before turning his eager attention forward again.

Jamie found himself smiling too. This was a good lad. For a moment he wondered how his younger brother Simon was doing, keeping the smile for a brief while as he recovered first from his memory those good times when he had been followed all about by the other boy. . . . With a frown, he got back the rest of his memories of his home in a rush. Moraig, now; how was she? Once more he had forgotten. . . . But then, what man could remember such things all the time, with so much going on about him?

Master Antonio had taken the center space at the front of the room, facing the Archducal party itself, and had gone into his act once more. Jamie had seen him produce clouds of colored smokes and bunches of flowers before, and so he sat back without paying particular attention. The setting now brought other memories of similar events to his mind.

But no one will touch my shoulder this night, he thought ruefully to himself. The idea completed the job of bringing his spirits to a low ebb; and for some moments he felt heavy-chested, listless, and uninterested in anything at all; his mind raced futilely from topic to topic, never pausing long enough to complete a thought before grasping the next bad memory and holding it for inspection.

"Sir Jamie, is it you?" The voice came from above him and to his side, and he looked up to see the blond Sir Giles smiling down at him. Still glum, Jamie had to admit to himself nevertheless that he had seldom seen the Frenchman looking more happy.

"Indeed it is, Sir Giles," he answered. "Here with the Archduke's son, Carlo. Have you met the lad?" He indicated the small figure just before them.

"No, I haven't had that pleasure," Giles said. "Honored to meet your lordship—but how are you, Jamie? It's been some weeks since we've had a chance to talk. Have you heard the news from Savoy?"

They got lost in talking of the eternal war in the south of France, while Antonio continued his displays about the room; but eventually that, too, came to an end. Music resumed, penetrating the room from carefully screened corners; and guests began to circulate and talk, sampling from the lavishly heaped trays liveried servants were carrying about.

Carlo still looked interested in all that went on about him, but Jamie now noted a slight glaze in the lad's eyes. He signaled to the boy's tutor and the latter, after a conference with the Archduke's seneschal, returned the signal to Jamie, who stood up and turned to Giles.

"I'm sorry to leave you, friend," Jamie said, "but it's time the lad returned home and went to bed. I bid you good evening, and I hope we'll get a chance to talk more soon."

Giles bowed and smiled in reply, and Jamie rounded up his party and conducted the boy out of the building and homeward.

Carlo was asleep by the time they reached the old castle, despite the bumpy, drafty ride over the rude stones that lined the dark city streets. And to avoid waking him Jamie scooped him up, wrapped in a large cloak, and carried him through the door to the keep and up the stairs.

Near the top of the inside stairs Jamie had to pause while the boy's servants scurried about for lights and the lad's nightclothes; and the small figure stirred in Jamie's arms.

"Sir Jamie?" The tone was sleepy and quiet; and again the thoughts of Simon, orphaned young, came to the Scot.

"Hush, boy, sleep," he said in gentle fashion.

"Are you angry with me?" the boy spoke again in a mud-dled, sleepy tone.

"Angry? Of course not," Jamie said, looking down at the figure in his arms with some concern. He restrained himself from asking where the boy could have gotten that idea, not wanting to wake him further. But the boy spoke again.

"Are you angry at Brethin? Or Ned?"

"No, boy, of course not. Where would you get an idea like that?"

The figure stirred a bit; and a servant came by to take him, but Jamie shook his head and moved, carrying the boy himself in the direction of the now ready bed.

"You aren't with them anymore," the boy said. "You're always with the witch."

Jamie felt as if someone had plunged his body into icy waters; but he reached the bed and deposited the boy on it without incident.

"Sleep now," he said. "Just sleep. Everything will be all right." The figure murmured something and was quiet; and Jamie turned and went out, pausing only to check that the night shift of his guard was in place.

At the top of the outside stair to the keep, he stopped once more. It was his night to command the guard; but Ned had been with them at the palace, and Brethin had overseen the caretaker contingent here at the old castle; so they should both be off duty but still around. Perhaps he should talk with them both. He looked about, but didn't see them, and hurried down the steps and out the main gate of the castle. And, yes, he could see them, some way down the street, probably heading for the tavern that they all had been used to frequenting.

He paused, irresolute, pondering whether to run after and join them.

But what could I say? he said to himself. *Certainly they would not understand how it is with Irene. Or with me.*

He rubbed his chin. For that matter, how *was* it with Irene and with Jamie? Just what was it he was doing here? Was this something he could explain at all to a friend, or to someone at home . . . like Moraig?

The figures he had been watching had disappeared long before he turned his back toward the keep and signaled for the closing of the main gate.

Chapter Nine

"GOOD EVENING, MARIA."

"Good evening, Sir Jamie." These days the girl smiled at him more than she had before, but it seemed to Jamie that the smile contained a hint of some sadness. Was she sad for him? Could she now have somehow gotten the idea that he was no longer under her mistress's spell—that he still came at her call mainly out of the desire not to anger the most formidable woman in the archduchy?

Jamie shrugged his cloak off into the hands of the servant who was waiting to take it. He wondered if Maria remembered those early days when his high spirits had caused his cloak to dance about the room like some airy elemental just released from a bottle by someone like the Oxford doctor—or like Antonio. . . .

"You are the last to arrive," she went on. "Please come this way." She turned and moved slowly down the hallway in the direction of the same large entertaining room Jamie had been in so many times. He found himself watching her movements, admiring the grace that made her seem to float ahead of him with scarcely a movement to disturb the lines of her gown. Her hair was tied up on her head, held in place with bright blue ribbons that matched her dress. Her neck was slim and pale, and he found himself watching it as he moved behind her.

Better not let Irene get an idea of your thoughts, he told himself, and instead directed his attention to the gown Maria wore, which, although becoming, was not made of silk, as most of Irene's were. For the first time Jamie wondered just exactly what the girl's status in this household might be.

They came through the door into the great room, and once again Jamie was greeted by voices calling his name familiarly from all sides. He fell easily into his pose of easy good humor, and turned away from Maria as he tried to return each salutation. When he turned back her way she was gone from his view.

This night about forty people seemed to be on hand, and already Master Antonio was appearing at the head of the room. Jamie made a mental note to himself not to allow himself to be so late at such events in future—it attracted unnecessary attention.

As Antonio opened his act by causing another of the unfortunate guardsmen to act like a goat, Jamie spotted Sir Giles across the room; and he wandered over that way, hoping to engage the other in a conversation that could take his mind from this court life. But when Giles looked up on his approach, Jamie could see that familiar glaze of drink overlaying his gaze; and his heart sank a little.

"Good evening, Sir Giles," Jamie warily opened the conversation. It was too late to back off without any greeting at all, he felt—but something told him Giles was trouble this night.

Giles did not smile in return, and indeed seemed to be having a bit of trouble focusing on Jamie—looking at the Scot somberly, as if thinking slowly to try to remember just who it was standing in front of him. Jamie nodded politely and made as if to turn sideways to get a better view of the doings of Master Antonio, who was now producing a variety of popping noises out of thin air. But Giles moved his gaze with Jamie, and now reached out an arm to rest on the latter's shoulder, holding Jamie in place while he looked at him.

"It's Jamie," he said, badly slurring the initial consonant of the latter's name. "The big favorite now." He dropped his eyes to look down into his cup, as if he had gotten sly abruptly.

"Whatever you've got, it won't last," he said. And at that moment the lights in the room all turned a bright, eye-searing red.

Another of Antonio's tricks, of course, Jamie knew, although the color was not one he had seen before. And the effect seemed to have magnified the intensities of the flambeaux and candles in the room; and the brightness grew and grew until it pained the eyes. Jamie found himself beginning to squint against the glare, blinking as his eyes sought relief in the darkness behind his closed lids.

A final flare dazzled his vision, and then the lights winked out altogether and the room was plunged into a darkness that was welcome relief to all. Jamie could hear the wave of comment that welled up among the spectators, and he suspected that no small number of them would have caustic things to say rather soon. It was in fact unprecedented for one of Master Antonio's effects to cause any discomfort at all for his audience, and Jamie spared a moment to wonder if the man had somehow lost some momentary control of his art.

And at that moment Jamie became aware of movement about him; and he forced his eyes, pained though they were, to open. But the darkness about him was total, and he could see absolutely nothing except blurred green and red splotches that danced in front of his eyes in the darkness. He tried to listen for further indications of whatever had alerted him; but the crowd was getting too noisy and he could make out nothing.

After another moment, light returned to the room, growing slowly in intensity from the first small flicker, like a tiny dawn. It was greeted with relieved, excited whispers among the crowd—but Jamie noted that Giles was gone from the place he had been in before the darkness descended. Jamie looked about but could not see him in the room.

Later that evening, standing ignored at the edge of a group that was listening to a wry tale being told by the Greek, Michael—as his hands moved in the telling, Jamie noticed for the first time that he was missing the last joint of his left little finger—Jamie felt the customary touch on his shoulder. He turned—to find himself facing Irene herself.

"Sir Jamie," she said, smiling demurely up at him, "You are looking well. I'm sorry that I missed talking to you earlier this evening." Jamie looked down into her face, noting how undetectable her paints and powders still were.

"For that," he said, "I owe you a grave apology." He bowed low over the hand she had kept in front of her, brushing it with his lips; and as he did so, he caught the faintest trace of her fragrance once more. For a brief moment it made the breath catch in his throat again, and he paused.

"I was forced to chastise one of the oafs in my command,"

he said. He kept his head down, hoping the lie would not then be caught on his face. He kissed her hand once more.

She laughed softly and drew her hand back; necessarily, Jamie straightened up. He tried to recapture his customary blandness of personality before he looked her in the eye. But she was laughing, watching someone's reaction to the show they were putting on—someone behind Jamie.

When her eyes came back to him, he was smiling down at her—and having no difficulty at all in appearing to view her with lust in his heart. She was definitely a most beautiful woman.

She smiled dazzlingly at him now, and he smiled back unreservedly; then she moved off without a word, presumably to tilt with some other opponent in her own way. Jamie found himself laughing silently behind her—undeniably, she made life most interesting for all around her!

The touch on his shoulder came about an hour later, just as he was about to step out into the garden once more for a breath of cool air—and a little silence. And—apparently because they were already at the door—this time the servant took him on outside and along the side of the building to another door. He held it open for Jamie but did not himself enter, and the Scot again found himself left to make his way to the intimate chambers where Irene would expect to see him.

For a moment he speculated as to what her reaction would be if she came to those rooms and did not find him waiting. He laughed again, knowing that it would probably be dangerous, and possibly deadly, for him—but the expression on her face! His imagination supplied it for him, and he laughed again. But he continued into the building, and towards his rendezvous. She was, after all, most attractive and—in the proper setting—enjoyable.

In the early morning hours he woke from a light sleep. Careful to avoid movement that might rouse Irene, sleeping beside him, he turned his head to look at her. But the candles mounted along the wall, shining through a gap in the velvet hangings that swathed the sides of the bed, left the side of her face in shadow, and he could see her only in silhouette.

After a few moments he began slowly to sit up, still trying to avoid waking her. At last he was in position to look down at her, and he gazed at her—at all of her that he could see from where the creamy shoulders emerged from the covers that kept them warm in this cool room.

For a moment he felt the stirring of a tenderness he had never associated with this woman before. He could now see smudges in the powder on her face, in the coloration of her lips—and yet, somehow it made her seem more vulnerable, more human, more likable. Here in sleep she was relaxed, and he could look down at her and wish she was not such a determined manipulator of those around her.

He sighed; and with the slight movement of the bed that this caused, he saw her face change—tighten—slightly. He knew she was awake.

She had kept her eyes closed, but he put a smile on his own face and rolled more toward her. She was, after all, still beautiful—hadn't he said that some hours earlier?

He laughed softly, and the sound of that pleased Irene when she opened her eyes to see him. Her hands moved, hidden as they were under the blankets, and he jerked in surprise at what she did to him. Now it was she who laughed, looking up at him; and he joined her as they moved together quickly.

The darkness that filled the room from outside was beginning to turn a lighter gray when they moved apart again, and Jamie at least was puffing and sweaty. With some admiration he noted that Irene seemed to be as cool and composed as she always was in public—and yet it must be true, he thought, that she had been enjoying the night, too. Her smile as she rose and turned to look at him through the parted bed curtains seemed to have some reality to it, he thought.

"Rest," she said. "I'll be back in a moment."

She smiled again and turned away, fading into the darkness of a doorway in the far wall.

Jamie lay back softly, staring at the canopy that hid the ceiling from his eyes. He could not sleep now, he knew. He felt strangely emptied of thought, even of emotion; and his mind, never in his life inactive, seemed to be still in motion, but undirected—like a tiny weasel-dog, it seemed to be in the midst of so many trails that it could follow none of them for very long. He lay watching nothing, as if asleep with his eyes open.

Suddenly, without any apparent outside stimulation, he shook himself vigorously; and at the end of the movement he found himself sitting up at the side of the bed, head pushed out through the curtains which draped themselves about his shoulders.

What did that? he wondered to himself. Could he be coming

down with some ague? But that didn't seem right, either. . . .
He got up and, finding himself on Irene's side of the bed,
moved around to the other side, to where he had left his
clothes. But as he located them, he realized that Irene would
not be happy to find him gone. He had better stay.

He was restless now, not sleepy at all; and he moved about
the room a little, locating the remainder of wine they had
shared last night—drinking some. He stared at the door
through which Irene had gone.

At last he shrugged, and then grinned to himself; he was
beginning to notice that when in Irene's home—and several
others in this city—he seemed to instinctively act as if he knew
he was being watched by someone. Perhaps that was the case,
too—but he had begun to feel as if he were an actor or a
diplomat.

Still naked, he stood over his clothes a moment, debating
whether to dress; and having decided not to, he then fought a
battle over whether to carry one of his weapons in his hand. At
last he decided not to do that either, because of the effect it
would have if the wanderings he proposed were interrupted.
The decision left him very uneasy, but his mind told him any
excuse he might offer if found would be accepted more easily
if he were unarmed and naked. He managed to force a grin
again.

Ah, yes, he thought—*the wine.* He emptied the liquid that
was left out the small window into the courtyard.

*They'll believe that I wanted more, if they don't believe I'm
seeking to get rid of last night's,* he thought.

Pitcher in hand, he padded softly over the cold stone floor,
to the doorway through which Irene had passed.

The door was intricately carved, a nearly black wood, as far
as he could tell in the gray pre-dawn light; it seemed to have
many more brass fittings than an ordinary door would have, but
as far as he could tell they were mostly for decorative purposes. He grasped one of them, shaped like a lion's head, and
pulled the door toward him. It did not move. Now he pushed,
and the surface moved silently away from him. Quickly he
caught at the metal piece to hold the door after a small movement so that he could try to see if anyone on the other side
might have noticed the door moving. But the crack that had
opened at the side of the door showed only darkness.

Slowly he opened the door farther, and eventually stepped
forward into the next chamber. He had been here before, and

knew it to be a small room Irene often used for private purposes—and the other exit ought to be to his right. . . . He groped in that direction and finally found another doorway.

This one was curtained over, with another wooden panel behind that fabric—and he could see a faint light coming through the tiny crack at the side of this door.

After listening and hearing nothing for some minutes, he moved his fingers silently about the wooden panel, and eventually located the sturdy handhold. This door, too, seemed unlatched, and moved silently toward him a short distance before he stopped it. He put an eye to the wider crevice that had been created.

His first view was of a room that had been painted in some sort of geometric design in a variety of colors laid over a light yellow base. The light illuminating them seemed bright yellow, too—but soft, as if it were flooding the room from some great distance. He could not see any person, nor hear any voice. After a moment he pulled the door to him a bit farther.

Now he could see the entire room, except for the far left end of it—he had no idea how far the room might extend in that direction. But he was not concerned with what else might be there, because he could now see Irene herself.

She was still unclothed and was standing near the center of the space he could see. Bathed in the bright, soft light, she seemed at first to be a statue, still and unmoving. The light shone about her as if it were some sort of halo—or, he thought, as if it were somehow coming *from* her rather than *to* her. He was abruptly a bit uneasy with that thought, but he continued to watch her.

She was not after all standing perfectly still, he soon realized—he had merely caught her in a pose that she took for some reason having to do with her purpose there. In another moment she moved, altering her posture and position a slight bit, and froze again in place. After several more such changes he realized that she was watching herself in some mirror he could not see—perhaps that had something to do with the unusual quality of the light he saw about her.

She *was* beautiful, he realized. Her body seemed as unflawed as any statue he had seen in the well-adorned gardens of the nobility of Italy, where statues seemed to have been placed everywhere. Strangely, he realized that at this moment he felt no lust at all toward her.

A dark figure moved in front of him suddenly; and he very

nearly jumped backwards—he only just restrained himself from slamming the door and running.

The figure was the Greek, Michael, apparently pacing about the small room; and he had not seen the barely open door from which Jamie watched. Now he reached the right end of the room and turned about, presented his other profile to Jamie as he moved back, crossing in front of Irene—but apparently not interrupting her view of the mirror—and out of sight to Jamie's left. Jamie still had heard no sound, but now he tried to turn his head so that his ear could get closer to the crack through which his eye watched.

Frustrated, he moved his eye completely away for a moment, pressing his ear to the crack—but he still heard no sound. Either the room was soundless—no one making any noise at all—or there was some sort of muffling spell in action. The latter would not be any surprise, he supposed. He put his eye back to the crack in time to see Michael walk back into his view.

Yes, the man was definitely talking, but Jamie could hear no sounds; for a moment Jamie tried to watch his lips, to recognize the words. But he could make out no word that way, and he found Michael's constantly moving hands to be a distraction—so after a few moments, and as Michael again paced out of sight to his left, he returned his gaze to Irene.

In the interval, he knew, she had continued her series of poses, seeming to reserve her attention for the mirror. And for the first time since he had begun watching he found his gaze resting on her face rather than on her body and her surroundings.

He shivered—he had never seen such a face, such an expression, on her before.

He watched, suddenly aware that he was now seeing a side of her that had never come out in his presence—nor in that of most people, he suspected. This face before him was serious, and quite still—it reminded him of nothing so much as the expression he had seen once on the visage of a much-experienced executioner in France, as the older man had patiently studied the neck of a kneeling figure before him. . . .

He shivered. If Irene was indeed watching herself in the mirror, as he suspected, then she must have a strange opinion, indeed, of the body—of the person—she saw before her. As he watched, she raised a hand and brushed lightly at something she apparently saw on her left breast—although Jamie could

see no sign of a flaw. She lowered the hand and turned slightly
to the side, still watching ahead of her; and he saw that her
expression did not change at all.

Now she turned more completely to the side, almost presenting her back to Jamie, although her head remained turned to
face the mirror he assumed was there. Her mouth opened,
although Jamie heard no sound; and in a moment Michael
appeared again with a small, squat jar into which he dipped a
small brush and seemed to paint her upper back lightly. He
stopped, moved off to the left again, and then returned with a
gauzy cloth, which he used to rub her back gently once more.
Then he moved away again.

Her expression had remained still through all this; now she
turned and posed for herself again. If she was happy with what
she saw, she gave no sign of it that Jamie could see.

Deciding that he was learning nothing useful in this position—and it was dangerous to be here—Jamie softly pushed
the door shut and retraced his steps to the bedroom. There he
deposited the empty pitcher on a table, faintly regretting that he
had poured its contents out the window earlier, and crawled
back into the bed.

He had only been there for a few minutes when Irene returned—accompanied by a maidservant carrying a tray with
more wine as well as pastries. The servant showed no interest
in the fact that Jamie was in the bed, nor that her mistress was
moving about without benefit of clothing.

Maybe that's carrying her act a bit too far, Jamie thought; *it
is after all winter, and that floor is cool at best.*

When the servant had left, Irene gracefully reentered the
bed, moving under the covers to snuggle next to Jamie again;
and she waited for her flesh to warm up under the blankets
before she began to caress him, touching him here and there in
ways that would have excited any man Jamie could think of.

After a few moments she stopped to reach to the bedside
table near the head of her side of the bed, handing him a cup of
wine and then a small, spicy meat-filled pastry. It was very
good, and he found it had the added effect of making him
thirsty. He drank more wine and was presented with yet another pastry—this one sweet rather than spiced, but again making him thirsty.

He caught on quickly, but could see no way to avoid eating
and drinking as much as she wished him to take. The reason
for this would soon come clear, no doubt.

"Jamie," she whispered some time later, as he was feeling rather overstuffed and trying manfully to suppress a belch, "I am dreadfully worried."

He had forgotten, he realized, that he had always played the part of a simpleton around her; and that was the kind of man she was trying to deal with now. That would make it easier for him. He let the belch escape.

"Is something wrong?" he said tenderly into her ear. "What can I do to fix it?" He nipped the lobe lightly and she squealed a little and kissed his neck.

"I'm worried about Carlo," she said.

"Carlo?" he muttered, not having to feign some confusion.

"Yes," she said. "He's very dear to me, as to all of us—you know that." She leaned forward and kissed his naked chest, finishing with a tiny sharp bite.

"It has come to me that the lad is in some danger," she said. "You have heard that there is danger of war—perhaps a civil war or a rebellion—and there are those who think their cause would benefit if they could capture or harm—the family of the Archduke." She stopped, probably to let him think about it.

"But they are all guarded!" Jamie protested, trying not to laugh. He did not know where this conversation might be going, but it was going to be most interesting!

"Of course they are!" she said, "and no guard could be better than yourself." She stopped to nuzzle about in the hair on his chest for a moment, and he kissed her on the top of the head.

"But," she continued, "any guard force can be circumvented if people already inside the palace—*trusted* people—betray the guard. And that's what I fear." She stopped and eyed him, perhaps trying to judge how he was taking this. He nodded, trying to look as if he did not want to, but had to, agree that what she said was true.

"So, then," she went on, "you know that His Grace the Archduke thinks very highly of me—and I of him, never let that be doubted. And we've talked of my fears, and agreed on a scheme—a plan—to avoid such a problem."

She giggled, now—an incongruity that almost startled Jamie out of the character he was intent on portraying. He stared down at her, but she, thankfully, did not look up into his eyes; and in a moment she went on with her exposition.

"It is going to be very funny," she said. "We'll simply hide Carlo someplace where absolutely no one will be able to find

him—and only you'll help me do that, so it'll be a great secret
from everyone—including those who wish to harm him.'' She
laughed. ''And when they come to try to hurt him, they won't
be able to find him, and it *will* be funny.''

He tried to laugh dutifully, while his mind raced. Obviously
she was suggesting some plan whereby he would use his position as head of Carlo's bodyguard to allow her—or whoever
she might be working with—to take the boy. Probably the lad
would be kept alive, but certainly something political was in
the works. He wished he had been paying more attention as to
who was aligned with whom in and around the court. . . .

But could she really believe he was thickheaded enough to
believe this silly story? On the other hand, like most Italians,
she seemed to have a particularly low opinion of the abilities of
most northerners, and he had been playing to that opinion. And
if that was not what she believed of him, then this must be
some sort of elaborate trap—and what could be the point of
that?

At that moment he recalled the ornate, convoluted plans that
Pietro Claveggio was so fond of, and he realized that he might
very well be so far out of his depth that he could drown in this
particular plot—and not realize that he was doing so. He shivered.

Fortunately, Irene took the shiver to be a tribute to the
ministrations she had not ceased to lavish on his body; she
giggled again low in her throat and looked up at him. He
growled something incomprehensible—he was getting to be
very good at that—and pressed her down into the soft, yielding
surface of the bed. This sort of response would buy him time,
and perhaps take her mind off watching for his reaction—but
only a little, he was sure.

Shortly after dawn he left the palace, suitably tired after the
long, ardent night; anyone watching for his exit would perhaps
be satisfied, he hoped. He went home and slept for a few
hours, leaving word with Brethin to have Ned join them at
noon for some fighting practice. This was sufficiently different
from his practice of recent weeks that Jamie knew anyone but
Brethin would have had some comment to make. But there was
none, and when noon came the man came to wake Jamie,
silently still.

They got to the practice yard late and indulged in routine
exercises until most of the other fighters had finished their day
and left. And when the area was cleared, and with Brethin

standing nearby, Jamie suggested that they use practice swords and engage in fencing—without their helms. Ned's eyebrows raised slightly at this, but he made no comment; and soon, after they had traded the first few blows, Jamie explained briefly that he thought it probable that he was being spied upon, and that this subterfuge was thus necessary.

"I know a lot of that goes on in this city," Ned said. "But have we then become so important? What value can there be in watching us?"

"They watch me to see if I will betray them, perhaps," Jamie said. "I have something I must tell Pietro Claveggio, and that soon. We must find a way to arrange a secret meeting with him."

"I see." Ned frowned in thought for a moment, and then turned to Brethin.

"You've been going to the Archducal palace quite a lot lately, have you not?" he asked. "You can do it again this night, if I'm not mistaken."

Brethin grinned a little shyly, and nodded. Ned turned back and grinned at Jamie.

"Someone a little more attractive than Claveggio, I gather," he said. "But she'll have to wait tonight. He should be able to get a word with Pietro himself, never minding the underlings—and then I suspect we can trust that one to find his own way here—or wherever you may be—without being noticed."

Jamie nodded. He could wait that long, certainly. But he was wondering how long Brethin had been going off to the palace for his bit of dalliance—he, Jamie, had not even noticed.

He sighed. Somehow he felt he had lost a certain place in life. Beyond all doubt, he knew Brethin would always honor his commitment to Jamie and be at his back in any trouble—but it had been Ned who had known of his entertainment, and been able to offer the use of its appearance without the asking. Somehow Jamie felt vaguely left out of things again.

They continued to practice hard, for the sake of any watchers, and also to ease their own tensions; and when they were through Jamie wiped himself off, broke his fast, and fell onto his pallet.

When he woke the room was dark, and he knew that the early winter night had fallen as he slept. He had been awakened by a tap on the door of his chamber, and as he lay there it came again, soft—just one rap. This time the door opened, letting in light from a torch that hung on a wall in the corridor outside his door; and he could see that it was Brethin, alone, who stood there.

"What is it, Brethin?"

"A message—someone to see you, my lord."

"Who is it?"

Brethin made no answer, only looking at him with unmoving face.

"Ah!" said Jamie. "A moment."

He prepared himself rapidly, belting on his sword, which had been near at hand to his bedside, and then pulling on a cloak. He stepped out into the corridor, stopping in front of Brethin.

"Lead," he said.

Brethin nodded and moved off.

Together they went outside to the main gate of the castle, open to anyone's observance, and then proceeded down the street in plain view. At last Jamie awoke to the fact that they were heading for the tavern that Jamie and his friends had taken to frequenting in the days before Jamie himself began spending much of his free time around Irene. It seemed a good subterfuge for an appointment made on such short notice, and he was pleased. He would be ready for whatever move might next be required.

They rounded a corner and came to the door of the tavern, above which hung no sign, but only a carved wooden likeness—crude and unpainted—of an ox. One night, soon after their duties at the castle with Carlo began, Ned had taken a swipe at the figure with his sword, putting a small notch in its underside—and since then the three of them had taken to calling the place The Gelding. No one else knew what they meant by it, he remembered.

As they approached the door of the tavern, they paused, and Brethin gave a single very short whistle. A figure detached itself from the shadows of the opposite doorway and moved toward them—Ned, he saw after a moment. It was a cloudy, moonless night and the streets were very dark. No one else seemed to be about.

Ned went past him without a word, and Brethin pushed Jamie in the direction of the doorway Ned had just left; then both of them strode up to the door of the tavern. Jamie caught on in time to jump across and into the doorway before the two opened the tavern's door, lighting up the street to any observer.

He waited silently as the door shut again and darkness came once more—waited as his eyes once more readjusted to that darkness.

But it was his ears rather than his eyes that caught the small movement of the door that opened behind him—a door that opened on more darkness, so that no betraying light escaped. Jamie, who had been expecting something more to occur, restrained the impulse that had sent his hand to the hilt of his sword; he waited soundlessly.

"Inside."

The voice was just a whisper, but he knew it to be that of Pietro, and so he felt his way forward and down into the interior of the little building. After the first moment, Claveggio had taken his arm and was leading him, moving quickly, on through the building and out a back door into a small courtyard. They moved from this through a wooden gate and into a street so small that it was more properly termed an alley. Immediately across the alley they entered another building, and once there stopped their movement. Claveggio produced a small oil lamp from the next room, placing it on a crude table; both of them sat, facing each other.

"Not yet," Pietro said, before Jamie had opened his mouth.

Claveggio rapped sharply three times on the table with the hilt of his dagger, and in a moment a hooded figure appeared in the room from some interior portion of the building.

Claveggio pointed silently at Jamie, and the other reached into some fold of his black-seeming robes and produced what appeared to be a hand-mirror. This he held up in front of his eyes, as if seeking to look at Jamie through its surface—although from his side Jamie could easily see his reflection in the polished surface. But the figure passed the mirror up and down and about, as if seeking to reflect all of Jamie's figure. After several moments the mirror vanished back into the folds of the robe, and the figure bowed and left the room. Pietro looked across at Jamie and grinned.

"Considering the company you've been keeping," he said, "I wanted to know if you'd been spelled in some way by our enemies."

"There is at least one spell on me," Jamie said. "I had it put there myself."

"Yes, the one for the languages," Pietro said. "I've known of that for some time. We took that into account." He swept a hand through the air as if pushing the subject out of the way.

Jamie had always found himself distracted by the man's use of his hands in conversation, but now he forced himself to keep his eyes on Pietro's face.

"I have been approached by the Lady Irene—" Jamie began.

"Yes, you certainly have!" Pietro said softly; and then grinned as Jamie stopped speaking altogether.

"Forgive me! Surely you realize that it's all been most amusing!"

Jamie nodded after a moment, deciding that this would be a damned silly subject to come to blows with this man about.

"She wants me to give her Carlo," he said after a moment. He stopped there and watched Pietro sit back in his chair, a serious expression having suddenly appeared on his face.

"Ah," he said, drawing the syllable out, after a moment of silent thought. "That makes a sense of sorts, together with the few bits I've heard." He looked up at Jamie.

"Did she say how and when this is to come about?"

"Soon," he said. "That's all I know. She'll send a group of men in secret, I'm to turn the lad over to them, and they'll take him to some secret place of hers for safekeeping."

"It will be three days from now," Pietro stated. "Probably around midnight."

Jamie watched him steadily, knowing he would soon explain the statement—else he would not have revealed his knowledge.

"It hangs together with other things that I know are planned for that time," Pietro said. "One of them will be an attempt to assassinate the Archduke himself, and his heir, Carlo's older brother." He looked down at his lap, and then back up at Jamie, the shadows making his usually rakish face seem full of a sorrowful evil.

"You can see how important the boy becomes at that point," he said. Jamie nodded.

God in Heaven! Is there no honor in this country? Jamie thought to himself. *They war on children, and stab their rulers in their backs.*

"Do nothing," Pietro said, bending low now over the table-top toward Jamie. The grin was back on his face, but the light of the little lamp showed only half of it to Jamie, who felt as if he were seeing half of the actor's mask that meant comedy.

"Let them come as they plan," Pietro went on. "And when they are in your power—for they must be at one point, else they would not need you—take them. Try to get some of them alive, for questioning, and for witnesses—we will need them to do for their chiefs, who will not come along.''

Jamie nodded again; and Pietro leaned over to blow out the lamp before taking Jamie's arm and beginning to lead him to the door. But Jamie shook off the arm that rested on his.

"No," he said. "I am no child. You need not lead me back home."

Pietro chuckled, but did not follow as Jamie felt his way to the door and stepped out into the street. Jamie saw no sign of any watcher as he made his way by a circular route back to the castle.

The next morning Jamie laid out the story to Ned and Brethin; and the three of them spent quite some time discussing how they would meet the threat. And the next day brought Jamie another invitation to see Irene at her palace.

It was a male servant who let Jamie in this time, and led him down a hallway—not to the great entertaining room he had gone to so many times, but off in another direction. Jamie watched the man's back as he walked, abstractedly trying to decide whether the man might be a danger to him if something went wrong with this visit to Irene—for this, he knew, had to be the great danger point of the enterprise for him. He did not underestimate Irene's abilities, and she might well see from him—his face or his reactions—that something was very wrong.

"Sir Jamie!" The startled feminine voice brought him quickly up from his reverie.

"What are you doing here?" Marie had just turned into the hallway from a cross-corridor and was staring at him in some astonishment. As he looked at her she suddenly blushed and brought both hands up to cover her face—although since the hands were clenched, only the reddened cheeks were obscured. She looked down at the tiled floor.

"Forgive me," she said. "You must think I'm awful! I—I was just so surprised to see you here. There's no party—" She faltered to a stop, and after a moment of silence looked up to see him grinning at her.

"This way, sir," said the servant Jamie had been following.

"A moment," Jamie said, not looking at him. He kept his eyes steadily on Maria, and her own eyes seemed to be caught by them. Blue and wide, they watched him as if fascinated by some mystery play that was being played out on his face.

He turned and moved off down the hallway behind the servant, who had begun moving again as soon as he did. He heard nothing behind him, and did not look back.

Irene had, it turned out, planned another intimate little dinner, much like the first he had had with her, although this time in a well-lighted, smaller room. The food was delicious, and her company at its most charming—she was creamy skin and big eyes, smiles and soft laughter, light touches on his arms and chest. . . . He drank a lot of wine and had a most pleasant evening, finding her worth enjoying to the utmost even though he was aware of the currents that flowed beneath the time. In fact, he became aware that he was deriving a certain satisfaction out of the awareness within him that he was as much in control of the situation as she was.

It was not until the very end of the dinner that she returned to the subject of Carlo.

"Have you thought about what we discussed some days ago—about protecting Carlo, I mean?" she said, cocking an eye at him as her head tilted, as if she were some young maiden beginning a campaign for a particular piece of fabric shown by the new trader in town.

"Certainly," he said; and retreated into silence as he refilled both their goblets, giving her a sly glance while he did so—he knew how she would interpret that.

"And will you do as I asked?" she went on after another moment. He pretended to frown as if in some confusion.

"Ah—just what is it you want me to do?" he said. "You want me to give up Carlo to you, so that you can protect him better?"

"Yes, that's it," she said.

"Right now?" he said.

"Oh, no," she said. "I can't protect him well yet—there are preparations to make. Tomorrow night, at midnight, men will come to you. You will order your men away and give Carlo over to our care. You may come with him if you wish—in fact, that would be a good idea, for then you would be with me more often." She smiled, and he grinned back.

"Will you be coming to get Carlo yourself?" he asked.

"Oh, no," she said. "I can't do that. If I'm seen the enemies will know where to look for the boy."

"That's true," he said. "But then how will I know these men who come for him?" *And how many will there be?* he thought to himself.

"You'll know," she said, smiling at him. "Just be ready. And now—no more questions. . . ."

She refused to return to the subject all that night, and he felt he could not press her far on it. But she certainly made the night memorable, he told himself as he left the palace the next dawn. Clearly, an inducement to cooperate.

He smiled. It had been a very good inducement indeed.

Jamie slept a good part of the day, and after dark fell moved outside, to lounge on the steps just within the main gate. It was cold, but he had dressed warmly, and was used to functioning despite cold weather. Passing Italians occasionally gave him the look they reserved for crazy foreigners—but no comments reached his ears.

The main gate had been closed for several hours when the hour of midnight approached; and he stood up and began to pace, trying to warm himself and take out any stiffness of muscle that might have developed while he waited.

He looked about him. He was standing in the courtyard of the small castle, on the steps that led up to the door into the keep. Carlo was in there, and with him Ned and Brethin, with a few more men. Hopefully, all of them had made their way in there undetected, and so remained unsuspected by the enemy.

The gate was centered in the wall that encircled courtyard and keep; and atop the wall could be seen the fires maintained for signaling, for lighting, and for keeping the sentries happy—they could warm themselves once in a while, at least. He wondered if the sentries were awake and alert—they had not been let in on the plan, at least not by him.

Jamie could not see any of his own men—but then, if they had done their jobs correctly, they were supposed to be out of sight.

He climbed to the top of the wall as if inspecting the guard—walking from one post to another and then making his way down by another stairway. At the bottom of the wall again he stopped and looked about. Not much had changed. The dimly lit gray stone of the outer wall and the keep looked bleak and solid, cold and grim. No one moved anywhere in his sight.

And then, there was movement! In the deepest, darkest shadows, there before the gate, suddenly he caught a glimpse of motion. He stood, watching, and saw that the gate was slowly and quietly opening.

How deep can treachery go? he wondered. This, he knew, was where he took his life in his hands—for if he was to be betrayed by Irene, this was when he would be most vulnerable to it. He took a deep breath and walked calmly across the courtyard toward the gate, leaving his sword in its scabbard.

When he entered the deeper pool of shadow, he was in control of himself, and his step did not falter at all. He walked up to the figures who were waiting there as if they were old friends—he even managed to ignore the fact that the two men who were supposed to be manning the gate were nowhere in sight.

Dead? Or gone with their money? It hardly mattered at this moment.

"Sir Jamie, we give you good evening." The voice almost stopped him in his tracks—undoubtedly, it was the Greek, Michael. He should have expected this, or something like it.

"Greetings," he said. *No names,* he thought. No use angering them by flaunting recognitions.

"Is all well?"

"Yes," he said. "It is quiet, and no one has been about for hours."

"Good," Michael responded. "Lead us to the boy, then."

"This way." Jamie turned and walked across the courtyard as if on the most calm of errands.

Jamie did not look back, although his stomach shouted its need that he should do so. But when he reached the stair in front of the keep and began to climb, he could hear the feet behind him spreading out, moving to the sides; and when he got to the top of the steps, near the door, he paused and turned. His companions had spread themselves out and were pressed against the wall, on the steps—trying to hide from the sight of whoever opened the door when Jamie called.

Probably, he thought, they were more anxious than he was. Certainly they had reason to fear some sort of betrayal.

Michael, near him on the right wall, nodded and pointed at the door. Jamie finished counting their heads, nodded back, and hammered on the door, using the pommel of his sword.

After a wait that seemed to stretch much too long, there was a fumbling at the other side of the massive sheet of wood; and the peephole swung open inward, emitting a weak beam of light.

"Who is it?" The voice was sleepy.

"Sir Jamie," he called. "Let me in." He did not recognize the voice—was it one of his men, or a servant? He hoped the man did not do something stupid.

The door opened, swinging outward in front of Michael. Jamie stepped inside immediately, locating the confused guard—one of the household staff rather than of the bodyguard—and turning him around with a rough hand on his shoulder. Jamie continued moving forward, pushing the man ahead of him at a stumbling, fast pace, until they reached the stairway that led downward to the first floor. Jamie pushed the man into it.

"Go down there," he ordered, trying to put real authority behind his words, "and stay there until I come back for you!" The man mumbled something, but Jamie had already turned about and did not catch the words.

"Lead on," Michael said. He had followed Jamie inside quickly, his seven with him. Now he eyed Jamie without further comment.

"I could go up and bring him down to you," Jamie said.

"No need for that," Michael said. "Let us go."

Jamie shrugged and turned to the door beyond which the upper stairway began.

The stair began at the edge of the great hall of the keep, which this night was only a large, cold, empty room. The room was also dark, with only a single torch mounted on the wall, halfway up the stairs, for illumination. And about the time Jamie climbed past that torch, he noticed that several of Michael's men had fanned out through the hall and were carefully searching through its shadows.

Not very trusting, Jamie said to himself.

He kept on climbing without outward comment, hearing the nearly silent feet that mounted behind him. At the turn up to the third floor he got a glimpse behind him, counting only four men. Apparently Michael was positioning his men to cover his retreat, if he might need such a thing. That, too, was wise, Jamie conceded. And it would make it tougher to ambush all the force without an alarm being raised.

The third floor was nearly dark when they got there. This was where Carlo's chambers were, down at the end of a corridor that ran directly away from the stairs. At the far end of the corridor a single torch burned; but the one close by had apparently died out in its mounting. Jamie walked past it calmly and on to the bedchamber door.

"Is there no guard?" Michael's voice stopped Jamie as much as the hand on his arm.

"Inside," Jamie said, managing to remain dull-sounding, he thought, despite the tension that was building inside him.

The hand left his arm and he reached out to the door, pushing it ahead of him silently. Ahead was only darkness. Jamie stepped inside, two quick steps and then another to his right, where he turned around.

He could see Michael's silhouette in the doorway, illuminated by the single torch in the hall. The man had stopped where he was, in the doorway.

Jamie waited, but Michael made no move, said nothing, for more than a minute. At last it was Jamie who spoke.

"Surrender, Michael," he said. "We have you."

The figure in the doorway had turned and sped down the hall even as Jamie spoke, and the Scot, startled by the man's quickness, lost a step or two in his pursuit. Behind him, as he ran back out the door of the bedchamber, he could hear Brethin directing a man to signal out the tiny window of the chamber, to alert the men hidden outside that the trap was sprung.

Michael was at the steps now, rounding to take them back down; and the three men who had followed him up had let him go by and were now lining themselves up to delay Jamie's pursuit of their leader. But Jamie confounded them by vaulting over the balustrade before he reached them, landing lightly on the steps somewhat behind Michael and tottering for a moment to regain his balance. Michael looked back at him and grinned, something wolfish on his face.

Below, in the great chamber, a couple of small battles seemed to be in progress; and even as Jamie moved down the steps he saw one of Michael's men go down to Ned's overhand sweep. Michael saw it, too, and realized that Ned and two more men would have the bottom of the stair before he got there. Jamie saw the man estimate his chances for a leap off the side of the stair, and give it up. The man's arm swept up, blade suddenly in hand, and he turned and suddenly was coming back up the stair at Jamie himself.

"Michael! It is over!" Jamie yelled, but the man made no response except to launch himself down low to come at Jamie's feet. Jamie leaped backward and almost lost his balance. Suddenly he was sweating. If he had to back up too much, he might encounter Michael's other men coming *down* the stairs—and he could not risk a look behind him, for the man ahead of him was going to be all he could handle.

Michael had launched into a barrage of blows, moving his sword in at Jamie, to clang off Jamie's sword or off the stone of stair or wall, and back out to be swung back again. Jamie had all he could do to dodge or parry the one-man melee the Greek had become, and found that he was slowly giving ground. But he could not afford to take his eyes off the other.

Michael seemed tireless, his arm like some infernal machine that would never stop moving. Jamie knew that he himself was tiring already. He had always thought of himself as a skilled and unusually strong fighter, but never had he met a man like this. His mind raced as he searched for some tactic he could use, at least to take off some of the pressure the other was exerting.

Behind Jamie, suddenly, he sensed movement—someone was coming down the stairs behind him. But he still dared not look back. Awaiting a blow from behind, he found that he had tightened his back muscles as if to better ward off the blade that might take him—but in doing so, he had almost slipped off his guard, and Michael nearly had his right leg. He pulled it back up, hating the retreat, and saw Michael looking up at him and grinning.

The man behind— The thought roared in his head; and then he leaped straight up and forward, directly at the Greek's face. The grin before him changed to amazement, and then Jamie was on it, feet first, kicking. The Greek tried to lean backward and ward off the Scot's assault, but his sword had been held low and to the side for his next blow, and he took Jamie's first kick right in the mouth.

It threw him off-balance, and as he leaned into Jamie, the Scot landed on the stairs before him, hard on his back, and Jamie's left foot caught Michael on the chest. The man's arms went up, though he made no sound, and he stepped back and down, trying to regain his balance—but the step took him off the edge of the stair, and he vanished from Jamie's sight.

Jamie had meanwhile begun sliding on his back down the stairs, unable to catch and stop himself until a hand reached down from behind him to grab a fistful of mail and slow him, pulling him in towards the side wall. He tilted his head back to see Brethin, leaning down from behind him.

"Brethin!" he said. "You took the others, then?"

"No," the other said. "Killed them. They wouldn't give up. Can you stand now?" At Jamie's nod he let go his hold on the mail, carefully watching for any sign that Jamie might start to go again. But Jamie sat in place on the step he rested on, breathing hard.

"I thought—" he began, and paused for a breath.

I thought it was one of them, he finished the thought to himself. *Michael almost had me with that smile of his.*

"Where is he?" Jamie said. "Can you see him?"

"Yes," Brethin said. "They've got torches down there now." He was looking over the side where Michael had gone over.

"My God!" he said abruptly, and then stepped back, crossing himself while beginning to mumble the same chant Jamie had been hearing since they had left the valley.

"What is it?" Jamie asked; and without waiting for an answer levered himself up and half-crawled over to where Brethin had stood back from the edge. Jamie looked down, to see the floor thirty feet below.

The floor was occupied by a loose ring of people, who all seemed to be backing slowly away from the figure that lay sprawled in the center of their rough semicircle.

Jamie looked more closely. That figure wore the armor, the clothes, that Michael had just been wearing—but what was in them now bore little resemblance to the Greek warrior Jamie had been having such a hard time with.

Inside the armor was only a skeleton, its bony grin looking out across the stone floor toward the doorway through which it had come some moments before. And as Jamie watched, the feet of the figure below him shook and trembled, as if—for a moment his gorge threatened to rise—something was inside feeding off the remaining flesh there.

Then there was silence. Stillness. Jamie at last managed to take his eyes off the form below him, sure—but not totally so—that nothing remained to be eaten—or to eat. He trudged down the stairs and headed for the doorway, knowing no one was going to be touching that form behind him for some time.

In the courtyard he encountered Ned, who had gone out some time before to look after the others of the raiding party.

"Did you get them?" Jamie asked.

"Oh, yes." Ned grimaced as he talked. "Only one was left when I got there, out by the gate itself." He spat over the side of the staircase.

"Dead?" Jamie asked.

"I suppose so," Ned said. "We had him surrounded, and he

threw his sword down—and then he just burned—went up in flames, before our eyes.''

"Burned—"

"Yes, just like that. I saw him do nothing, but he went up as if he'd been doused in Greek fire." He twisted his nose. "It smelled terrible!"

"Someone must have been watching," Jamie said.

"He screamed," Ned went on. "It must have been painful, because he screamed for several minutes." Jamie looked at his friend more carefully.

"Let's get a drink," he said. "We were up against sorcery, and lucky to get out of it." He clapped the other roughly on the shoulder.

"Get some wine—get it yourself; there may still be traitors in the castle. We shall drink in front of the boy's door."

And so they did; and when morning came and Pietro Claveggio himself came up the stairs, their heads hurt and their eyes were red and as sore as Jamie's back, where he had bounced on the steps. Inside the bedchamber they guarded, Carlo was pounding on the door, demanding to be let out, and the noise had Brethin burying his head between his knees.

"Come," Pietro said, "it is time to go now."

"Go?" Jamie said.

"My men control all this castle," the other answered. "You are relieved of your duty here." He grinned. "The Archduke wants to see you."

"The Archduke?" Jamie echoed. After a pause he went on. "Now?"

"Now."

This time, as Jamie met the Archduke again, he knew that the man really saw him. In truth, everyone saw Jamie, for the Archduke received him in a well-attended ceremony that took place at the front of the great ballroom of the Archducal palace.

"Sir Jamie," the Archduke said—speaking more loudly than necessary for Jamie's ears, but it was after all a grand ceremony—"your actions have saved the life of my dear son Carlo. For that alone I owe you a great debt. And know further that the plot you uncovered also constituted a danger to my eldest son and heir, Enrico, as well as to myself."

At this there was a murmuring among the crowd of courtiers, for which the Archduke paused a moment. Then he raised a hand slightly, bringing instant silence, and continued.

"By means of your information, our good friend and protector Ser Pietro Claveggio has been able to root out and destroy a veritable nest of vipers that has been nestled here in our midst."

He turned to Pietro, who was standing beside Jamie. He smiled like a father, Jamie thought.

"Ser Pietro," he went on, "know that in thanks and recognition of your services, we are settling on you and on your heirs the title of Marquess di Castello Lorenzo, with estates pertaining thereto. We shall be informing our dear brother the Emperor himself of your worthy service."

Pietro bowed deeply as the Archduke turned to Jamie.

"And you, Sir Jamie, must accept our most heartfelt thanks. We hereby endow you with the lifetime use of the Estate Polino, which we are sure you will find most agreeable." He nodded, and Jamie bowed as deeply as Pietro had.

"What is this Estate Polino?" Jamie asked Pietro as they got into an unobserved room after the ceremonies.

"It's a farm," Pietro said. "It's located in the south, near Roma, and it's a rich one. You'll live well all your life with that under your control."

"But my children don't get it?" Jamie asked.

"No," said Pietro. "When you die it'll revert to the Archducal family. But until then—"

"I don't want to be a farmer," Jamie said.

"No need," Pietro answered. "There is a resident manager who'll run it for you. All this appointment means is that the income each year comes straight to you instead of to the Archducal coffers." He grinned.

"I have an idea you'll never get time to get down there anyway," he said. "You'll be in some demand for your services from now on."

"Are there new threats we have to watch for?"

"Always," Pietro said. "And of course Irene and her party remain, weakened but as cunning as ever."

"Irene!" Jamie looked at Pietro in amazement. "Is she still free? She hasn't been arrested?"

"Oh, no," Pietro said. "She has most powerful friends in Constantinople and at the Imperial Court itself—it would be terribly dangerous to arrest her without strong proof of her complicity in such a plot as we have smashed."

"But I told you what she asked of me—"

"Alas, there's no proof of that, except your word. And your

word weighed against hers. . . .'' Pietro shook his head sadly.
"All the men who came for Carlo—and for Enrico and the
Archduke, too, for that matter—died—sometimes rather nas-
tily, in truth.''

"But Michael was known to be Irene's man!'' Jamie said.

"Yes,'' Pietro said. "But his face was not clearly seen by
anyone besides yourself, and the body you said was his was
not recognizable.''

He paused, looked about, and then went on, in a lower tone.

"And Michael was seen to have boarded a ship that left
Genoa the morning of the attack. We cannot fight that proof.''

"We all know that magic has been used in this!'' Jamie
protested once more. "Can't we get the services of some potent magicians to work out the proof and expose their devices?''

"Yes, we could,'' said Pietro. "But we will not. The Archduke will step on no more toes than he has to at this point.''

He looked at Jamie more closely.

"You understand why I am telling you this, my friend,'' he
went on. "You're now a marked man yourself.''

Jamie nodded, staring at him.

To have Irene angry with him—undoubtedly she was that—
was one of the things he wanted least in this world. He shivered slightly. For a moment he saw again the vision of her as
he had seen her early that morning, posing for herself in the
room when she did not know he saw—it was that woman who
would foster a cold, unrelenting revenge, in her own good
time. However long he might live, he was in grave danger.

On the other hand, he reminded himself, he was now rich
and well-known, well-thought-of—and had powerful friends
of his own. He would protect himself, too. He walked on with
Pietro, down the hall to the graveled walks of the main garden,
where friends awaited them. And he felt as if he were walking
out towards the valley that his family lived in, bringing with
him the wealth and power he had always known he would
bring to show them. He grinned as they stepped into the pale
gray light—he could see that the sun would beat its way
through these milky clouds soon.

"Jamie,'' Ned said as they approached the group that had
been waiting outside. Jamie's heart fell a little—Ned's expression was unaccustomedly serious.

"What's wrong?'' Jamie asked.

"It's Maria,'' Ned said. Jamie stared at him, fear suddenly

alive in his heart even as he puzzled how Ned had even known that the girl existed.

"Yes?"

"We got a message that she was someone you were fond of," Ned said.

"A message? From who?"

"We don't know," Ned answered. "But the message said that, and then said to remind you that the girl was still in the Palazzo Visconti." He shrugged. "It's not much, but it sounded like a warning to me." He looked Jamie in the eye.

"It is," Jamie said. "And meant to worry me in my hour of triumph. It's devilish!" He frowned, trying to think what he could do.

"Pietro," he said after a moment, reaching over to touch the shoulder of his friend who had been conversing with some of his men who had come to greet him as they stepped outside.

"What is it, Jamie?" the other said. "I saw that your man brought you bad news."

"What can you tell me of the position of Maria—the girl who resides with Lady Irene in the Palazzo Visconti?"

"Well—as I recall—" Pietro began; then caught Jamie's eye on him and grinned. "Of course I know," he said. "Just my habit to dissemble, that's all." His expression faded into thought.

"She is the younger sister of a man named Andrea Matteleone, who is a powerful banker and trader of Genoa," he said. "Matteleone has political ambitions and wants to get his family ennobled. He has made some sort of alliance with Irene and her party—possibly he bankrolls them, I'm not sure of that—and in token of that sent his sister to live with Irene. No doubt she will be the prize in some useful marriage scheme one day."

He eyed Jamie as he said this, an eyebrow raised; but he said no more.

"Maria is in trouble because of me," Jamie said. "She is in that house at Irene's mercy, and you know that woman will be able to think of many small tortures for her. Is there not some way we can get her out of there?"

"Let me think on it," Pietro said after a moment, his eyes still on Jamie. "This is important to you?"

"Very," Jamie said. Pietro nodded.

"Come to me tomorrow, at the cathedral, when the Archduke goes to worship,'' he said. He turned away, and Jamie watched him go.

The man would come up with something, he knew. But for all that it rankled a bit—dealing with Pietro was a little like dealing with the devil himself. He would get what he wanted, but it would probably cost him a great deal in return one day.

On the great steps before the massive, unfinished—and very ugly—hulk that was the Cathedral of St. Ambrose, Jamie stood beside Pietro and thought about the course of action the other had just outlined to him. The idea was simple, and he was sure it would work—especially since Pietro had probably had time to do a little advance work with the Archduke.

Inside, the Mass was just over, and crowds of hangers-on had begun to swirl about the massive wooden doors; since the Archduke had the place of honor up front, it would take a few moments before his party arrived, even though all other attendees would be delaying their own departures until the Archduke had preceded them—Jamie wondered for an idle moment where all these people had been, then, if not at the Mass?

Now the great main doors swung outward, the guards who had opened them providing the force that pushed many of the crowd backward—some even fell a short way down the stone steps, and the cries and yelling increased in volume for a moment or two. And here, at the head of his own little procession, came the Archduke, accompanied by his intimates, as well as by the Archbishop, a red-faced, white-haired man of middle years who was known to be a political appointee himself.

The Archduke, eyes roaming boldly about the crowd and the great square beyond them, stopped his forward movement as he reached the top step's edge. He spread his feet far apart and planted his hands on his hips, which caused his elbows to push his cloak back and to the side. It opened at the front, revealing that he was in his ceremonial armor inlaid with gold, partly covered by a doublet. The contrast with the fur-collared deep brown cloak was striking, and Jamie found himself making a note of the effect.

Pietro nudged him, a solid blow in the ribs that caused Jamie to sway slightly for a moment before he recollected what he was to do. He strode boldly forward, moving from his place halfway up the steps to stand directly before the Archduke. He looked upward to find the Archduke looking back down at him.

A Prince need not ask, Jamie told himself, *but a knight may have to.* He began to mount the great steps, still looking up as he moved. And the crowd, perhaps sensing a great occasion, moved out of the way so that he could step right up before the Archduke.

No word was spoken, and at last Jamie found himself two steps below the figure that still surveyed the whole square— and himself—as if its proprietor. Jamie got down on one knee and bowed his head, and at last the Archduke spoke.

"Sir Jamie," he said. "You are welcome in our sight, indeed, for we are ever mindful of the services you have done for us. But why do you now approach us in this fashion?"

"A boon, Your Grace," Jamie said. He had been warned to let the Archduke do most of the talking.

"Ah," the richly wrapped figure said, "and what is it you would ask of us?"

"I crave this favor not for myself, but for a lady," Jamie said. *That should appeal to any chivalrous instinct he may have left,* he told himself silently.

"A lady? And how may we aid some lady in need?"

"The lady is lonely," Sir Jamie said. "She is required to remain far from her family, and I fear she will pine and sicken without their presence. I beg of Your Grace to give your aid to return her to them in all haste and safety." Jamie stopped himself from going any further than Pietro had advised, but only with some effort.

"Why, most gladly will we do so," the Archduke boomed out, happy with his role at this point. "We will see this lady home safely, and that immediately. Pray, who is this lady who so needs our aid?"

"The Lady Maria Matteleone," Jamie said, and bowed.

Chapter Ten

"ACTUALLY, SHE SEEMED a little unhappy to be leaving," Ned said to Jamie as they ate in The Gelding three nights after the meeting with the Archduke. "Perhaps it was because you weren't there to see her off, but the young lady seemed rather vexed."

He shrugged and threw a bone over his shoulder.

"Still, with the Archduke's public promise, there was nothing Irene could do to harm her," Jamie said. "And that's the important thing. She's well on her way by now, then."

"Yes, and in the midst of a goodly caravan," Ned added. "The Archduke said 'safely' and he'll not take the chance of letting some bandit play loose with his own word. She's well guarded, and no one would trifle with a caravan being run by the armorer Mazetti, anyway."

"Yes, I've met this Mazetti," Jamie said. "He's a most formidable fellow, big and hearty. And he seems to do very well for himself, for he wore most rich clothing, even in the midst of his workshop, when I visited him to be measured for better armor some weeks ago."

"Rich he is," Ned added, reaching for the chicken before them and pulling a portion of it loose in his hand. "He is known as the best armorer in a city that produces the best in the craft that there is to be had. He's good, and it has made him rich. And he's not reputed a man to be mishandled."

"You said that before," Jamie said. "Why?"

"There are tales," Ned said in a lower voice. "They talk of him using magics in his work."

"And what of that?" Jamie said. "You've seen magic in

use, Ned, and you should know that it's only another tool that a skilled craftsman may use if he can. Why must we fear that?''

''Oh, that's true,'' Ned replied. ''But the stories say there's something different about this Mazetti's use of magic—something about a demon that makes itself look like a man.''

Jamie's eyebrows raised a bit, but he made no further question on the subject. He had another topic he preferred to pursue.

''And was the Lady Irene there as Maria left the Palazzo Visconti?'' he said. At Ned's nod he went on.

''Could you tell her feelings from her face?'' Jamie asked.

''That face?'' Ned shook his head. ''No. That one is a lady through and through, and was a perfect picture of grace and beauty. There was nothing to read there.''

Jamie said no more, musing silently as Ned finished eating; and then they both drank for a while. Nearby, three more of Jamie's men sat quietly eating and drinking, but not in the usual wholehearted fashion normally expected of them.

The chill night was clear as the five of them left the inn, turning right and up a slight slope toward the turn that would put them on the street for the castle that was their headquarters. In the light of the three-quarter moon, frost glistened on the bare stones; as they moved, their footprints showed up in dark patches amid that silvery sheen.

About them in the street Jamie could see an occasional trail in the frost—but not often, for the night was early yet and few people had yet begun to make their ways home from whatever evening had taken them to. Jamie kept his eyes on the street before them, knowing that his companions could be trusted to watch about them as they went—Jamie preferred to avoid turning an ankle in some pothole.

Here, he noticed as they turned the corner, came the trail, very fresh, of a group of men—perhaps it was the watch making its patrol down the center of the street. No matter; they would not dare to accost Jamie and his men after the events of recent days—he was well known around here now.

Eyes still on the ground, he stopped abruptly, and behind him one of the men trod on his heel, not having been expecting the stop. Jamie wasted no breath in a curse, though, but pulled his sword; the others, seeing this, hastily did likewise while Ned, at Jamie's left, hissed under his breath.

''Lord Jamie, what is it?''

"Look at the tracks, Ned—see? This group of men split up
when the watch came by, and some went into each alley to
hide."

"Ah! I see—then we're between them."

"Yes. Let's move."

Jamie began walking forward again, still up the sloping
street towards the castle. But they had only made another three
steps before figures moved out from each alley mouth.

But Jamie's action had gotten them away from their position
directly between the two alleys, so that the dark figures all
came at them from slightly behind. Jamie and his men formed
into a rough circle, back to back, but kept moving, slowly,
because of the men in the rear having to walk backward. The
dark figures that pursued them followed, spreading out in a
rough semicircle, the men on the ends of the semicircle slowly
working their ways forward in an effort to draw the line into a
full circle to hold their prey. Jamie counted seven of them.

And now another figure stepped out, this time from a doorway ahead of them. This figure was not hooded or muffled as
the others, and his blond hair shone in the pale moonlight. His
sword was still in its scabbard as he walked forward slowly
toward Jamie.

"Giles!" Jamie said.

"Yes," said the other. "I have come for you, Jamie. I think
you know why."

"You do her bidding so easily then—even to murder?"

The French knight snarled a little, his teeth showing in a grin
that had no humor in it at all; and his right hand crossed the
front of his body as he reached for his sword. Then he relaxed
with a visible effort.

"Ah, no, Jamie," he said. "You seek to make me lose my
temper then? You see I do no murder here—my sword is still
covered, while yours is out. We will fight, yes—but it will be
a fair match. And when I kill you she will see there is yet worth
in me."

"No murder?" Jamie asked. "What do these masked men
around us?"

"They will keep your friends out of my way," Giles said.
"There is no reason for your friends to die."

"You delude yourself," Jamie said quietly.

Giles made no answer, but reached for his own sword. Jamie
continued to stand in place as Giles did so, watching as the
Frenchman pulled up his blade and settled into a fighting

stance; plainly he was waiting for Jamie's attack, but when it did not come he was left by himself, waiting.

The masked ones made no move, Jamie knew, although he was keeping all his attention on Giles—Ned and the others would have warned him if the dark ones made some attack. So Jamie simply waited for Giles to carry the attack further—it seemed somehow right that the blond knight should be the one to open hostilities. They were both knighted and it was an affair of chivalry, for all the bandit trappings to it.

At last Giles straightened from his crouch, looking across the space between them at Jamie.

"You will not attack me, then?" he said.

"It is you who desires this fight," Jamie said. "I simply wait and defend myself and my friends." Giles seemed to flush, his mouth widening in a grimace.

"I said they were in no danger," he said harshly.

"Then you are a fool, for you keep bad company," Jamie said coldly. He watched Giles narrowly, knowing the man would move at any instant.

He did. With a yell—perhaps some native phrase that Jamie could not trouble to translate just now—he raised his blade into the air over his head and ran forward. Two steps, three—Jamie stepped slowly forward to meet him. At least it seemed a slow advance to Jamie, but suddenly he was in close to Giles, and the other, sword still above his head, looked at Jamie with a sort of amazement beginning to dawn on his face as he found he now had no room to make his downward swing. And at that moment Jamie stepped directly to the side and buried his left hand in Giles' midsection.

Or at least he tried to: Giles was wearing mail under his doublet in that area, and Jamie's gloved hand felt the impact against it painfully. Even so, the force behind the blow stopped the Frenchman in his tracks; and as he brought his sword down it had no force behind it, and missed Jamie completely.

Jamie stepped back and watched the other closely. Behind him he could hear shuffling movements and quiet comments among his own men—he interpreted that as meaning that the dark figures were closing in, and Ned was coordinating their defense of Jamie's back side. He grinned a little as he heard Ned curse one of the attackers for getting too close.

"Gods! You smell bad!" Ned said.

Without warning, Giles attacked again, this time not so rashly, his sword across his front in a position from which he could either parry or take a backhanded swipe at the Scot. Jamie stepped across in front of the blade, taking the position from which it could reach him least easily, and took a backhand swing of his own, coming under the other's sword.

Giles met Jamie's blade with his own, and the sound of the two blades meeting rang across the night. Almost immediately it was echoed by an encounter that Jamie could hear behind him, but he could not spare a glance to see what had happened.

Jamie kept on moving as Giles instinctively froze after their blades met, rounding behind the other's arm while he brought his blade up into the air over his left shoulder and swung it in the direction of Giles' head. Late to parry, Giles ducked instinctively, moving right into Jamie's arm as it reached for—and hit—his shoulder, pushing him back off-balance.

Trying to reset himself, Giles flung his arms a bit too wide, and Jamie stepped back left again, all his body's weight lending momentum to his blade as it swept from over his right shoulder and took Giles's head off.

Without taking the time to watch what happened to the body after that, Jamie turned to see how his men, outnumbered, were doing. At a glance he saw that two of his men were down, along with four of the attackers. Ned was trying to deal with two men, and the other of Jamie's men—he could not tell which it was—was fast being beaten down by a big man. And even as Jamie stepped forward, that big man's sword clanged off the soldier's and caught him in the shoulder; Jamie's man went down with a cry.

The dark figure stepped forward with sword raised above the soldier, and at that moment Jamie reached them, swinging his sword fast at the other's head. He jumped back, pulling his sword back into position for a new attack—but as he did so, he stumbled over a body on the ground behind him. Jamie lunged low, savagely fast, and his blade knifed into and through the man's thigh.

The man made no sound, even though Jamie's blade tore forcefully through the flesh as he pulled free; and Jamie watched as the other, still masked, pulled himself up straight.

"That's a bad wound," Jamie said. "Surrender."

"Look out!" Ned yelled from Jamie's right; and the Scot ducked and turned, finding that one of Ned's opponents had abandoned Ned to try to take Jamie from the side. Jamie parried the swing that came his way by only the narrowest of margins, and backed away, trying to keep all possible opponents in front of him. As he did so, Ned's man backed away with a wound, then turned and ran for the dark alley from which he had come. Instantly Ned turned and slashed savagely across the back of the man who was still facing Jamie. The man cried out and bent backward, dropping his sword and falling in a heap.

Jamie turned to look at the man he had wounded in the thigh a moment before. The man had evidently been hit in an artery, for a bright, shining pool was spreading on the ground at his feet.

"Give it up," Jamie said. "You haven't got long."

The other cursed—it was a language Jamie did not recognize, but he understood the words because of his pentecost spell—and raised his sword to shoulder level. He seemed to take one step forward, then to slip in his own blood and, still with arm raised, fall heavily on his back and left shoulder. His right arm held the sword in the air for a moment, and then it tumbled out of the hand that had held it, seeming to lose some life of its own as the moonlight that had shone off the polished blade was lost in the twisting, tumbling fall. It clanged on the stones of the street, and the arm fell behind it, limply.

"Are you all right?" Ned said. He was gasping a little as he spoke.

"Yes," Jamie said. "How about these others?"

They attended to their own men, finding two wounded—one badly—and the other dead. Of the eight men who had attacked them, one had fled and the others were all dead—some after suffering rather minor wounds.

"Just like at the castle, in a way," Ned said.

Jamie nodded.

"Jamie! Look!" Ned had pulled up the mask from the face of the man who had bled to death before them.

"Lucas Morhacs." Jamie nodded. "That makes some sense—who else would Irene send but men who are smitten by her? I wonder if these others are former lovers, too, or just hirelings?"

"She keeps busy," Ned said.

"Perhaps," Jamie went on. "But it could be that she doesn't know of this attack—these men could have been trying to impress her."

"Then why did they all die? Is it she who works the magic, or someone else?"

"More can work magic than one," Jamie answered. "And

while these died, it was not in the same way as those others we fought in the castle.'' He shrugged. ''I don't know if we'll ever find out.''

The watch, drawn by the sounds of their combat, came running up; and it was with some difficulty that Jamie managed to keep them from assuming that he and Ned were bandits, to be attacked immediately. But with their help the wounded men were taken to the castle for treatment; and as that was attended to, Pietro Claveggio showed up, with a guard of his troops behind him, waiting in the courtyard as Pietro climbed the stairs to greet Jamie at the door to the keep.

''The watch reported to me,'' he said. ''You're all right?''

''Yes,'' Jamie said. ''But I lost one man, and maybe another.''

''You're able to travel if you have to?''

''Yes,'' Jamie said. ''Do I have to?''

''Maybe soon,'' Pietro said. ''I'm not sure yet. But you'd be wise to be prepared to move quickly.''

Jamie frowned. It sounded like Pietro was giving him a strong warning, but he was not sure he understood exactly why he should be in danger.

''Why?'' he said. ''I defended myself and my men on the street when attacked, and there were obviously more of them than of us.''

''Yes, but not too many more,'' Pietro said. ''No, I'm guessing there. But one thing you don't know—Lucas Morhacs was the son of the favorite sister of the Archduke.''

He stopped, and Jamie watched his face in the torchlight as the man seemed to struggle not to say more. The thin face twisted before him as he watched, and at last settled into quiet.

''Think about that,'' Pietro said. ''And about the gratitude of kings.''

''I've heard,'' Jamie said, with an emphasis he had not intended. He saw Pietro staring at him for a moment, oddly. Then the older man nodded and turned away, striding down the stairs and climbing back on his horse. In a moment he was gone.

Jamie watched him go, and then turned to direct Ned and Brethin to prepare the old comrades of their lance to go at a moment's notice, if need be.

By noon things were falling out much as Pietro had hinted. A castle servant returned from the Mass in the cathedral with a word that the Archbishop himself had preached a sermon against foreign barbarians who savage loyal citizens in the streets—and the Archduke had reportedly listened without comment.

At midday Jamie gathered the members of his lance about him in a corner of the courtyard of the castle.

"We'll split up," he said. "I may have to run, but if I do I want you all ready to leave. So Ned will take you out into the hills. Brethin and I will wait here; and I'll send Brethin to you when I know what will happen."

"You can't send us from you, Lord Jamie," Ned said, and the men around them murmured in agreement.

"I must," Jamie said. "If we have to run, many of us will move slowly, while one may move fast. And you will be reponsible for guarding my treasure."

That seemed to mollify them, until Ned spoke up.

"What treasure, Lord Jamie?"

"The one we're going for right now," Jamie said. "I have word that they're holding the service for Morhacs in the Cathedral right now, and Irene will certainly be there, deep in mourning. Come!"

He led the way out of the castle gate and they rode at a sedate pace to the palazzo he had visited so many times. At the door he dismounted and rapped loudly with his sword hilt; and when it was answered by a male servant, he pushed his way by, followed by Ned and three men.

"But the Lady Irene is not here!" the old servant protested. He followed Jamie, clasping his hands as he tried to walk sideways beside the Scot.

"I know," Jamie said. "Hold him." He pushed the man to the side and one of the others held onto him, sitting him on a bench in an alcove halfway down the hall. Jamie and the others kept walking, and Jamie led them to Irene's chambers. There he directed one of them to the area where the table silver would be kept; and then led Ned and the other man to the cabinet in which, he knew from his many visits, Irene kept her jewelry.

It was there. She had evidently been careless while preparing for the funeral, and had left much of her silver and gold chains out in plain sight rather than hidden in the secret compartments Jamie had expected to have to search for. They tore down curtains and rolled them into bundles with silver, gold and gems inside; and hastily made their way back down the hallway to the front door.

"How can we do this?" Ned asked. "This is robbery!"

"It is retribution," Jamie said. "She killed. And now she may cause me to lose the estate I have only just been given by the Archduke."

"I'd forgotten that," Ned said. "All right."

They remounted their horses.

"All right," Jamie said. "All of you except Brethin will go out of the city, hiding in the hills to the north. Brethin will know where to find you when I send him." He waved his hand and they rode off without a word.

"Now, Brethin," Jamie said. "Let us go back to the castle and wait for developments."

"I don't like that," Brethin grumbled. "It's a good place to get trapped."

"I know," Jamie said. "But I have to take that chance; I can't look as if I'm in hiding, or I'll lose this war automatically. We must hope we get word somehow, before any troops show up."

But they never got to the castle gate—as they neared it, a shrill shout from the wall made Jamie look up. He saw the small blond head of Carlo atop the same tower they had used for practice so often.

"Flee, Sir Jamie!" the boy yelled. "They await!"

A figure appeared behind him, and the boy ducked and vanished from their sight. Jamie waited for no more, but jerked his horse and pounded back out of sight around the corner nearest. There he stopped and turned to Brethin.

"Split up!" he said. "I'll lead them away while you go to Ned and the others."

"Never!" Brethin said; but Jamie snarled at him.

"You must!" he said. "You and Ned are guardians of my wealth now. With that I can go home and be a success, and there's only the two of you to preserve it for me."

Brethin grimaced, but was silent.

"Alone, and without the weight to slow me, I can get away from all of them," Jamie continued. "So you wait for me to do so. Wait only four hours. If I'm not back by then, make your way back to Ned's home and wait for me there. Use what you must of the treasure. I'll get there somehow." He turned to ride off, but Brethin quickly stopped him.

"My lord! Here!" he said, handing over a small inlaid wooden box.

"What's this?" Jamie asked.

"I don't know. An old man came from the house while we waited for you outside the lady's palace, and said I must give it to you before you left the city."

"An old man?" Jamie echoed. The box, about the size of four of his fists together, seemed a rich-looking prize; it was intricately carved, and the detail work was filled with silver or pearly substance. A glistening red stone adorned the center of what appeared to be the top; but the box would not open immediately for Jamie.

"Not now!" he said, and thrust the box behind him into a saddlebag.

"Go!" he roared at Brethin, waving a hand; and then he rode off at a gallop himself, hearing the sound of the other's horse—and the sounds of pursuit as well.

Jamie galloped recklessly through the middle of the city. He could have hidden easily, but he knew that by drawing the pursuit to himself by a noisy ride, Brethin and the others could be safeguarded.

Once his horse knocked over a burly peasant who did not manage to get out of his way quickly enough; but in general his ride was noisy enough that everyone gave him plenty of room. And when he got to the south gate, he found that no one had apparently been given orders to try to stop such a one as he— for he rode without slackening speed directly at the guards, and they dived out of the way, landing in the muck left by the day's passing traffic in animals. Behind him as he left the gate he could hear one of them screaming curses down upon his head. He grinned, hoping the man had no magic talents of his own.

Then he was off down the road, and behind him as he turned he could see a large party of horsemen coming through the gate. They spotted him, and an arm raised in his direction; then he turned back and bent over his animal's neck, riding fast and hoping for the shelter of the trees and the rough country, which he knew fairly well from the weeks of training his company in it, and from rides with Carlo.

Around a bend he turned from the road into rough country; and in an hour or so he could hear only distant pursuit behind him. He pulled up his gasping horse in a clump of stunted trees, climbing off it for a rest—despite the chill, they were both hot and sweated up.

When he had cooled a bit, he took the saddle from his horse, rubbing it down with an old tunic, talking to it softly and soothingly. Its eyes watched him steadily, and he patted it softly on the nose. The palfrey was an older horse, and a trusting one; he had liked it for some time, since picking it up in France. It was unusually large and strong for a palfrey, he thought, but he supposed its gentle disposition had made it unsuitable for a destrier, which otherwise probably would have been its destiny.

He looked down to see that the tiny inlaid box Brethin had handed him had tumbled from the open top of the saddlebag when he had put the gear from the horse down on the ground at his feet. He stooped to pick up the box, and then put it aside while he resaddled the animal and put the rest of the gear on its back.

Seating himself at the base of a tree, he decided not to tether the palfrey—he'd be up and moving in a moment anyway, and the animal was not of a disposition to go galloping off without him. He began to play idly with the little box, searching for the way to open it—it was evidently one of those oriental boxes that have hidden catches, he thought.

After a few moments of prodding and pulling about its surface, he heard a tiny click, and the top surface seemed to loosen in his hands. He grinned, and slid it open. . . .

His head seemed to explode into pieces with a great roaring noise, and he heard himself screaming and he tried to grasp it with his hands and hold it together. He was on the ground, there was a great roaring noise between his ears, and the pains began to shoot through his eyeballs and down to the interior of his nose; his teeth chattered and the sounds of that echoed and reechoed in his head. . . .

He awoke in the darkness; and wished he had not done so. For long moments he was unable to move, every attempt to do so causing a new roar in his head. Periodically he found himself on the verge of throwing up, his stomach subject to nausea attacks that seemed to come from the darkness about him like the waves of the sea—and at the thought of that sea, he *did* throw up. . . .

When morning came the horse was gone, and with it all Jamie's gear. He never knew what had happened to it, but theorized that his moanings and thrashings had scared it off.

His head still hurt but the nausea had ended, and as he gathered himself up and trudged off downhill—unsure where he was, that seemed as good a direction as any—he found that

he still had bouts of dizziness and roarings in the ear. He tried
not to think about it, but simply walked.

After a couple of hours he was feeling better, but almost
walked into the midst of a party of mounted soldiers that was
apparently searching for someone—for him, no doubt. He
managed to duck into some bushes and remain unseen; and
while he waited for them to end their rest break and move
away, he considered his situation.

Already he had thoroughly missed the rendezvous with Ned
and Brethin and the others; moreover, without a horse he
would be unlikely to catch up with them soon. And since he
had lost his gear, he was virtually penniless in the bargain. No,
he would have to make his way to Cornwall by himself.

This search that was going on was bigger than he had imagined possible, and that was an additional complicating factor.
It was insane to contemplate swinging around the city to head
north—too much chance of being caught. He would do better
to get away from the city in whatever direction he could, and
try to find some other route to Ned's home. So, continue
downhill then—that was how to find the sea eventually, he
supposed.

He wondered if that would prove to be a good way to find
food also.

The soldiers moved off, chattering a bit among themselves;
and after an interval he picked himself up and wandered over
to where they had rested, hoping perhaps to find scraps of
food. But there were none. He moved off into the bushes and
continued, trying to make a downhill journey coincide with
one direction according to the sun—he had to make some
distance between himself and Milan.

It would be nice to come to a stream, though; he was thirsty.

In the early evening he found a tiny stream, and managed to
drink his fill—he almost made himself sick—and wash a bit
besides. But he had come across no food at all. He kept walking as night fell, finding it too cold to stop—he now realized
that he had also lost his flint and steel and had no way of
starting a fire.

He walked through the night, thankful for the nearly full
moon that kept him from bouncing off trees and once from
going over a modest cliff. And in the very early morning he
saw the lights of several fires in a valley below him.

Making his way down the hillside, he almost wished he had

not seen the fires—the moon had gone and visibility was almost nil; it seemed that he would wander forever in this darkness and cold. But finally he found that the fires were a good deal nearer, and after that progress seemed faster. But he had enough sense left, he told himself, to be cautious on his approach—he did not, after all, know who these fires belonged to.

The sky was graying fast in the east as he neared a fire, and he moved from one to another, inspecting the sleeping forms and the various equipments he could see. It seemed to be a merchant caravan with a guard of the Archduke's soldiery. He plotted ways of stealing food, and decided that it was wiser to go hungry for a bit longer.

At that moment he saw a familiar figure rise from a pallet near the fire he was watching; and for a moment he racked his brain trying to remember who the big man he was watching might be.

Mazetti! The answer burst in his mind, bringing with it the realization that this had to be the caravan that was taking Maria to Genoa. Hope flamed in him, and he began to move from fire to fire, searching for the one that she might be beside.

Eventually he settled on the fire that had a small tent nearby; and he worked his way through the shadows to its rear wall. When he reached it, he stopped, momentarily stumped for his next step. But then, exhausted and hungry, he decided to take the bull by the horns—he scratched on the tent fabric with his fingernails.

After some moments he heard movement inside, and eventually a voice that he knew.

"Who is it?" There was a tremor in the voice, but it had to be Maria.

"Jamie," he whispered; and when it seemed she had not heard, he whispered his name louder. This time there was a startled cry, and then the fabric bulged out towards him as her hand struck it.

"Jamie, is it really you?"

"Yes. Be quiet."

"Quiet? Why? Is something wrong?" Her voice was already lower, he noted. Good.

"I'm being pursued," he whispered again, "and by the Archduke's men. I need someplace to hide."

There was silence for a moment, and then the fabric before him lifted slightly. He could see her hands as they lifted the cloth, one hand using a knife to saw at its lower edge and make the lifting easier.

"Come in," she said.

He wormed his way under the edge as she held it, and eventually found himself inside. It was darker in here, he realized—that meant it was rapidly getting lighter outside. The camp would be up and packing to go on its way soon, so he could not stay long. He said as much to her and she stopped him.

"No," she said. "We've been in this spot for two days, waiting for the caravan master to come back with replacements for several horses that were killed in an accident. We probably won't move at all today. So rest here. In a while I'll go for some food."

He fell asleep immediately. But it was not a satisfying sleep, since Maria had to keep waking him because he was snoring. During one of his wakeful moments, he wondered what she had done with her maid, but was too tired to ask—perhaps she had not brought one along. It would be in character for Irene to send her home without one.

In the early evening Maria stepped out, and he nodded off again. It was full dark when she returned, and he woke as she stepped through the flap, accompanied by a big man who was carrying a torch. Jamie leaped to his feet, ready to fight—but relaxed when Maria held up a hand to quiet him. At the same time, he recognized Mazetti again.

"This is Master Mazetti," she said. "He will help us hide you."

"How can he do that?" Jamie asked. "There aren't any hiding places in caravans like this. It would be better if I simply went out into the darkness again."

"That's wrong," Mazetti's voice rumbled at him. "The Archduke's men have come about us, and you'd be likely to stumble upon them out there. Better you stay with us."

"How can I do that?" Jamie said. "And why should you risk the Archduke's displeasure for my sake?"

"I have a way," said Mazetti. "And I have my reasons— anyone who is hunted by the Lady Irene as you are is my friend."

"You've had a run-in with the lady?" Jamie asked.

"Oh, yes, that I have," the man said. His barrel chest seemed to swell while his gray whiskers lifted, and his deep-set blue eyes looked into Jamie's squarely.

"She has brought her magics into the politics of my home city," he said. "She not only keeps a tame magician but dabbles in the Art herself, and that well. And once she tried very hard to extort the secret of Nessuno from me."

"Nessuno?" Jamie echoed.

"Yes." Mazetti smiled. "And Nessuno is also how you will be hidden, here in the caravan." He reached behind him and peered from the tent flap; then held it open for Jamie to see what stood before it.

He saw, at first, only a man in a suit of armor—a man completely covered by the plate, mail and cloth, so that almost none of his flesh could be seen. Somehow, as he watched, the figure disquieted him—and after a few minutes he realized that the figure before him had not moved at all in that time. No human could do that.

He turned to Mazetti, a question on his lips; but was silenced by an upraised hand.

"Nessuno, come inside," Mazetti said. And the figure stirred and walked forward into the tent. The hairs on the back of Jamie's neck seemed to stir of their own accord—and at the same time he felt a buzzing in his head, between his ears. He felt dizzy and faintly sick again.

The figure called Nessuno stopped at Mazetti's command, and the armorer began to take the pieces of armor and cloth from it.

"Perhaps the lady would step outside," he said after a moment. Maria turned without protest and left. Jamie eyed the older man in curiosity.

"It is not a pretty sight," the man said, "nor modest, in some ways. You will see."

He continued to remove armor, to reveal, eventually, the form of a manlike creature. Jamie stared at it in awe.

The creature seemed to have no life of its own, and looked like nothing so much as a clay figure grown to man-size. And it did not seem to be alive, for it never moved except when Mazetti told it to—at which times it did exactly what Mazetti said it should do.

"This was created for me by a magician, a doctor from Oxford, in England—one of the truly great ones—for whom I once made a clever array of instruments. This mannequin, as he called it, can be directed to take the shape and size of a man as I indicate to it—which makes my task of fitting armor much easier. And it also serves to carry things around for me—such as this suit.'' He indicated the armor now lying on the ground.

"Nessuno, go outside," he said; and followed his creature. "Put that on," he added, looking back through the flap at Jamie. "I'll be back in a moment."

Jamie found the armor a bit difficult to get on, a bit short for him, and wide at the waist. But by the time Mazetti returned, he was completely dressed—war-experienced knights had to know how to suit themselves when necessary.

"Good," Mazetti said. "And so you see how we will get to Genoa with you safely. The guards with this caravan are used to seeing Nessuno following me about, or waiting silently with my wagon—and they are a bit afraid of him. So you will simply follow my bidding, be silent, and patiently wait. Can you do that?"

"Of course I can," said Jamie.

"The not moving will prove more difficult than you think," Mazetti warned.

"For a knight," Jamie said, a little nettled, "many things are possible."

Chapter Eleven

"AND WHO IS this man, that I should offer him employment, sister?" Andrea Matteleone, scion of a wealthy Genoese banking family, looked at his sister Maria with some distaste. He was totally ignoring Jamie except as an object of discussion, and the young Scot was trying to control his own tendency to either bristle or stamp out of the interview.

Since Jamie had lost virtually everything in his flight from Milan, Maria had offered him work with her brother or one of his friends. Matteleone, however, was proving difficult about it.

"He befriended me in Milan," the girl answered. "He has proven himself as a warrior; and he was well-known in that city for his abilities."

"Then why is he not in that city, but here, and penniless?"

Jamie stirred on his feet; the man was apparently intent on trampling on any pride that Jamie might have left. And as he made that analysis, Jamie realized what the merchant banker was doing—he was trying to provoke some incident that would enable him to turn down his sister's request in good face.

Jamie, with that realization, found his temper cooling rapidly. He was ahead of Matteleone in this game they were playing now, and would not be baited.

"An unfortunate accident," Jamie said at last, smiling at the other man.

The graying beard the other wore shifted a bit as if he had clenched his jaw in anger, but Jamie ignored that, looking pleasant.

"Accident? What sort of accident?" Matteleone said, his voice harsh.

"His horse ran away with all his possessions," Maria said, "when someone attacked him."

She carefully neglected, Jamie noticed, to mention that the attack had come in the form of the magic spell that had been an antitheft device on a small box.

Matteleone looked up at Jamie with a sour expression on his face—he was shorter than the Scot by some four inches, although almost as wide as Jamie across the shoulders, and carrying, Jamie estimated, a good forty pounds of unnecessary weight. Jamie felt that the man looked more like the sergeant of some free company than a merchant banker—except for the fact of his impeccable dress, rich and colorful, and his manners and language. But the bulge at his waist suggested that he was living the good life entirely too well.

"I will consider," Matteleone said; and stalked off out of the room. Jamie and Maria watched him depart in silence.

"I must apologize for my brother's manner," Maria said bitterly. "I didn't realize he'd react with so much hostility. I'm afraid it's my fault."

"Why?" Jamie stared at her.

"He fears you, I believe," she said. "That is, I believe he does not want someone like you around me."

She blushed.

"You mean he thinks of me as a fortune-hunter?"

"Yes," she said. "Remember he's a banker and a politician. His aim is to bring a title into the family, and to use it to increase his wealth even more. I'm really only a piece in that game he plays."

Jamie nodded.

"I'm unmarried, and will bring a large dowry to the man who is chosen for me," she said. "So that's a man he wants to choose very carefully." She blushed again. "I think he fears your presence will cause trouble in his plans for me."

"It might be so," Jamie said, looking down at her. She was smiling up at him, standing close. He did not remember how she had gotten that close, but he found he liked it. She was pleasant to look on, and to be with, and she had undoubtedly saved him from the Archduke's men there in the hills.

"What are you thinking?" she said. Her smile had widened, and it seemed as if her eyes had taken on a certain mischievous glint. Could she be reading his mind? he wondered.

"I was thinking of my home," he said. "It's in the mountains, and it's cool."

"That sounds nice," she said. "Do you have a family there?"

"Yes," he said shortly.

"I'd like to meet them," she said.

"Perhaps you shall," he said. "But it's a long way."

"That's all right." She looked away for a moment, and then back. "It would be a most enjoyable trip, I'm sure."

With the wealth Ned and Brethin were guarding for him, he was sure he would be able to live well in any of the lands near his father's kingdom. But first he was going to have to find a way to get as far as Ned's home in Cornwall.

"Do you think your brother will find me employment?" he asked now.

"I'm sure of it," she said. "It's partly a matter of family honor, since I, as his sister, have offered it already. Then, too, he is always bemoaning the shortage of dependable men for his enterprises."

"What enterprises are those?" Jamie asked. "Trading?"

"Some of them," she said. "And he has interests in many parts of the country, and outside Italy as well—Spain and France. I don't know all the businesses he has a hand in. I'm sure there'll be a place for you."

Jamie kept his silence, uncomfortably. He was a warrior, and a warrior only. It was all he had ever trained for, and all he knew or wanted. He was skeptical that such a one as Matteleone could have any good use for him—but then, he had few options at this point. And it might allow him to stay near Maria.

He smiled at her again. She reminded him of his own sister, who had been so adept at knowing and influencing him. Maria was smaller, of course, and softer. . . .

Jamie returned to spend that night with Mazetti at his inn once more. The burly armorer was being most generous, allowing him to sleep on a pallet near Mazetti's goods—not that anyone was likely to try to rob the well-known craftsman, anyhow, with Nessuno known to be around. But in fact Nessuno was still hidden in a crate among the other's bales of goods.

"Come on with me," Mazetti said as the evening grew late. They had been sitting in the common room, talking and drinking. The armorer had been interested in Jamie's comments, as a knight, on styles and purposes of armor—and somehow they had gotten off into the philosophy of armor.

"I'll show you what I mean when I say that the man in armor is dead, or at least dying," Mazetti said.

Jamie thought this a strange remark to come from the best armorer of the age, but he followed along as the other stepped outside into the cold, wet night. He enjoyed Mazetti's company and found this talk most interesting.

"I'm going to introduce you to a man who frequents the dockside area," Mazetti said. "His name is Alessi—Guido Alessi—and he is, to be blunt about it, a thief."

"A thief?"

"Yes. He leads a gang that lives by preying on the ships that come into port, and the unwary among their crews. From some they extort a sort of 'tax'; from others they simply steal. It's a low life, but Guido does it very well. And he's a good leader to his men."

Jamie shrugged uncomfortably; somehow this did not sound like the sort of person either he or Mazetti would normally associate with. But the armorer had already shown a predilection for unorthodoxy, in many ways. He wondered just how far the other's interest might extend.

In an unlighted alley near the docks Mazetti stopped before a door that appeared no different from any of its neighbors. Putting one hand lightly on Jamie's upper arm, he said softly that the Scot should learn quickly to keep his mouth shut.

"They are touchy of strangers here," Mazetti went on, "and while I am known to them, you may quickly find yourself looking at a half-dozen knives. Be prudent."

Jamie nodded; and Mazetti put a hand on the door and pushed it open.

Inside, dim light from a guttering fireplace and a couple of smoky torches illuminated a straw-floored room and several groups of disreputable-looking men. The room was totally silent as Mazetti led Jamie inside and pushed the door closed behind him.

"It's me, Mazetti!" the man said. "You know me, and I vouch for my friend here." He walked across to a large table near the right side of the room and sat down on the bench beside it. Jamie followed and sat with him.

A dirty-looking little girl appeared from a door in the other wall and walked across to Mazetti, waiting sullenly but saying nothing. He told her to bring them both wine, in a goodly quantity; she turned about and vanished without a change in expression. In another moment she was back with two leather cups.

"Drink!" Mazetti said. "It's terrible stuff, but it's wine." It was, indeed. Wine, but very bad wine.

"Guido!" Mazetti roared as he put down his cup. Jamie saw a large, tanned man with his back to a corner look across at them.

"Guido my friend! Come drink with me!" Mazetti said loudly.

The man rose silently and stepped out from among the half-dozen men who had been sitting around him. Jamie saw that Guido was a large, swarthy man, tall and wide and very nearly bigger than Jamie himself was. His hair was short and curly, glistening black; and below it he wore a short black beard that appeared to be little more than a vastly overgrown shadow.

The big man sat across from them and examined Jamie closely with his eyes, saying nothing; and Mazetti waved a hand negligently in the air, that quickly produced another cup—for Guido—and more wine for them all. Guido took a large drink and wiped his mouth with the back of his hand, shifting his attention to Mazetti, who had been watching him without saying anything.

Jamie took in the sight of the rounded muscles in the dark man's huge arms, that sprang naked from the ragged holes at the top of his dirty, rough-cloth tunic. The other seemed to be dressed as the poorest of peasants, but he carried himself like a leader of men. Jamie found himself watching the gang leader with more than ordinary curiosity—as if he were sizing up a possible opponent, one who might become a possible friend.

The broad, rounded face turned and looked into his eyes at that moment, and Jamie saw that they were evaluating him, too. He wondered what the man thought of what he saw—and Jamie had the presence to recognize the strangeness of his own reaction, that he, a knight and a prince, should be at all concerned over the reaction of a peasant to him.

"You see what I mean, Jamie?" Mazetti was saying to him. "This man has never worn armor, and probably never will. It is not right that he should. But in time he and his type of men will be the rulers of this world—and to do that they will find the ways to kill the armored men. Is that not so, Guido?"

"Perhaps it is already so," the dark man said; and then a shy grin appeared on his red-cheeked, round face. "Is that why you call me over here, Mazetti—to show me off?"

"Of course it is!" Mazetti bellowed. "What other good is there in you?" He laughed, and Guido roared with him.

Later that evening, when Mazetti had stepped out the back door to locate the bog, Jamie found Guido looking at him once more. He returned the look coolly, and at last Guido spoke.

"You're a strong man," he said. "I think you are a knight, too. Am I right?"

"Yes," said Jamie.

"And perhaps even more than that. But strong, first of all. Wrestle with me."

At that the whole room quieted, and Jamie realized that he had been set up—that they had all been waiting for some such contest to be suggested. Probably if Jamie had been smaller, some lesser opponent would have suggested himself for Jamie's trial—but as it was, he had drawn the chief himself.

Jamie wondered whether Mazetti was part of this. The man had not yet returned.

Apparently it was to be a kind of arm-wrestling match. Jamie had done similar things before, in camps and in the squires' hall when he had been in training; and so he settled himself across from Guido and rested his elbow on the table—avoiding a puddle of wine that had been there longer than he had. Guido took his hand in a firm clasp and—

Wham! Jamie's arm had been twisted and slammed down, splashed through the very puddle he had just tried to miss. He had been relaxed and so had not been hurt, but the back of his hand stung a little from the force of its hitting the table.

"Guido!" The voice was Mazetti's, from the door at the back of the room. "You have to use the signal, you know." The big man grinned sheepishly at Jamie and nodded, holding his hand back in position, tacitly waiting in agreement to do it correctly this time.

Jamie rested his elbow and once again clasped Guido's hand in his own. They waited, and Mazetti counted down from three and yelled.

"Go!"

Instantly a great pressure built up in Jamie's hand and spread down his forearm to his elbow; it continued moving back up his arm to the shoulder. And there it stayed, growing greater and greater. Jamie felt his muscles bulging and straining as he pushed with his hand at the other man's hand, there at the top of their forearms—but the other hand did not move backward at all.

For long moments they strained, and Jamie could see that the cords were standing out on his arm and hand. Across from him he could see Guido—the man looked up into his eyes at that minute—whose face had reddened and who had developed several vertical creases between nose and cheeks.

Jamie realized that the pressure being put on by the other man was continuing to increase; and as he watched, the dark face opened in a laugh—and Jamie's hand swayed backward a tiny amount. Reaching deep into his reserves of strength, he concentrated all his attention on his hand, taking his eyes from the Italian; and slowly his hand recovered the tiny amount of ground it had lost.

But when that had been accomplished he heard Guido laugh once more—and his hand was pushed back.

This time there was no stopping it; and with increasing force his arm leaned back, until finally the back of his hand slammed down onto the tabletop. Instantly Guido released Jamie's hand and sat back, breathing hard and still laughing. Jamie moved his hand and watched the other man; and at that moment Mazetti slipped down to sit beside him once more.

"Bravo!" he said. "That was a fine contest. No one has made Guido work like that for a long time." He shoved a cup of wine across.

Around them the regulars of this tavern were talking among themselves and congratulating Guido on his victory—and he reached out and took the cup of wine from before Jamie. He took a large swallow from it and put it back down in front of the Scot, watching him steadily with sober eyes above a smiling face.

Jamie looked into his eyes a moment; then smiled and reached for the cup. He drained it, and Guido smiled at him and slapped him lightly on the shoulder.

Mazetti laughed too; and the laughter spread among all the crowd in the dingy little tavern, even though most of them had no idea what was so funny.

Much later, Mazetti and Jamie set out again for their inn—accompanied by a small group of men from the tavern. To escort them, Mazetti had explained; it was a rough neighborhood.

One of the men, a small, dark-skinned fellow, laughed loudly at something his companion said. He turned to Jamie and laughed again, saying something. Jamie found he could not understand the words.

"What?" he said. "Say that again." The other looked up at him and said something again.

This time Jamie was concentrating, and as he did so his head buzzed, a roar that grew from nothingness inside his ears and reverberated about his skull. Sweat broke out on his face and he swayed in place, fighting the attack of nausea that threatened to make him throw up on the spot. He clutched at Mazetti, who grabbed his forearm and held him steady, looking at him in concern.

"I can't understand him," Jamie muttered. "Something's wrong; I can't understand him!"

"Of course not," Mazetti said. "He's drunk and lapsed into Siciliano dialect—none of us can understand him."

"You don't understand," Jamie said. "I've got a pentecost spell—I'm supposed to be able to understand anyone—"

He broke off and leaned away from Mazetti, against a wall.

"I think I see," the other said. "You have a spell, but it's not working, eh? Maybe something's gone wrong with it. Are you all right?"

"I will be," Jamie said.

Chapter Twelve

THE FOLLOWING DAY Jamie received a terse note from Andrea Matteleone, directing him to the establishment of a man named Giacomo Renaldi. Mazetti, busily packing for his return to Milan was able to tell him a little about Renaldi.

"A merchant of the middle sort," he said. "He does well but he started from nothing and grew fast—and the stories have it that he is not overscrupulous in his methods."

"What do they want me for?" Jamie asked.

"Who can say?" Mazetti shrugged. "He is of the class that always has a use for a bravo or a thug—" He interrupted himself with a grin. "Now don't get upset with me! I'm not calling you a thug! But you'll have to be careful, because you may find yourself being told to do bad things."

Jamie frowned.

"But wait till you get there," Mazetti went on. "Why borrow trouble until you reach it?".

Jamie nodded and made his way out, after bidding Mazetti a safe trip home and thanking him for his help and his friendship.

Renaldi's place was a dingy, ramshackle building in the merchants' quarter, very near to the docks. In fact, Jamie thought as he made his way there, it was probably quite close to the tavern in which he and Mazetti had met with Guido Alessi.

"You are the man Andrea sent, eh?" the man identified to him as Renaldi said. Despite the appearance of the building, Renaldi was prosperous-looking and dressed well. He was large-bodied, but seemed to carry the weight easily; and he kept a short, well-trimmed graying beard, above which small eyes twinkled at the world. Here in the building he wore rich, colorful clothing, with an apron over it all to protect his finery; and he kept his floppy cap on inside.

"Yes," Jamie answered. It seemed as if he should have more to say, but nothing seemed called for. And undoubtedly it would be good for him to get into the habit of terseness, since in his servile position he would have to be controlling his tongue throughout the foreseeable future.

"Do you know your duties, then?" the man asked.

"No," Jamie said. Renaldi frowned.

"No?"

"I was told only to come here," Jamie said.

"Ah, I see." Renaldi nodded. "All right. Simply put, you're to be my bodyguard. That means you will stay near me day and night, watching for those who might attack me." He paused.

"You're big enough," he said. "Are you a trained fighter, then?"

"Yes," Jamie said. When the man seemed to be waiting for detail, he went on.

"I've fought in the wars of France for several years; and lately I've been in the bodyguard of a great noble in Milan." No use going into too much detail, Jamie thought.

"Good," the other said, seemingly satisfied. "Bodyguard to a noble, and now you work for me, eh?" He nodded, smug at some importance this fact seemed to give him. Then he caught his head in mid-nod, jerking it up to look at Jamie.

"Why did you leave Milan?" he said. "Did your client— die?"

"No," Jamie said, unable to completely hide a grin. "Quite the opposite—he was in fine shape when I saw him last."

"Very well." Renaldi frowned for a moment or two, but seemed satisfied once more.

"You'll stay near me, even in the night," the man went on after a moment. "And eat with me, too—tasting my food first." Jamie almost turned away at that remark, but managed to stifle his anger quickly.

"Ah—one more thing," Renaldi said. "Can you read or write?"

"No," Jamie said. It was not true. He could write tolerable

Latin, some English, French and Italian, and read them all with
varying ease. But with his pentecost spell giving him trouble
these days, there was no point in borrowing trouble. He believed it was best to not give too much of himself away to such
a man as this—he would not be expecting one of his bravos to
read or write; that was rare even among the upper classes, the
nobility.

For several days Jamie followed Renaldi about like some
tame sheepdog; and he quickly found that any plans he might
have had to see Maria in his time off had to go by the boards—
he had no time for himself. He ate when—or just before—
Renaldi did; he slept when Renaldi did, but on a pallet laid
across the door to the master's bedchamber. He wondered what
would happen if Renaldi took a wench with him.

After several days of wandering around behind Renaldi,
though, Jamie began to become acclimated to the ways of this
particular trading establishment, at least—although one of the
first things he noticed was that little or no actual buying or
selling seemed to be getting done here. The dim, spacious
interior of the old wooden building was busy all day long, but
Jamie quickly noticed that all the activity seemed to involve
goods being carried in from somewhere else in the town, in-
ventoried, and then repackaged and moved elsewhere. Strange
business, this merchanting, he thought to himself.

But eventually Renaldi left the building to do something
besides go to his home; and Jamie followed quietly along
behind him as he went with a small pack train to a small
residence on the northern edge of town. There the goods on the
train were unloaded—but not unpacked—and left with a
goodly pile of similar packages. And the train turned and came
back to the main warehouse.

By now Jamie was sure that something most unmerchantlike
was going on, but he was not about to make any comment—to
his employer or to anyone else. In fact, he had managed not to
say anything at all to anyone in Renaldi's establishment for so
long that everyone there seemed to ignore him as a part of the
fixtures. And then one day a few familiar faces turned up once
more.

Eight days after he had gone to work for Renaldi, Jamie
awakened in the middle of the night, sure he had heard an
unusual sound. He lay on his pallet in the doorway, listening—
but at first heard nothing. The dark corridor in which he lay
was silent, still. He lay back down on his pallet—and as his

ear reached the level of the bottom of the door to Renaldi's bedchamber, he once again heard something.

This time he was sure it was the sound of voices he heard; and he moved over to press his ear more firmly against the door, as near the crack at the bottom as possible. But he could not get down low enough for direct access to the crevice, and so could not make out the words. But there definitely were voices to be heard, and they definitely were inside his employer's bedroom.

For a moment he puzzled over how someone had gotten in: as far as he knew there were no other openings into that room than the one he blocked with his body. But he quickly gave that up as a profitless speculation and began to ponder just what he should be doing about the events he had discovered.

If Renaldi was in danger then he should burst in and try to rescue the man. But what kind of danger could he really be in, with all this talk still going on? No, it seemed more likely that some secret conference was being held—and since Jamie had not been invited, his unsolicited presence would probably be most unwelcome.

He debated going back to sleep; but then rose silently and padded down the hallway to the stairs that led down to the outside doorway; and he took up station in an unlighted portion of the tiny garden that Renaldi took no care of. He waited for almost an hour, until a brief flash of light told him that some door or window had opened for a short moment on the second floor level, near his employer's room. He watched closely, trying to discern whether someone might be coming down in some way—and suddenly he heard a rustling, tearing sound. Someone had come down somehow into the garden!

The light above flashed again briefly, and Jamie froze in place, not wanting to be seen by the second man if he accosted the first—and so he stood silently in place as the shadowy figure of a man crossed the rustling garden and went out the rusted gate across from Jamie.

In a moment the second man was crossing the garden too; and Jamie watched him go without moving.

When the figure had gone out the gate, Jamie leaped to grab the top of the wall behind him and levered himself up, in time to look down on the form of the man who had just left by the gate as he came around the corner and headed in Jamie's direction. Jamie let him get by and then pulled himself up onto the wall, letting himself down as silently as possible into the street. The figure he was following was just vanishing around a corner just ahead, so he headed in that direction.

When he rounded the corner, though, there was no one in sight; and Jamie stood there for a moment, puzzled. But then he nodded to himself, deciding to take a chance, and he began to run, heading down the street and ignoring all diverging avenues until he came to the square at the street's end. There he settled himself in a misshapen shadow at the base of a statue, where water flowed calmly; and he waited.

After a moment or two a figure walked into the square from the next street over from that down which Jamie had come—a figure that whistled a little as it walked, and which Jamie felt he had seen before. And as it passed close by him, the figure's face was illuminated by the dim light of a distant torch. It was Guido Alessi.

No need to follow further, he thought. He now had plenty to think about. He sat for several moments in the silence of the square after Guido had vanished into the darkness of a street on the other side. Then he got up and walked silently back to his post before Renaldi's door.

Knowing something unusual was going on, Jamie realized that if Renaldi was involved in something illegal or dangerous, it could have serious consequences for the man's bodyguard. And so the young Scot began a campaign to find out just what might be occurring.

The flow of goods into the warehouse for reshipment began to slow down, he noticed; and the men who had been working at that job idled about the place. Jamie tried to strike up conversations with one or two of them, but found none that were willing to talk—or perhaps it was that none of them knew anything to talk about.

Renaldi himself, however, began to give Jamie more opportunities to learn; for he was spending more and more of his time out of the warehouse, moving about the town and doing odd pieces of business with a variety of the more prosperous merchants. Always close, Jamie eventually figured out that what Renaldi was doing was selling to them various pieces of property that he seemed to own in the heart of the city—in fact, he owned a surprising portion of the merchants' quarter.

But he was converting it all into cash, it seemed.

In the next days Renaldi led him out of the city and into the hilly countryside above the town, to four separate farmsteads.

Jamie was not privy to what occurred inside the farmhouses when Renaldi was there; but it was more food for thought.

He wished Mazetti were still about; the man had a good insight into human nature and might be able to tell him something about what was going on. For Jamie's part, he only knew that something was indeed going on—something at least illicit—and that it was probably going to be dangerous. He debated running away, but felt that he could not do so—he had no money yet. Besides, then he would not be able to come back to see Maria. . . .

Not having seen her since the day of his interview with her brother, he nevertheless found himself thinking of her each day. Perhaps she could give him some idea of what was going on.

Now that was a good idea, he realized. If only he could get some time free to go and see Maria—and her brother.

"You, Jamie!"

Renaldi had turned and addressed him directly for the first time in several days, he realized.

"Master," he responded, hating it but knowing the man liked to hear the title.

"I'm going out," Renaldi said. "But I won't need you this time. Wait for me at the warehouse—I should go back there in four hours."

"Yes." Jamie nodded. Inside he felt a species of elation; only yesterday he had been hoping for some time to go and see the two Matteleones—and now this. He waited until Renaldi vanished up the street, and then headed out across town towards the palatial residence of the banker Matteleone and his sister.

"Jamie!" Maria was obviously happy to see him, and it warmed his heart strangely.

"Good day!" he said, and continued to smile down at her. She was certainly a pretty little thing, he thought. And strong in her way, too. She smiled back at him.

"It's been so long!" she said at last.

"Yes," he said. Now, for some reason, he could not think of much to say to her. He thought about holding her hand, but decided that that might be too presumptuous in the event anyone else walked in—like Andrea, her brother.

"Maria!" Yes, there he was now. He had just come in through the door that Jamie could see over the girl's shoulder, and he was distinctly glaring in their direction. Clearly, he had little liking for Jamie or the attachment of his sister to the Scot.

"Master Matteleone, I am glad to see you," Jamie said. Seeing a distinctly scornful look beginning to appear on the man's face, Jamie continued hastily.

"I've come upon some information that I don't understand," he said, "but I fear some mischief may be coming from it, and I'd like to ask your advice as to what I ought to do."

He had hooked the man now, he saw; no banker or merchant could refuse the offer of new information like this—it was often the lifeblood of a business. After a moment Matteleone nodded coldly but in a civil manner.

"Come into this sitting room," he said. "We'll have some wine and discuss what you've found." He turned to his sister.

"Maria, would you call for some wine, please?" And he turned and led the way into the sitting room without waiting for her answer. Jamie smiled at the girl, nodded, and followed.

Sipping his wine, Jamie briefly told the story of the strange things he had seen done by Renaldi, and of his connection with Alessi. Maria listened in awe, interjecting a question now and again—most of which Jamie could not answer.

Matteleone, however, listened in a stolid silence, sipping at his wine. And when Jamie had finished, he made no response except to put down his wine cup and call for the servant.

"Alessandro," he said when the man appeared, "find Giacomo and tell him to come to me with several men." The man nodded and disappeared. Matteleone turned to Jamie.

"We'll wait a moment," he said. "Perhaps the men I sent for can help us." He paused, and then went on.

"It seems obvious to me that Renaldi's removing his goods from an area that he believes will become dangerous," he said. "Did that occur to you too?"

"Dangerous?" Jamie said, falling back into his Milanese court character of the stupid barbarian. "How so?"

"Wait," Matteleone said; and in a moment he greeted the three men who entered the room at his command.

"Take him," he said, pointing at Jamie.

Maria stared openmouthed as the three men charged at Jamie; and the Scot barely had time to throw himself out of his chair before they were on him. He got a hand up, and the first one ran straight into it; but the other two came around that one and were on Jamie at almost the same time, pinning his arms before he could draw sword or dagger and wrestling him to the ground. They were strong and experienced men, and they had him down and powerless in mere moments.

"Andrea, what are you doing?" Maria was standing now, staring from her brother to Jamie and then back.

"Sister, you've had to learn something unfortunate through this man," Matteleone said. "Unfortunately, what he discovered is something I happen to have a vital interest in. And I cannot afford to have his tales floating about the city right now."

He looked at the men holding Jamie, who had begun to tie the Scot's arms behind him.

"Take him to the wine cellar," he said, "and keep him there until I say otherwise."

He turned away, and the men hauled Jamie to his feet.

Bruised, Jamie lay for some time in the corner of the cellar where the men had thrown him; and when he had eventually struggled to his feet, he found it did him no good. There was no way out of the windowless, locked room; and his hands remained tied behind him. He paced, finding his balance a bit unsteady now that his arms could not swing freely at his sides. But he was full of a certain restless energy—perhaps the energy of indignation—and he was not happy to merely sit in a corner and wait for his fate.

For, thinking about it, he was sure that was what would be coming to him. Matteleone would not let him live to tell about whatever was going on—either beforehand or afterward.

After some hours the door opened quietly, letting in a beam of light. In its center, silhouetted, he saw the slim figure of Maria.

The girl stood there quietly while her eyes adjusted to the darkness; and Jamie merely stood where he was, waiting. At last she strode forward, finding him in the dimness and putting her arms about him as she leaned on his chest.

"Oh, Jamie!" she said, in a voice very near a sob. "I'm so sorry! What my brother does, I knew not—or I would have warned you!" She trembled a little against him.

"Help me get out of here," he said, almost roughly. She represented his only chance now.

"Oh, of course," she said softly, and she produced a small knife. He turned about to present his arms, bound behind him, to her; and for a moment he felt in the pit of his stomach a small fear for his back. But that was nonsense, he knew; and he disciplined himself to stand still while she sawed at the tough cords that bound him.

At last he could turn about, rubbing at his wrists to renew his circulation; and he looked down at her once more.

"I'll have to leave right away," he said. "If they discover us, we'll both be in great danger. Come with me."

He was surprised to find that he had asked that of her.

"Where?" she said, blinking at him in some surprise. "Where could we go?"

He had not thought that out clearly himself, so he paused a moment before answering.

"To my country," he said. "If we can find a passage to England, I can get to my men in Cornwall, and they have my treasure waiting for me." He paused again and looked down at her.

"I'd like to take you back there with me," he said. "Will you do it?"

"Yes," she said, almost inaudibly. But he heard it. And she hastened on.

"But we'll need money to get there. So I won't go with you now."

"No?" He blinked in his turn. "But then what?"

"In a week, when the riots start, I will be able to get my hands on a great deal of my brother's money," she said. "I think he is even sending a ship to England. I know he got a letter from the Archduke through me when I was at court. It recommended him to the King of England for license to set up a branch of his business there. If I can be on that ship at the waterfront, you can come for me there, and we can smuggle you on board and get away that way."

"Riots?"

"Yes," she said. "That's what's going to happen, that he and Renaldi will cause. He told me just now."

That would be ideal—but he would have to stay alive until then, he thought. But who was there who could hide him from Matteleone in the meantime?

He went off down the dark streets by himself, thinking about this. He was only aware at the last moment, then, of two dark figures that seemed to materialize out of the shadowy walls themselves, one on either side of him—and that was the last he remembered.

Chapter Thirteen

JAMIE CAME OUT of semi-consciousness to the awareness that his hands and feet were uncomfortably numb. Waking, it took him a little time to gather his senses from the partial oblivion into which he had retreated from the pain of his bonds and the rough handling that had followed Guido's signal to his men.

Slowly, it came back to him. He had been tied and hauled off like some large sack of grain, to be thrown down onto the hard floor in a dim corner of some underground storage room. That had been . . . when? Certainly some time since, possibly several hours.

Fury and panic began to kindle together within him, but he fought them down. Physically now, tied as he was, he was helpless. It was not a time for muscle, but for mind.

He experimented cautiously, moving his arms and legs. He thought he could manage to squirm himself into a sitting position if he had to—but it would make noise, and for the moment it would be common sense not to draw attention to himself, at least until he had some plan of action worked out. Noises of any kind could draw the gang's attention back to him; for he could hear them, close by, talking among themselves; and now, with his returning memory, he remembered with grim humor that he had bruised more than one of them before they had managed to truss him into immobility. After which, of course, they had taken the opportunity to pay him back for his resistance with kicks, the effect of which he could feel sharply even now on his ribs and thighs. But he had left marks on some few of them first.

Still, he hardly felt the need now for more of what they had

handed him in retaliation; and drawing the gang's attention to
him before he was ready might just do that. What was necessary first was to examine his situation in more detail.

He raised his head and looked about himself. This room was
some sort of underground vault, perhaps the cellar of some old
warehouse. He could dimly make out the ceiling, high above
him in the near-darkness of the vault; it appeared to be very
solidly beamed, made of wood, and could well be a warehouse
floor overhead. But it was much too far above him to do him
any good at all.

His head was near the intersection of two of the walls, so he
could inspect them easily, but he got little good out of that.
They were of an unhandsome yellow-brown stone construction, solid enough to keep him in; and the mortar between
them, while rough and possibly crumbly—could he touch it to
find out—also seemed stout enough.

The floor was quite a different thing; the stone it was made
of was a dirty gray in color, smoothed by use—probably the
present building had been laid down over the ruins of an older
one, even more solidly built.

So much, then, for the place in which he was being held.

Jamie managed to roll himself silently over onto his stomach, though he scraped some hide from his right elbow and
knee in the process. Rolling, he considered, was at least one
method by which he might be able to propel himself about the
room, but since he had just bumped into a mound of casks and
boxes—of which there were no small number scattered
about—he did not think much of that method of grinding dirt
into the fresh scrapes on elbow and knee.

The level of light in the room flared up as he lay on his back,
catching his breath. He smelled the odors of cooked food suddenly, and from the fresh upwelling of talk among Guido's
band, still too distant and low-pitched for him to make out the
subject of their conversation, he guessed that they were either
settling down to a meal or had gotten into a serious discussion
of some sort, possibly both at the same time.

Jamie rolled onto his right side once more, ignoring the
protests his joints made; and stopped there balancing himself
on his left arm, which was bent back under him. Gingerly he
levered his upper body forward, bending at the waist so that he
was doubled forward toward his knees. Taking advantage of
the raised level of noise at the far end of the room to hide what
sound his own movements might make, he tried to throw his

weight back to his left, as if to roll onto his back again—and after a bit of rocking and swaying he found himself sitting up on the floor.

He was breathing heavily now, if as quietly as he could; and he quickly found that he had to be careful of his balance in this new position, since the constriction of his legs made him likely to sway and fall helplessly backward once more. He wriggled about and finally managed to put his back against one wall, holding himself upright.

From this position he could at last see the members of Guido's band gathered around a small fire they had made in a part of the vault near the only door, which was at the top of six stairsteps and set ajar to let the smoke out. Jamie's position was as far from that door as possible. He sat at the rear of a wide ledge at the back of the room, while the gang occupied a much larger area, whose floor was about three feet lower. From somewhere above him a cold draft blew down on his neck, probably from some ground-level window, small or barred undoubtedly, but large enough to provide ventilation and drive the smoke out the farther open door.

The gang sat about on casks and sacks, Guido among them; and Jamie could hear their talking, but not well enough even now to catch more than an occasional word. Beyond them he could see the ironically open door that was his only hope of escape—a large, battered-looking, but still solid slab of wood.

The important question, he told himself, was why he was still alive. It would have been much easier for Guido and the others to cut his throat and dump his body off a wharf than to struggle with him as they had and tie him up like this. Someone less bright than Jamie might have had illusions about his own value to the gang—Jamie had none. He could think of no reason right now why Renaldi should want to keep him alive; and none—except the friendship that had seemed to exist between himself and Guido—that could cause the gang chief to refrain from killing him unless he, in turn, had a specific personal need for Jamie.

So—which was it? Some unknown need of Renaldi's or Guido's, or simply and improbably Guido's friendship, that was responsible for the fact that Jamie's heart was still beating? The necessary thing for him to find out now was which it was—need or friendship. If the reason was need, there would then be the further necessity of finding out what the need was, and how to make the best possible use of it to ensure his

continued survival. If friendship . . . that was another game
entirely. . . .

Meanwhile, was there any chance of his getting loose in any
way? His wrists had been tied behind his back—but with
seamen's rope rather than landsmen's leather thongs—and the
rope felt thick enough so that he might try stretching it without
cutting his wrists to ribbons in the struggle. Silently, Jamie
tensed his arm muscles against the ropes, but there was no
perceptible give to them. Seamen's knots as well, undoubtedly. . . .

Unexpectedly, he saw Guido get to his feet, say something
to the men about him, and come toward Jamie. He stepped up
to the ledge where Jamie lay by means of a box placed in front
of it. Jamie sat motionless and watched the big man come
toward him, noting that the other carried a long, slim-bladed
dagger—not in its sheath, but naked in his hands. The Scot felt
his stomach muscles tighten in reflex, and made an effort to
relax. His mental condition was more important than his physi-
cal preparedness just now, if he was to get out of this at all.

About three feet before Jamie's legs, Guido stopped his
approach and squatted in place, disdaining the use of a box or
keg. He looked relaxed and comfortable in that position—no
doubt, like most men of peasant stock, he had been used to it
all his life. He said nothing, merely looking at Jamie for several minutes. Finally he spoke.

"Would you like to see a priest?" he said.

Jamie had been half-expecting that his fate might be upon
him, but for some reason this particular form of announcement
very nearly had an unnerving effect on him. Realization of his
helplessness flooded through him and he had an instant vision
of himself lying still in a pool of blood, in this dim corner. But
at the same time he found that some impulsive part of himself
had taken control of his mouth, causing it to spit loudly—not
at Guido, but off to Jamie's right. Guido laughed softly, still
watching him.

"No, no . . . I just asked because you never know what a
man might hide inside. A drink, then?" At Jamie's nod, he
called to his men and someone brought him a wineskin. Guido
helped himself thirstily.

"Renaldi told you to do this to me, didn't he?" Jamie asked
the big dark man before him.

The other nodded soberly and held the wineskin down to the
Scot's lips so that Jamie could drink. He did so, ignoring the

sour wine that spilled out the sides of his mouth to run down his chin and onto his chest. While making a production of gulping and then belching, Jamie considered asking bluntly whether Guido had been given orders to kill him; and then decided against it. After a moment he looked up again.

"How about something to eat?" he said instead. "I haven't eaten since yesterday—or maybe the day before, I'm not sure."

He watched as Guido, now on his feet, looked down at him silently for a moment.

"Sure," Guido said, "why not?"

He turned off toward the fire; and Jamie leaned back against the wall, finding that his breath was coming fast and his stomach muscles had cramped slightly. Jamie tried to ignore them and think—if he got out of this, it would be thanks to his tongue and his mind. . . .

When Guido returned he was accompanied by several of his men, who carried among them a large wheel of white cheese, a jar of more wine, and a cold roasted fowl of some sort. All of these items were put down directly on the dirty floor to the right of Jamie's bound—and numb—legs; then Guido waved his men back from Jamie by a few feet, taking himself out of possible reach as well. He squatted again and looked into Jamie's eyes levelly.

"Be careful," he said quietly. The dark blue eyes below the bushy black brows were most serious, and Jamie nodded silently.

Not that his agreement would make any difference if he got a chance to escape, of course—Jamie found himself tempted to laugh silently, and knew instinctively that if he did, Guido would be able to see that in him, too. He kept his face expressionless.

Guido lifted a hand and waved to one of his men, who stepped to Jamie's side and reached down behind him with a knife. In the dark and constricted space between the Scot's back and the wall, his moves were clumsy, and he managed to nick both Jamie's wrists somewhat. But the bonds fell away, and Jamie made no complaint, only bringing his arms about in front of him and beginning clumsily to rub his two benumbed hands together like the frostbitten paws of some wintering forester in the north.

"Toad!" Guido's harsh voice was followed by a variety of more colorful curses. The gang leader had noticed that Jamie's

wrists were bleeding, as the latter's clumsy rubbing movements spread the blood about. For several minutes Jamie and
the rest of the band enjoyed Guido's colorful castigation of the
unfortunate rope-cutter, being taken to task primarily for his
lack of control with his blade, and secondarily for damaging
someone belonging to his boss, whom he had not yet been
given an order to damage.

His legs still bound and stretched out uncomfortably straight
before him, Jamie began to eat from the food placed awkwardly to his right, well out before him. He was indeed hungry, he found, and for a while he attacked the fowl like a
starved man, picking it up whole in his still numb hands and
tearing chunks from the bones with his teeth. As the immediate
pangs of hunger eased at these attentions, he began to move in
a more leisurely fashion, and to make use also of both the jar of
wine and the cheese. For the moment, in the satisfaction of his
hunger and thirst he forgot the watching men about him, including Guido himself, who had moved back a little to seat
himself on a cask and now sat, also watching Jamie and still
with his dagger in hand.

After a few more moments Jamie looked up at Guido, saying
nothing while he chewed a large mouthful of fowl out of his
tongue's way. Then he drank from the jar, finding this wine
also sour and bitter, but strangely enjoyable for all that. He
grinned a little and looked at Guido.

"When do the riots start?" he asked, and laughed silently
but openly as Guido's eyes opened a little. Two or three of the
other men started to speak, and were silenced by a glare from
Guido.

"You didn't know I knew about them?" Jamie taunted
them. "You should have guessed. You knew I worked for
Renaldi."

Guido nodded but continued to say nothing. Jamie continued
to grin.

"And for Matteleone, of course," he added. Guido's spine
straightened as he sat up, his eyes going to the men around
them. But then he shrugged. It was too late to do anything
much about the revelation now. It was proof of what Jamie had
suspected all along; the underlings had no idea who the real
controller of their organization was.

Best be careful not to get Guido too angry with you, though,
he warned himself. Watching Guido's face carefully, he con-

cluded that the man was not going to say anything he did not
have to at this point. The initiative remained with Jamie.

"So you'd better be very careful," he said, almost con-
fidentially, to Guido. "You and your men are going to be out
on the streets taking all the risks—and you're going to find that
you've been set up to take the blame for the riots, as well."

Some of the men muttered again, but Guido did not look at
them; he merely sat quietly in his place, looking calmly at the
prisoner. He was, of course, aware that Jamie's voice had been
getting louder as he spoke, and that the men remaining at the
fire had heard and begun to make their way over to join the
group already about him. Guido would not appreciate the apparent fostering of rebellion in his ranks, but he was too intel-
ligent not to realize that something vital to him might be
occurring. He would realize that it was too late now to send his
men out of earshot without arousing their fears and suspicions.
He would have to accept the situation Jamie had brought about
and make the best he could of it.

Now he squatted down beside Jamie, so that their faces were
only inches apart.

"Explain yourself," he said quietly.

Jamie shrugged, took another bite at the fowl in his hand and
followed it with a gulp of wine from the jar in his other hand.
The wine stung the back of his throat as it went down, and it
occurred to Jamie that he was in truth back in battle, although
this time he was fighting with his tongue.

His body was responding as it always did when he went into
battle. His arms and legs seemed on fire, burning with some
internal energy. His eyes seemed to see more clearly, his ears
to hear better. His mind was racing, moving faster than it ever
had before, so that he felt as if he were thinking of things to say
more quickly than his tongue could get them uttered.

"What I mean," he said after a moment, "is that you've
been told by your employer—Giacomo Renaldi—to arrange
for crowds to gather on his signal—and yours—to riot, beginning in the dockside area and then moving through much of the
city. You've been told to take your own men out with the
crowds, to use them for cover, and to make sure certain establishments are attacked and destroyed. Am I right so far?"

He looked Guido in the eye for a moment, and then turned
his gaze on the other men standing about him. All of them

were clustered around now, looking uneasy. The silence was ominous.

"You worked for Renaldi," Guido said, "so it's no surprise that you know this. And of course we all know it. So why tell us?"

"Because you don't know all the plan—the rest of it."

Guido stared at him coldly. He would, Jamie knew, be knowing he had no choice but to ask, and resenting his loss of control of the situation. Like his men around him, now Jamie had him hooked.

"And that's what you'll tell us now?" Guido asked ironically.

"Yes."

"Yes," Guido said. "You will most certainly tell us something. But how can we tell it's the truth?"

"Because you have orders to kill me," Jamie said, "and the truth will keep me alive. Because you're going to need me to save yourselves from this trap."

"Perhaps," said Guido. "Go on."

"I've already shown that I know as much as you do about your employer's plan," Jamie said, "and more about your employer's associations than most of you do. So it's reasonable that I would know even more. And since I'm in danger of my life, then surely what I tell you is going to be the truth, for you'll undoubtedly check what I say and keep me alive only if I am right."

"Perhaps," said Guido again. After a second's silence he went on, still looking without expression at Jamie, although now he was rubbing a hand through the dense thick beard at his chin.

"Tell us then, what you think we need to know," he said, "and we'll check it. You can stay alive while we do so. And if it checks out . . . fine."

The other men gathered more closely about as Jamie looked up at them, preparing himself.

"Have you asked yourselves why all this is being done?" he asked.

Most of those there looked bemused, but Guido nodded.

"Of course," he said. "Our work is to damage the merchants who compete with Renaldi, so his business will get stronger. It's a good plan." He looked about at his men, who nodded with him.

"Yes," said Jamie. "But isn't that what you and your men have done so often before?"

"I see what you mean," said Guido, "and it is true. We work for Renaldi, and we would attack his enemies if we could—but they have men like us who will do the same to Renaldi if we aren't careful."

"And where will those men be during this rioting?" Jamie asked.

"Inside their establishments," Guido said, "defending them, as we would be . . ." He stopped.

"But you will not be defending Renaldi's establishments," Jamie said. "And what's to stop the rioters from destroying them?"

He stopped, and there was silence. Jamie went on.

"But Renaldi has moved all his goods out of the city, and sold his buildings, has he not?" The faces about him were blank.

"Check on it," he said. "You'll find Renaldi's got nothing left to lose here in the city. And certain others, too."

The silence continued. "That's smart of him," said Guido thoughtfully after a moment. "His competitors will be hurt, but he will be safe."

"Yes," Jamie said. "But how safe will all of you be?"

Guido looked at him with an enigmatic expression, and then shrugged.

"There is always danger," he said. "We know that."

"But what about the soldiers?" Jamie asked.

"Soldiers?"

"Certainly," Jamie said. "Think about it. The magistrates and the nobles can ignore you and your men when you fight other bands like yourselves. The damage you do is small; and that's the way things have always been. But this riot is going to cause great damage to the merchants' quarter, large enough to be a threat to the city authorities themselves. That, they can't allow; and so they'll send in their soldiers to deal with the rioters."

Jamie paused and took another drink of wine; the silence about him was complete.

"Of course, the greater the damage in the quarter, the more Renaldi and his silent partners can profit when they come back in after the riot is put down, with their own goods undestroyed or looted. And whatever damage your riot can do, an attack by

the soldiers upon the rioters will cause much more.'' He
looked about at the men.

"Do you think the soldiers will come in without a great deal
of killing and burning, to say nothing of a little looting on their
own?'' Heads shook solemnly about him—these men knew a
little about what the soldiery were like, particularly the free
companies generally employed by the Italian cities. Only
Guido remained expressionless, uncommitted.

"If you didn't know they were coming—as you did not—"
Jamie said, "you would have been among those attacked,
probably killed, like other rioters.'' There was more silence
about him, and after a moment he went on, pressing the advantage he sensed.

"One more thing,'' he said. "Did it never cross your minds
to think there will be an investigation, perhaps by the Duke
himself? And do you think Renaldi—or his associates—would
want men to remain alive who knew their names and their parts
in this?''

Jamie looked steadily now at Guido rather than at the other
men. After a moment the gang leader cleared his throat.

"It's not a pretty story,'' he said. "But you could have just
made it all up.''

"Hold me here,'' Jamie said, "and begin to look about you.
You'll be able to find out some things that I have said—you
will see some of them are already true.''

At that moment they were interrupted by curses and a scuffle
at the door to the room. Jamie's view of the area was now
blocked by the standing gang members about him, but most of
them turned to see what was going on. Guido cursed himself
and rushed away, jumping down from the ledge and arriving
quickly at the doorway—as Jamie could tell by the sudden
cessation of sound. After that, most of the other members of
the band moved quickly in the same direction, and Jamie could
see further—but still little more than their backs as they
grouped about whatever action was taking place.

There was some muffled conversation—Jamie could hear
Guido's voice, deep and demanding, and another, shriller
voice that rose plaintively in response. Shortly Jamie heard a
deep-voiced exclamation and the sound of a blow, which was
immediately followed by the sound of a body hitting the floor.
In a few minutes Guido was back, while several of his men
engaged in something that involved their stooping below
Jamie's eye level and moving off with something. Jamie took

his eyes off them and watched Guido, wondering if he had lost the big man's attention or belief.

"You were saying?" Guido said.

Jamie shrugged.

"If you only look at what your employers are doing, and think about what they may be doing—then I think you'll have cause to wonder a little," he answered. "And if not, you'll still have me and you'll have lost nothing but a few hours and a little effort."

"Except for that fool you scared enough to try and run off just now," Guido growled.

"Did you really want to keep such a one?" Jamie challenged him, sure he knew his man on this subject at least.

Guido mumbled something unintelligible, but seemed satisfied by the answer.

For the next three days Jamie remained a prisoner in the cellar, although he was no longer tied up. The freedom was an illusory one, however, because Guido's men were uneasy at his suggestions, and, feeling vaguely threatened by something they did not really understand, tended to watch his every move as if only waiting for an excuse to slip a dagger into him.

By the middle of the third day, however, their suspicions began to relax; and on the fourth day Guido returned from a short absence with a strange companion, whom he led directly to Jamie. Jamie's heart sank when at first glance he took the companion for a priest or monk of some sort.

But as they drew near, Jamie's apprehensions eased somewhat, because the other, at close quarters, looked ever less like a priest. He—Jamie thought it was a male person—was wearing a long gray-blue robe, so large for his small, wizened body that it seemed to hang shapelessly from high, bony shoulders. The wrinkled face that peered out from under the shadowy hood was either brown in color or deeply tanned; it was hairless except for white eyelashes, as far as Jamie could tell, and the eyes between them were small, beady, and dark brown—to Jamie they looked like the eyes of some animal.

The man looked down at Jamie without expression; but as Jamie met those eyes he sensed something behind them that caused his ears to buzz once more, his head to ache slightly.

The man continued to stand and watch Jamie while Guido once more squatted and addressed Jamie.

"We've been checking," he said, and paused, perhaps to watch Jamie's reaction. "We found nothing to prove what you say, although it is true that Renaldi has moved all of his goods elsewhere—and others have, too." He shrugged.

"So there is no proof—" Jamie said.

"No." Guido smiled slightly now. "But it is a very good story indeed. And this man will check *you* now." He waved a vague hand at the little man beside him.

"He is very expensive," he said, "but he is the best in the city for the weaving of the truthteller spell. And so we will see about you." He waved at the little man as he arose, this time by way of telling him to get on with his business—giving Jamie no time to protest or comment. But Jamie could think of nothing to say, anyway.

"I am Bandras," the wizened man said, squatting in his turn before Jamie as Guido and his men moved well out of the way, back to the door side of the room. His voice was deeper than Jamie would have expected, and there was that in it which seemed to expect no answer. Jamie watched him.

Still squatting, the little man pushed his cowl back, revealing a hairless brown skull and little else. But it seemed to make some difference to the little man, for his movements quickened now and he began to mutter a nearly silent chant under his breath and he stared into the space immediately before him and began to dance about in it with his hands—the rest of his body remaining virtually unmoving. The hands, small and scrawny, with dry-looking brown skin stretched over what seemed to be bird's bones, moved in rhythmic patterns whose beat Jamie could not seem to catch, but ever faster and faster and more demanding—until Jamie felt he could not possibly look away. Faster and faster they seemed to move, and some part of the young Scot thought that they should surely have begun to blur before his eyes—yet he thought he could see and follow every movement. . . .

The abrupt pain in his head snapped his eyes closed and rocked him back in his place until he cracked his skull against the wall behind him. He felt himself straining at invisible bonds that seemed to hold his arms helpless at his sides as his hands tried to go up to cover and hold his head; and through the roaring that grew in his ears he could hear his own moaning. He leaned sideways and threw up, partially upon himself and partially on the floor. And he was only vaguely aware of being straightened in his place and made to take some wine.

An unknown time passed, during which Jamie was aware that things were being done to him; but he seemed to have no will of his own, and no interest in doing anything other than hiding somewhere within himself. And after a time even that went away, and he slept dreamlessly.

He awoke to find Guido shaking him by the foot, from his customary squatting position well out in front of Jamie. Guido looked at him without speaking, and the big black-haired man handed him a wineskin, smiling.

Chapter Fourteen

"BANDRAS SAID YOU told the truth," Guido said, as Jamie took several deep thirsty pulls at the loose mouth of the skin. For once, it was good wine. After a moment Jamie put the skin down, and looked at Guido, grimly.

"What did he do to me?" Jamie asked.

"I don't know," Guido said. "I try not to watch the truth-teller at work, even though I hire him at times. It hurts the eyes."

He paused a moment.

"But there was something strange he had to say," Guido went on, frowning. "He asked me to apologize to you for him. He said you had other spells on you—and one in particular that had been by accident damaged already. His work further destroyed it, he said. He said I should tell you he was sorry about that."

For a moment what Guido had just said made no sense to Jamie, then he became aware that some of the other men in the cellar now seemed to be talking together in words he could not understand—and the truth jumped at him.

"The pentecost spell," he said aloud, without thinking, "yes, it had been damaged. And now it seems gone completely . . . but wait—" he looked up at Guido again, "I can still understand *you*!"

Guido's face showed his incomprehension.

"It was a spell that allowed me to speak any language perfectly," Jamie explained. "But . . . I suppose if I've once used the spell to work with a language, maybe I can learn that language in the process and not lose it when the spell goes away.'' He looked up again. ''How do I sound to you?''

''You have an accent,'' Guido said bluntly. ''You had none before. Is that part of it?''

''Maybe it is,'' said Jamie. ''Maybe it is.''

He fell silent.

Guido shrugged.

The rest of Alessi's band now accepted Jamie, at least to some extent—it helped that they had known and tested his strengths before. And in associating with them about the cooking fire in the little room, he made another discovery about his now extinct pentecost spell.

Several of the men were from various regions located some distance from Genoa or Milan, and apparently spoke among themselves any of a number of dialects—some of them incomprehensible to even the native Italians among the group. These Jamie found he could not understand at all, even though he had apparently once communicated with one of the men quite successfully.

''I didn't use it enough to learn that language,'' he mused to Guido, who stared back at him without saying a word. ''And now I never will unless I find a way to get that spell back.''

He chose not to mention the follow-up thought he had just had, which was that when he left this area he would have a great deal of difficulty making himself understood—unless he went back to France or England. He did not think Guido would want to hear of his possible leave-taking at this stage.

Even the Italian he could speak was harder for him now. He had to work at it, striving to pick up what was being said to him, searching his memory for the right words with which to respond. What had been a comfortable, easy habit—one requiring no exertion at all—had suddenly become a great deal of work: simple talking.

In the middle of the fourth night in the cellar, he awoke suddenly, knowing he had just had a simple nightmare. But the fear of it could not be erased from his heart, for it was a nightmare that was based totally on real life.

In his dream he had been returning from a night at some festivity in Milan to his quarters in the palace Carlo lived in. And from a dark alley mouth something had attacked him— something he could not quite see, but which squalled in his ear as it reared to close abruptly with him, wrapping terribly hot, smothering arms about him, seeking his neck. . . . And in his dream, unable to move his arms to grasp his sword, he had looked about him for Ned, for Brethin—and found no one. Whoever had been with him—surely he remembered there had been someone with him—was gone. He was alone.

Shivering as he woke now on his pallet near the fire, despite the fact that it was not that cold at all, he realized that the dream had a lot of truth in it. It might, in fact, be taken as a kind of warning, if one believed in that sort of thing.

For it was true: he *was* alone. And he had never been so before in his life, for all practical purposes. As a king's son, there had always been someone about who was watching out for him, who would back him up, if only for the sake of what his blood made him. And later, he had been a knight with a full lance behind him, and with comrades sworn to him, whom he could trust. His back would never be bare; he would never be alone.

No more. He was as alone as any man could be, surrounded by strangers who were thieves and murderers.

He did not know if he was shivering because he was afraid, or because he was lonely. But he knew he was going to have to guard his own back from now on. And he supposed he would have to be his own friend, too. . . .

"The order has come," Alessi said the following day. "The riots begin this day." He looked at Jamie.

"Have you thought of any more places?" he said.

"No," Jamie said. "I think that is all there were. Have you located them?"

"Yes," Guido said. "And I have men watching them." He smiled. "We will have to leave the city, but we will do so as rich men. Now come." He turned and led the way, and so Jamie left the vault for the first time in over a week.

By the time their party had reached the gate out of the city, the tumult of the ordered rioting had begun behind them, some of Guido's men having been left behind with orders to start it off before racing to catch up with their fellows. Jamie supposed that they would make Renaldi and Matteleone feel better as they listened secretly for such noises, there in their palaces behind high walls and augmented guard forces.

Their group climbed into the hills above the city, into an area at the edge of the farmlands, where rich men sometimes maintained richly furnished villas just as the Romans had done centuries before. But as the group moved, it avoided the villas,

keeping to more hidden ways and moving ever upward from
the sea, until at last they entered a copse of withered trees that
occupied an aged ravine in the side of a large hill.

Under the trees the remainder of Guido's band waited for
their arrival; and Jamie noted that the greetings among the
reunited group were quiet, subdued. Guido, he reflected, might
have done well training mercenaries for the Archduke—certainly these men seemed to be concerned with the job at hand,
and seemed to know how to go about it properly.

The band did not loiter, but set out once more uphill, managing to move in relative silence for all its size. Jamie moved
with them, in a position directly behind the gang leader—he
had even been given his sword back, and suspected he would
be expected to make good use of it soon. He wished he had his
armor and his destrier, though.

He caught himself in what he was doing and laughed silently—might as well wish for Ned and Brethin, too, while he
was at it!

His spirits were raised a little by the thought, strangely; he
followed Guido as the man came over the lip of the hill and
halted behind a tiny bush, signaling with an upraised hand for
everyone else to stop where they were. Only Guido could see
what was ahead of them, but that did not seem to bother
anyone else in the long column.

After a moment Guido raised his other arm and swung it
sideways in a horizontal fashion. Behind him, several of his
lieutenants hissed softly at their men, and the entire column,
slowly and with some raggedness, swung sideways and up the
hill to form a ragged line along its length, with Guido at the left
end. They were still just over the hill from whoever might be
watching on the other side, and could not be seen.

Guido looked down the line at them—there were about
twenty-five in all, Jamie thought—and nodded; then he raised
his sword arm straight into the air and lowered it straight
before him, beginning to walk forward as he did so. The line
moved with him.

So did Jamie, slightly behind and to the other's right. After
the past few military years Jamie was startled at the silence—
no voice was raised to shout a battle call.

They topped the crest, and now Jamie could see their target,
a farm located about halfway down the hill from their position,
in a small grove of tall, thin trees. The buildings were no more
than a house of old stucco behind a low, yellowing wall; a

barn, of wood and somewhat worn; and several outbuildings, in varying sizes and states of repair. These were clumped together about two hundred yards down the hill from their position as they topped the crest.

Despite the downhill grade, Alessi kept his pace to a steady walk, and the men seemed disciplined enough to be able to hold that pace with him. Their silence continued, except for an occasional curse as someone stumbled or brushed against a thorn.

Watching the farm ahead, Jamie paid little attention to the ground under his feet and did some stumbling himself; but the experience of the last few years was pushing him and he did not really pay attention to his own missteps. He could see a few figures visible in the open area of the farmyard, several men, a woman, and two children. Were there more inside? Probably, he thought.

The information he had gleaned from Renaldi's papers had suggested strongly that this place must be where the merchant had hidden much of his treasure and trading stock—and rather than hide it with a strong guard to advertise that something was being hidden, Jamie and Guido believed that he had tried to hide it in a place where no one would think to raid or rob, for the few weeks such hiding might be necessary—a place with only a few trusted people to guard it. Jamie hoped he was right. He would be in trouble with Guido and his men otherwise.

They were only fifty yards or so from the farm now, and— apparently for the first time—someone saw them coming. There was a yell, and all the figures turned to stare at the silently moving line of armed men which continued its steady voiceless pace down through the dust and dried vegetation. The silence of the movement, Jamie suspected, was probably deliberate, for the purpose of disquieting the people below, if they were not worried enough already by the mere sight of the intruders. None of Guido's men would prefer to fight, if they could gain their loot without a struggle. In this, they were the very opposite of the knightly class, who sought battle on any pretext.

Down below, the figures in the farmyard were moving, except for the woman, who caught up one of the children, yelled something at the other, and began to run away from the farm down the hill.

Clever of her, thought Jamie to himself, and silently wished

her luck. None of Guido's band broke ranks to go after her—
there was larger gain in the farmhouse.

In fact, it was the farmhouse that the men below had all
instinctively headed for, so that told the raiders where their
goal was—if indeed it was here at all.

And now the raiders had reached the grove of trees, were in
among them. The unevenness of the trees caused the line of
men to bunch and separate, spoiling the unity of their advance
somewhat. But it did not really matter, Jamie realized—there
was no real battle about to be fought here. No one was coming
out of the house to challenge them, to contest them. For a
moment disgust stirred in Jamie. Was this what he, a knight,
had come to? A brigand among brigands, about to loot a farmhouse?

In mere moments Guido's men had surrounded the farmhouse and examined all of the outbuildings, which turned out
to contain little of value. The leader stood beside Jamie and
discussed the situation with him. It was merely an exercise,
Jamie suspected, since the man had already called for axes to
be brought up. Meanwhile, a few errant crossbow bolts had
come from the house, and all the men had taken cover.

"Have you any idea how many there are?" Jamie asked.
Guido turned and waved forward the two men who had appeared over the hilltop with two axes each.

"If they were more than us, they would have come out
already," he said, turning back.

"They will probably have armor," Jamie said.

"It matters little," the other replied. "We are used to taking
down men in armor. They are fewer than us, and we can
surround them and move more quickly than they, and pull
them from their feet to hack them apart like turtles. We will
have them now."

Jamie felt his hackles raise instinctively, but had sense
enough to keep his mouth shut. He thought to himself, as he
cooled down in the silence, that there was no point in his
arguing on behalf of the armored class when he himself was
out here without armor. . . . Rearing died hard, of course.

The men with the axes arrived, and with them a group that
had located a couple of small farm carts near the outbuildings.
These had been loaded with miscellaneous collections of items
from the outbuildings, so that they were standing more than
full when the men began to push them backward into the open
space around the farmhouse. Jamie soon saw that they were to

be pushed in front of the windows from which the crossbowmen were shooting.

The men inside the farmhouse could see what was intended
too; and the volume of crossbow fire aimed in the direction of
the carts quickly increased. Two of Guido's men took bolts and
were dragged off; but replacements were available, and the
carts continued to move toward the building.

The next step was fire, of course; and makeshift torches
began to drop on and around the carts. But for this, too,
Guido's men had been prepared, and the carts had been wetted
down thoroughly before the movement began. Buckets of
water were also available to douse torches that could not
quickly be dislodged by pikes.

When the carts were in place and the crossbowmen neu-
tralized, the axmen scurried across the open space in front of
the farmhouse and crouched beside the door. Guido grinned at
Jamie while his hands checked at his waistband for sword and
dagger.

"Our turn, now," he said. "Maybe we'll get to see how
well you knights can do without horse and armor."

"If you're worried about how well I'll do, why take me
along?" Jamie responded. Both of them laughed, and then
Guido turned and ran across to the door, dodging to escape
crossbow fire from other windows.

One bolt whirred through the air near the big man, but he did
not seem to notice it. Jamie watched his run, at first to watch
for obstructions or patterns in the fire of the crossbowmen—
but in a moment he was admiring the grace of the big man's
movements, the economy with which he got his large body
across the open space in a short time. He did not even seem to
kick up as much dust in his running as the other men did.

Guido had reached the door now, and turned to look back,
laughing and beginning a gesture to Jamie, one that probably
meant that it was the Scot's turn now. And at that moment the
door of the farmhouse slammed open, smashing into Guido
from behind and knocking him forward, off balance, into the
dust. Quickly, he caught himself on an outstretched arm; and
even as Jamie and the three men with him began to run toward
the house, had drawn his sword while rising and turning. The
man's arm was swinging his sword in a vicious backhanded
low blow even as he turned, so that the momentum of his
whole body was behind it; and Jamie saw that the blade
slammed into the ribs of the second man who had come out of

the farmhouse. The man was wearing mail, but the blow bit through it and opened the man's side like a bullock being hastily slaughtered for hungry warriors. The sound of the blow was tremendous, but Jamie did not hear the man cry out.

Around him, more of the raiders were gathering, and now they were shouting. Jamie, in the lead of the group sprinting toward the sortie that had suddenly developed at the farmhouse door, was only a few yards away now—he could not remember if he had been dodging while running to avoid possible bolts, but it did not matter now.

He was cursing himself for not having foreseen this happening, though. Any trained warrior, or hunter, for that matter, should have been able to see that a trapped foe who sees the noose tightening about him is likely to make a mad effort to avoid it. The sortie from a place besieged was a time-honored tactic.

The men in the farmhouse had done what was all but inevitable. Knowing that axmen would soon be battering down the door that was their last protection, they had chosen to go out and try to cut down some of those enemies while they were unprepared. And so they had attacked while only Guido and three of the cart-pushers were there to back up the axmen. It was brilliant timing.

The first man out had slammed the door into Guido entirely by accident. The blow had thrown him off stride, and while he recovered the second man had slipped around him and skewered an ax-wielder—just in time to take Guido's back-handed blow in the ribs. But Guido had not yet had time to recover, and his side was still toward the door when the first man thrust at him.

Jamie watched as the blade seemed to slide into Guido's own ribs; Jamie could see that the entry was deep and probably fatal. *Armor would have helped a lot, Guido*, he thought to himself.

The big man was folding over as he stood now; but he seemed to have locked his arm about the other's sword, preventing its withdrawal. And the foe made the mistake of trying to keep his grip on his weapon while Jamie ran up—the last few yards seemed to go by as if they were mere inches—and swung a two-handed blow from over his shoulder, right to left. His blade caught the defender at the jointure of neck and shoulder, and came close to taking the man's head off.

Four more men had come out the door, but at the sight of

their first two fellows showing gaping wounds, they slowed in their charge. The first of the four got under the guard of another gang member and gutted him, but as he did so he stepped too near the cart on that side, and a hand reached out to hamstring him with a short, sharp little blade. The man cried out and went down, dropping his sword, and was quickly pulled under the cart, where he cried out for a moment or two even more loudly.

Two more of the attackers had moved to their left, where the two unmolested axmen still crouched; and as the first swung a clumsy blow his opponent seemed to melt away in front of him. At that moment the men behind Jamie arrived—Jamie was just pulling his own blade from the still-falling body of his victim—and used a pike to pin the second of the two men against the wall to the side of the door. Its point did not pierce the man's mail and leather armor, but he was immobilized enough to be easily reached, and in another moment one of the axmen had lopped off the man's left leg above the knee. The man stepped back and let the fellow fall, giving him a blade in the throat as he went.

The other defender had managed to wound the man in front of him, but he was outnumbered and took a wicked blow from each side at the same time. He staggered and looked dazedly about, lifting a hand to push his helm back on his head; and then fell to his knees. An ax took his head off, and the raider wielding it tittered in a sort of manic glee.

Jamie, meanwhile, was now facing the lone survivor of the sortie, the last man out the door. This man had seen Jamie pull his blade from the trunk of the first man, and had stopped in shock. Staring wildly at Jamie, who at first made no move toward him, the man—a red-faced blond fellow of about twenty-eight—tried to pull the door back closed. But it was blocked by the body of both Jamie's man and Alessi; so he let go of it and began to back into the farmhouse, watching Jamie with wide, staring eyes.

The man had no mail but only boiled leather armor, as well as a metal skullcap that apparently rested atop a turbanlike cloth cap. It was the least sophisticated armor among the defenders, and Jamie suspected it meant that this man was considered the worst fighter among them.

Jamie stepped forward one step toward the man, and looked into his eyes.

"Give it up," he said. "You have been beaten. Surrender to

us now.'' He stopped, trying not to look so menacing as to frighten the fellow. The other stopped too, and looked at him. Jamie saw that there were tears under the man's eyes, and that he had apparently soiled himself down the front of his legs.

The man said something, but coughed, his voice a croak; and Jamie could not make out the word or words. The man's nose was running now, and probably his throat was full too. Jamie paused to give him time to clear it—and from the sound of the snuffling and grunting the fellow emitted, that was just what was occurring.

The man lowered a hand that had gone to his mouth, and now he dropped his sword. He opened his mouth, looking at Jamie—and then turned sharply. In the room behind him there was rapid movement, and the man had just begun to scream when three men jumped on him from behind and to the side. They pulled him down to the floor, and even as they did so their daggers were rising and falling—and the scream was quickly cut off, first to a low, bubbling moan, and then to silence.

More of Guido's men had gotten in one of the windows. Jamie watched as they picked themselves up, all of them stained with the dead man's blood; and then those behind Jamie crowded into the doorway.

In moments the gang had scattered through the house, apparently sparing no thought for either Guido or Jamie. Yells and shrieks came back out to Jamie's ears, but he could not tell if that was because more of the farmhouse's staff had been discovered, or because some of Renaldi's treasures had been uncovered.

He turned around and looked down at Guido, who was lying almost in the doorway, just in back of him. After a moment Jamie got down on one knee, turning the man over onto his back. Unquestionably, the gang's leader was thoroughly dead. Jamie looked at his face for a moment. It had no secrets to tell.

Jamie stood and turned back to look into the dark doorway of the house, from which much noise still emanated. Then he turned again and stepped across Guido's body. He set off across the dusty farmyard, but after three steps he halted.

He thought for a moment, and then turned back to Guido's body and knelt beside it. He lifted the hem of the tunic the man had been wearing and poked about in the man's waist area until he found a small leather purse. It clinked, but he did not look into it before inserting it under his own waistband. He stood up once more and trudged across the farmyard toward the barn and outbuildings.

The only horse left on the farm that he could see was old and appeared tottery, but he untied its halter rope and leaped astride its back, kicking it into motion. He was sure the animal would not be able to handle the steep route by which he and the gang had come, so he directed it off down the front of the hill on the only trail he could see. After a half-mile or so he found a small, little-used road, barely more than a track with dead vegetation growing between the ruts made by cartwheels. While he sat on the horse at the intersection of trail and road, wondering which direction to take, he heard a snuffling noise from the bushes across the road from him.

"Come out of there," he called.

There was no answer. He called again, trying to send his voice over a wide area while seeming to direct it exactly at whoever was there.

"I know where you are, and I'll come for you if you don't step out now."

He lowered his voice, gentling its tones.

"I won't hurt you," he said. "I'm a knight, not one of those rabble, and I only want to ask you a question. Come out."

He waited. The sense of disgust with himself he had felt during the attack on the farmhouse had returned. Before him, the silence continued, but he still waited. The sun beat down. After a few long minutes, with a faint rustling sound, a woman stood up right in the midst of the undergrowth at the edge of the trees. She was holding a child, no more than a couple of years old, which had obviously been crying.

"You ran from the farm," Jamie said. "Where were you going?"

The woman said nothing, staring at him. Her face was red, and he suspected she had been crying too. She rubbed her brow with the side of one hand, smearing around the dirt already there; and a lock of dirty black hair fell from under her kerchief across her eye. She blinked but otherwise ignored it, continuing to watch him with a look that reminded him of nothing so much as a wild animal that had been slightly spooked.

"Do you know this road?" he asked. Still she made no answer. She did not even seem to be understanding his questions, and he wondered if she understood his version of Italian. He looked at her with growing exasperation for a moment.

"Answer me!" he yelled suddenly, bouncing on the back of

his horse as he did so. The woman started, crouched a little, but continued to say nothing. When he made no further movement, she began to straighten up again a little. He watched her, and then sighed.

"Genoa?" he said, trying to put the questioning inflection into his voice. He also pointed with his sword, in both directions up and down the road, and looked at her.

"Genoa?" he said again after a moment.

After a long pause, she raised an arm and pointed down the road to his right. He looked that way, then back at her. Then he bowed slightly in her direction and kicked his horse into motion once again.

Chapter Fifteen

THE OLD HORSE went lame short of the city, and Jamie left it at the side of the road, cropping grass, after it refused to move any further. He saw no point in beating the animal, and set off down the road at a trot, heading for the wall he could now see ahead of him. Even before he reached the gate, he could hear the deep roar that was the voice of the riot, apparently still alive somewhere near the waterfront. He wondered if the guard would let him into the city, or if the gates had been closed.

As he trudged up the slope in front of the gate, his question was answered—he could see the big doors standing open. There was only one guard in sight, and he was spending more of his time looking inward towards the city than outward along the road.

Within the city's walls, streets were largely deserted, although twice he caught sight of a solitary figure moving through the shadows. Three streets further on he saw a pack of boys yelling and howling in pursuit of someone else he could not see at all. There was a beastlike menace in the tone of the yells, and he thought of the hungry wild dogs he had seen in one famine-torn province of France. He began to keep closer to the shadows himself.

He took a circular, sideways route that kept him away from Renaldi's headquarters and Matteleone's palace, but led him down to the waterfront by way of a quiet residential area. As he neared the docks he began to move even more slowly, although there was no one visible, working his way through the narrow, twisted streets, trying to watch down them in all directions, while keeping his eyes open for possible sidestreets that he could use for escape routes if he had to.

"Jamie!"

The rather loud whisper came from a narrow street he had just passed, and he jumped and turned, drawing his sword.

Sword in hand, he watched the mouth of the street from which the whisper had come. He watched warily, knees slightly bent and body alert, ready to run away or spring forward. No one appeared.

"Who called?" he asked in his own loud whisper after another moment.

"Jamie," the voice came again; but this time it was less a whisper and closer to a normal speaking tone.

Jamie felt himself relaxing at this release of tension, and his sword point lowered a bit.

"Show yourself," he said. For a moment there was no sight or sound, and then with a small scuffling sound a thin figure appeared in the mouth of the sidestreet.

"Bandras!" Jamie said, surprised in spite of himself.

"I have other names, too," the figure said, while the line where eyebrows should have been raised in something that might have been amusement on another face.

Jamie felt the beginning of a familiar ache in his head.

"I know you," he found himself saying; but his sword point lowered further; and as Bandras moved forward in his long robes, Jamie made no move to back away. He watched as the wizened old man moved up to him, until he found himself looking down into the brown, lined, hairless face, that he had once seen looking down into his.

"You hurt me," he said. "And you destroyed my pentecost spell. Can you replace it?"

"Of course I can," said the other. "But not here and not now. Later you will need it again."

"But how am I to leave—" Jamie began to protest, but found himself hushed by an upraised hand which seemed to appear from nowhere out of the wide gray-blue sleeve.

"There is no time," Bandras said. "You must go back around the docks and approach from the other side. You will find two ships. Either will take you away."

"That's what I was hoping," Jamie said. "To find a ship to take me home. But why tell me this?"

He sheathed his sword but he heard in his voice a sort of challenge.

"Always you brim with questions, young man." Bandras' voice changed, and the particular, rich inflections of it made Jamie look again at the little man. Jamie felt his eyes widening.

"The Oxford doctor!" Jamie exclaimed; and took an involuntary step backwards. Then his face registered his confusion; he knew he must be mistaken, and yet the sound of those words had been so like them when uttered by Septilos. . . .

The brown face smiled up at him now, perhaps enjoying his discomfort.

"Yes," the voice said, "it is I. It has always been I." Bandras stopped and looked at Jamie; but Jamie found no words to say.

"It is a spell, like any other," the little man said. "It is useful for me to have many forms."

His tone changed again. "Do you recognize these tones?" Jamie stared at him, hearing the voice of Antonio.

"Hobie . . ." he almost whispered, "were you Hobie, too?"

The form that still looked like Bandras shook its head.

"Not Hobie, no," it said. "But there are associations among all those who work with magic. We aid each other; and there are some things, James of Illareth, that touch on the lives of not only all who work with the magical arts—but on all men and women. In time you may learn more of that."

His eyes burned into Jamie's so brightly that Jamie tore his own gaze away from the little man and looked instead down all the streets he could see in case trouble was coming.

"Are you following me?" Jamie asked, still without looking back at he who had been Bandras. He was not sure what he would do if the answer turned out to be yes.

"Go!" the other said. Jamie looked back then and saw Bandras pointing a finger back the way Jamie had come. And Jamie found himself moving that way.

"Oh, and Jamie—" The voice came again, stopping Jamie, who had just looked away from the little figure. Jamie turned and looked back, stopping.

"Don't go back for the sapphire," the wizard said. And while Jamie was still looking at him wordlessly, he stepped back around the corner of the little sidestreet, out of Jamie's sight.

Jamie stood in place for a few seconds more, but had just

decided *not* to go back and look around the corner, when a voice whispered in his ear.

"Get moving!" Jamie started, knowing that no one was near enough to be able to do that to him. Then he laughed and turned on his heel. He walked—in fact, he sauntered as he went.

Returning to his tactics of hiding, skulking, and sneaking, keeping always to the shadows, he worked his way through the core of the city, circling around the dock area and the merchants' quarter. And as he neared the far side of the circle he had been circumnavigating, he almost ran headlong into masses of soldiers that had suddenly appeared in the streets.

He ducked back into the alley he had just come out of and ran back down it some distance, unsure if he had been spotted and pursued. He stopped to pull himself to the top of a one-story shack, and from there again pulled himself to the top of the adjoining, two-story building—fortunately he was both tall and able to leap upward with some facility.

He could not see very much from his position on top of the two-story building; but at least he could not be easily found himself. He kept low, virtually lying down on the slightly sloping roof, watching and listening for whatever he could perceive. For a while he could hear nothing except the rioting noises off in the distance near the harbor and the distinctive noises of armored troops on the move, much more near at hand. Then the latter ceased.

After some moments he slipped back down from the roof and returned up the alley to the position from which he had spotted the soldiers; but now there was no movement at all on the streets before him. He began to move faster, sure that the situation was about to come to a boil and that it was imperative that he get himself away as quickly as possible. He darted across the wide main street and into the shadows on the other side, striking up a narrower sidestreet he did not know, but which seemed to be tending in the direction he wanted.

A bit later, as he was peering around the corner down the length of a wider street, at the end of which he could see the sea—he heard a sudden change in the welter of noise being emitted by the rioting mob, somewhere off near the docks. He had been able to smell smoke for some time now; and now as he looked up he could see a shapeless smudge of black hanging above the city, some distance to his left. It was a calm day, and the smoke seemed to hang in the sky low above the rooftops, unmoving and menacing.

The roar of noise from that area suddenly increased in volume, until Jamie almost thought he could make out individual voices. And with it he thought he could hear the clink of weaponry—the troops had found the riot and were handling it in their own way, he supposed.

If he was going to head for the docks, this was the time to do it. But another possibility held him to this spot. It was a gamble if he stayed, but a good one—he thought. In any case he could spare a few minutes, now that the troops were driving the rioters away from this area, a fact that might well be of interest to others beside himself. He would wait half an hour where he was. If nothing happened in that time, he must move while Bandras' promise of the two ships still held good for him.

He waited. The minutes passed and no soul stirred in the streets. There was no sense in risking any longer wait. He was just about to step out and run down the street toward the sea when his ear caught the sound of someone on horseback. He stopped and looked about hastily, then stepped to the side and into a deep doorway whose gate swung loose.

A mounted figure came around the corner of the street ahead of him—if he ran, he would plunge headlong into it. It paused at the corner, then turned and cantered slowly in his direction; but it did not stop as it came by him, and he saw, as he had hoped but had hardly dared to expect, that the figure on the horse was Andrea Matteleone. This would be the moment for Matteleone to return secretly for whatever treasure of his was secretly kept—kept even from his most trusted servants. The man was wearing a cloak with its collar turned up, and a loose, floppy merchant's hat, but Jamie recognized him easily. A feeling of triumph warmed Jamie.

Letting Matteleone get a bit of a lead on him, Jamie followed. He thought again about the ships, about Bandras's—the doctor's—warning to get away; but this he would not let pass.

Around several corners, keeping to doorways and the shadows, Jamie followed his man easily; and it was only a short distance to the place where Matteleone reined in his horse and jumped down from it, tying its reins to a tree at the edge of the small garden he had ridden up to. Jamie watched from the nearest corner, and then, as the man moved into the garden a few steps, presenting his back to Jamie, the latter dashed silently across the open street to take a position in a doorway across the street from the park.

Matteleone located a small bench about fifteen feet from the street where his horse was and turned around, sitting down; he was now facing Jamie directly; but the latter was in deep shadow, and well hidden as long as he did not move.

After some minutes another figure rode up—and Jamie was now not at all surprised to see that it was his erstwhile employer, Giacomo Renaldi. Renaldi remained on his animal, pulling up beside Matteleone's horse; and the other, seeing him, rose and moved forward, mounting his own animal but saying nothing. They moved off in the direction from which Matteleone had come, not talking at all.

Matteleone, slightly ahead of Renaldi, led them around several corners and into a smaller street that seemed to be lined by windowless buildings. Here he pulled up and got off his horse, to be joined on the ground by Renaldi. They tied their horses at a ring on a nearby house and moved back in Jamie's direction as he peered around the corner they had rounded earlier. He was prepared to scamper out of the way should they return all the way, but they did not, instead crossing the street to enter the shadows of an archway there. They had been talking, but Jamie could not hear any of their conversation.

As Jamie watched, the men finished their conversation, and Renaldi turned to leave—and as he did so, Matteleone reached down with his right hand to pull a dagger from behind the leg of the arch the men were standing under.

As he rose back up Renaldi started to turn around again, and Jamie could hear his voice. But Matteleone had position, and he stepped sideways as Renaldi turned, grasping the man by the other shoulder and pulling him backward, off-balance, as he punched the dagger up and down and into the man's back between the shoulder blades. The point seemed to hesitate, caught for a moment on bone, but then slipped in, and the beginnings of a scream broke from Renaldi before Matteleone's left hand moved swiftly up from Renaldi's shoulder and around his neck to stifle the murdered man's mouth. They swayed together for a few moments, the dagger being withdrawn and driven into Renaldi yet again and again—until the other crumpled to lie at Matteleone's feet.

Matteleone knelt beside the body, his position obscuring Jamie's view while he bent and did something to Renaldi.

Then he stood up again, dropping the dagger and apparently looking up and down at himself, examining himself, perhaps, for bloodstains. And while he was doing that Jamie arrived silently behind him and worked one forearm about the man's neck, his knee in Matteleone's back, his other hand holding the wrist of the forearm pressuring against Matteleone's windpipe.

Matteleone gurgled slightly as Jamie's arm pressed inward and began to crush his larynx. The townman struggled weakly against the grip. But Jamie's arm strength was vastly greater than that of the other, and Matteleone only seemed to be dancing while he hung from the Scot's powerful grasp, his hands clawing feebly at the arm that was strangling him.

Standing behind the other, Jamie saw the back of Matteleone's head inches before his eyes, as if at the end of a short tunnel. His attention was all on his own arm, which he could see folded around under Matteleone's chin. The loose sleeve on that arm had fallen back and the muscles were standing out under the tanned skin along the top of that arm. He thought he could count every little reddish hair all the way down the length of it. . . .

After a while he noticed that his shoulders were beginning to ache a little, and he came back to himself. He relaxed his grip and the Italian dropped at his feet, crumpling in a heap and landing in a pile, to look as if he were kneeling with his head on the floor and his arse in the air. But he did not move at all.

Jamie stood for a moment, looking down at the two bodies. He bent his arms at the elbow slightly. They were a little sore and stiff as if he had been clenching some weapon throughout a long afternoon of fighting practice. He flexed them slowly several times, as if to stretch the sore muscles, once more looking down at Matteleone's back.

So. He had killed Maria's brother after all; and not in honorable battle, either. He thought he should be feeling sorry about it on both counts, but he did not seem to have that emotion in him. Truly it was not in the code of chivalry to strangle a man from behind—but then, Matteleone had never lived by that code. And Jamie could not believe that Maria would spare much concern for her brother's demise, even if she should ever come to learn the way of it.

He, Jamie, was still a knight, for all that. But he knew he had seen too much to remain the deluded, naive man of war he had started out to be. His dream had been of a life in which fighting—killing—was a pure and noble affair, and where the

motives of men had not been of concern—because all men's
motives were the same.

But now he knew it was not that way—it never had been.
Little by little, the dreams with which he had left his home had
been whittled down by his experience with life as he had
encountered it. War and life—neither one was the stuff of
which dreams were made. Life was compromise with what was
possible.

He was not in love with Maria, for example. But she was
rich and he had made a vow not to return home until he was
rich enough to laugh in the faces of his father and his brothers,
who had thrown him out. She was not only rich, but she had
connections with the Italian cities that would make him a great
man in his own distant and primitive land. Beside those advan-
tages, what was love? What was personal success? What were
the ideals of knighthood and kingship? A small nagging guilt
ate at him that she should care so much for him and he so little
for her, beyond what she represented in the way of his own
personal gain.

But on the other hand, if she was willing to settle for that
sort of marriage, what had he to reproach himself about?

The hard thought reminded him of another of his illusions
that had not stood up to reality. Knights cared for glory, not for
loot—he had believed once. Well, he knew better now.

He bent down and quickly rifled through the possessions of
both bodies. He had kept the battered old sword he'd gotten
from Alessi before the battle at the farmhouse—the swords of
the townsmen seemed light, fragile, and too heavily orna-
mented for his taste. But he did take Renaldi's dagger, tucking
it in his waistband, and also located on Matteleone a small boot
knife that reminded him of the *skein dhu,* the "black knife" of
his homeland. He slid it into his own boot-top.

Finally, after some thought, he began to strip the corpse of
its outer garments. Matteleone was several inches shorter than
Jamie—almost everyone was that, at least. But he had been
wide-framed and the years had thickened not only his body
with good living. His knee-length gown of rose velvet amply
covered Jamie's drab doublet, yet the slit sides of the borrowed
finery would still allow easy access to his sword. The merchant's hood and blue riding cape completed Jamie's disguise.
He pulled the cowl of the hood well over his face as a final
touch.

He also found five purses that clinked in his ear satisfyingly—each man had carried more than one. Opening the largest one he had taken from Matteleone, he stared at its contents. They consisted of some dozen golden coins and also five great emeralds Matteleone had apparently found and retrieved from his private hoard by the time Jamie had seen him.

Jamie stared at the emeralds. They represented no small fortune, if he could find honest dealers—whom he knew of already in Bordeaux. He could turn them to usable gold on his way home, for there was no reason not to head home now. He had what he had sworn on leaving he would return with—wealth and, in Maria, a bride not only beautiful, but with rank and wealth in her own right.

As the vision of his homecoming rose in his mind again, he began to stuff the gold and gems back into their purse; and one large blue stone he had not noticed previously rolled from the purse and onto the stones of the street, tumbling some distance before lodging, plain to his view, in a small crevice.

He looked at it, frozen in his place. It was a sapphire—twice the size and many times the worth of even the emeralds. He bent automatically toward it and the warning given him by Bandras returned to his mind. He was pulling the purse's drawstrings tight even as he leaped away from the bodies, away from the sapphire, and across to Matteleone's horse. With his momentum built up by his run, he was on it with a quick leap, leaning forward to slash loose the reins with his recently gained dagger, catching them up and turning the animal about—just as a party of horsemen came around the corner in the other direction.

He held himself down to a trot as he moved away, and the party—they looked like a party of warriors who had probably come into the city with the soldiers who were no doubt still slaughtering rioters in the merchants' quarter—maintained their even pace for a while, although one of them yelled something Jamie could not hear.

He reached the nearest corner and turned down it; and as soon as he had gotten out of sight, he kicked his heels into the ribs of the horse, galloping in the general direction of the docks, the sea to his right visible now and again through open spaces in the rows of buildings. He thought he heard a yell behind him, and turned to look back. Six men had just rounded the corner far to his rear and were galloping after him. He turned, taking the first right he came to, and then the first left and a second right.

Suddenly he was at the bottom of a small hill and flashing out of the narrow street he was in, into a small square. As he burst into it he narrowly missed running down a party of pikemen who had been engaged in picking over the bodies that were lying about the square. Jamie's horse shied from the waving hands of two of the men, who were trying to grasp his reins; but then the horse found itself moving over a group of the dead. Frightened—even the best warhorse dislikes stepping on a body—the horse reared; and as it did so it slipped on the stones of the square. It began to fall over backward and to Jamie's left side, and so he slipped from its saddle and threw himself the other way, landing on his feet directly in front of a startled soldier. Jamie raised his sword over his shoulder and the man backed away three steps and then sidled off to his own left, beginning to call for help.

Jamie turned and ran for the nearest street mouth; and the two men who might have stepped in front of him only stood and watched him go. There were a few yells behind him but no one seemed to be following.

He ran on down the street to the next right turn, taking that and following it down a gentle slope toward the docks. There was no one at all in sight at first, except for a couple of bodies. Several wooden buildings were burning feebly, and every door that he saw had been battered down or was completely gone. There were pieces of wood and torn chunks of food and cloth lying about in the street, and occasional wet stains. Once from an open doorway he heard a woman crying. He closed his ears to such sounds.

Breathing hard, with Matteleone's sword in his hand, he turned the corner of a building and ran out into the open space of the docks.

He was at the far downriver end of the docks, the place to which he had been headed. Directly before him was the long dock itself, stretching out from the shore with the dark, scummed water of the harbor at its left and a row of warehouses built on top of it on its right.

Only two ships remained tied to this dock, with a good fifty yards between them. Bandras had been correct. All others had evidently chosen to prudently remove themselves into the open water of the harbor where gangs from the shore could not easily get at them—at least not without a number of small boats, which were hardly likely to be found lying around for the taking in this neighborhood.

The far ship was a large, round-bodied, cargo-carrying vessel, built to sail outside the Mediterranean waters, brightly painted, clean, and with the golden lion which was the Matteleone emblem painted on its single large, square sail. It looked ready to sail at any minute; and Jamie suddenly remembered the letter in the purse with the gems, introducing Matteleone to the King of England, with a petition that he be allowed to set up trading headquarters in that country. The gems, Jamie suddenly realized, had undoubtedly been the capital with which Matteleone had intended to set up a branch of his business in the south of that island from which Jamie himself had come; and this ship would have been waiting—was, in fact, still waiting—to transport him across northward for that purpose.

It was well planned, Jamie had to admit to himself. Following the riots would be a clever time for Matteleone to absent himself from Genoa, just in case suspicion on the part of the Archduke should happen to drift in his direction. This, then, would be the voyage Maria had said could take him home again—could take them both to his home, if he wanted her as she wanted him. Now it all made sense. Matteleone undoubtedly had plans for his sister at the court of the English king. Moreover, he would hardly want to risk leaving her behind to be held against him by the Archduke as a hostage.

Just now the gaily painted ship swayed at its moorings; and the metal helmets of soldiers twinkled in the sunlight above its side railings. Matteleone had made sure the vessel would be well protected. By the same token those same soldiers were making no effort to come to the rescue of the only other ship tied to the dock and closest to Jamie, where a pitched, hand-to-hand battle was going on between a group of what seemed to be Genovese city militia and a thin line of sailors who were trying to keep them from boarding and looting the nearer vessel.

This nearer vessel was a small galley, with a bank of hardly more than a dozen oars to the side. On board, preparations to get under way were at work, but it hardly looked as if the sailors could hold off the eight or nine militiamen long enough to let this be accomplished.

The fighting group was clustered close to the ship's side. It was even odds that Jamie could slip by them and get to the Matteleone vessel. Even as he watched, he saw a helmetless head join those wearing metal at the cargo ship's side—and he recognized the blonde hair of Maria. So, she was already aboard.

All this went through Jamie's head in a sudden instinct of recognition. If there had been time, he would have shaken his head in wonder at the arts of Bandras that had directed him here. Before him lay all he had searched for ever since he had been unceremoniously thrust from his home. He had sworn then to Brethin, as they had ridden off, that he would return with more wealth—and more fame—than anyone in the kingdom, from his father on down, had ever dreamed of.

Now here it was, waiting for him. Maria was not the sort to weep over the brother who had treated her as no more than a pawn in his own search for wealth and power. All Jamie had to do was reach the ship where Maria waited, join her, and travel home to become a power in England, a man whose money and connections would quite overwhelm the small, impoverished kingdom from which he had been outcast.

All he needed was to slip by the fighting militia and these were too deeply engaged with each other to pay any attention to someone moving swiftly, moving quietly, and passing them without any offer of threat.

He started forward to the Matteleone ship, drifting along the face of the warehouses, his back against their sun and water-dried planks, Matteleone's sword in his hand. He was sure Maria could see him, but she would have no idea that it could be him coming. She would probably assume him to be, from the rich new clothes he had taken from her dead brother, some merchant-gentleman who had hired the militia to seize the other vessel for himself, and who now came to take command, now that that seizure was all but accomplished.

He pictured her surprise after he had passed the fighting men and at last approached her ship. How she would welcome him; and how they would work together to make a success for themselves in the land from which he had come to find such as her. What use or need for the pentecost spell now? Shortly, he would be among English-speaking people again; and, if his tongue came to hunger for the Gaelic occasionally, there was no reason he could not use his new power and money to have young Simon, and perhaps even Moraig, sent down to him—where he could further their path in life much better than his father could.

He slid silently along the front of the warehouses, waiting for the explosion of joy and triumph that should have been burgeoning inside of him at last. He could even send to the continent now, to find Ned and Brethin, to bring them both back to him and make them rich as well. But the feeling did not come—and his first impulse was to blame its absence on Bandras. That damned magician had put a spell on him after all—had he not hinted that there were purposes at work among magicians that had uses for Jamie?

But then Jamie rejected the thought. Hobie had told him once that the one thing workers of magic were unable to do was to use another human being against his or her will. They could offer glittering inducements, or choices, but they could not force. So, he was not being forced now. Of his own free will and desire, he was choosing Maria and what she offered him. . . .

Or was he?

He paused, back against the wooden planks, very close now to the fighters, who still had not taken notice of him.

What was wrong with him? He had left home an innocent, believing that all he desired waited for him at the point of his sword, which would, of course, never be used for other than knightly and honorable things. But the wars in France—and the intrigues of the Milanese court, plus those of the Genovese merchants—had given him a more realistic view of life. There was no place in the real world for the sort of knight-errant he had originally conceived himself to be. It only made sense that he should take what he wanted, by any means available—that he should marry and use Maria, for example, because her love for him would permit that use—when, in truth, he did not really love her, only liked her, as he had used to like Moraig.

There was nothing wrong with what he was about to do, or what he had done, he told himself fiercely. Irene had shown him the way. The means were nothing—only the end mattered.

And yet . . . the memory of himself marching like a brigand, with brigands, upon the helpless people of the farmhouse earlier; and what he had felt then—dirty and unknightlike—came back to him. Must this be what he must always choose? Must there be no other way to what he had dreamed of but raiding and murder and robbery, and the callous use of a woman who honestly loved him?

Something within him exploded, with all the old Jamie-like fury, at the thought of it. Suddenly he was outrageously angry. He would not be dictated to—no, not even by fate, not even by all the magicians in the world, not even by the world itself. His life would be as he had dreamed it should be, or else there was no meaning to it.

Now, with that anger to trigger it, the explosion of joy and triumph did come to him. It burst into life within him. He thrust himself away from the planks at his back. In three long strides he was at the back of the militia fighting the sailors. His sword cut right and left, savagely into them, striking down one, then a second, and then a third with three hard over-the-shoulder cuts delivered with all the force of his arm. The next militiaman on his right caught sight of him, turned and ran, yelling—and panic struck the whole group, which turned and milled about uncertainly, then backed away and ran from the sailors and this armed madman who had suddenly appeared among them.

But there was the sound of hooves galloping toward him from behind. Jamie, about to smile at the sailors, turned to catch out of the corner of his eye a vicious cut being aimed down at him by someone he had not seen before—apparently a dismounted knight for he was wearing belt and spurs—a slim young-seeming fellow whose face was obscured by his helm. Jamie rebounded from his parry and moved to his left, swinging an underhand blow into the ribs of his opponent. But the man was wearing good armor—thick mail with a few plates—and Jamie's blow did no damage. The other turned, swinging his sword in a heavy two-handed blow that Jamie had to leap backward to avoid.

Jamie was faster than his opponent, but unarmored, and he knew better than to stop moving. As he danced to his opponent's right once more he looked over the man's shoulder, to see that the sailors had all run to their ship, stopping only to cut or cast off the lines. Jamie shifted his stance and faked an overhand blow at his foe's head—then slipped to one knee as the man raised his sword for a parry at head level, and threw himself at the other knight's knees, knocking him down.

He rose as the man fell, and ran across the width of the dock as the ship, oars working, began to pull away from it. He had to leap about four feet from the dock's edge, but he was moving fast and had little problem doing so, tumbling over the bulwarks and sprawling on the deck as the gap between ship and shore widened rapidly.

There was rapid movement near him, and he raised his sword before him as he tried to scramble to his feet, seeing two

sailors running toward him with large wooden pins in their
hands. But as he reached his knees someone stepped across in
front of him, back to Jamie, and said something loudly that
seemed to stop all the movement in their direction. The oars
kept working, Jamie noted.

After a moment another man stepped up to his side. watching Jamie intently and then addressing the man whose back
was still to the Scot—the man who had stopped the new attack
on Jamie. This man now turned, and Jamie saw that it was the
same man he had looked at over the bodies of the soldiers on
the docks when he had come to the relief of the sailors. This
burly, hook-nosed individual looked up at Jamie—he was a
good deal shorter than the Scot—and said something in a
scratchy, raspy voice; but Jamie shook his head and scowled
mildly to indicate that he could not understand.

After a moment the man turned to the other who had come
up on Jamie's right and said something in lengthy explanation,
gesturing expansively as he got rolling with his tale, pointing at
Jamie and at the shore. The other man listened silently, eyes
watching Jamie from under graying brows that contrasted with
his deeply tanned face. After some moments he raised a hand,
receiving instant silence from the talker. He kept the hand up
in the air while the other—his left—patted his large front
gently. He looked pointedly at Jamie's sword; and after a
moment Jamie eased it into its sheath gently. As he looked
back up the man nodded and smiled; then said something—
still in the strange language—to Jamie's benefactor. The other
sailors all turned away, and the man in front of Jamie smiled
and gestured him toward a cask. Jamie sat as all the sailors got
back to work.

The oars were working, but the sails had now picked up a
strong breeze and begun to fill. They were moving fast enough
now that Jamie could feel the coolness of the breeze they were
making in their forward movement. It was cooling him off
rapidly.

As he sat there his skin seemed to get more sensitive, and he
could feel the winds ruffling the hairs on his arms. His skin
seemed to be tightening, and while his face still seemed hot,
his arms and legs and chest seemed to be getting cold. He
began to be aware of all his bruises and scrapes, but he dismissed them for a moment.

The edge of the land was falling away rapidly, and he could
see all the city spread out before him. Fires still apparently

smoldered, here and there, to judge by the dark smudges over the city; and on the dock and shore they had just left, clusters of troops were gathering. But they could be ignored—there still seemed to be no ships about that would be capable of pursuit. Probably most captains had left port quickly soon after the disturbances started.

Probably he had better not plan ever to return to this city, he thought; unless he became very, very powerful, he would be remembered with much ill-feeling—although, now that he thought of it, they might never actually identify just who it was who had cut the swath through them.

It was strange to think that a second's impulsive decision had turned him away from that ship bearing Maria, with all it promised him. Strange that his life should turn and change so quickly upon a moment's feeling. . . .

But it was not a moment's feeling, he realized suddenly. It was a feeling toward which he had been working ever since he had left home. He had ridden forth with Brethin, sure that life was a matter requiring only to be dealt with by the point of his lance and the edge of his sword—and that given these things and a steadfast mind, fame and fortune would be his, and from fame and fortune would inevitably come all he would ever want to seek.

But it had not turned out that way. The way it had turned out, knighthood had developed to be something other than what he had thought it was. Not all knights were knightly. Nor were all wars honorable—or even reasonable. Nor was beauty—as in the case of Irene—necessarily good. Nor wealth and rank guarantees of happiness and all that might be desired.

Slowly, he had come to realize all this. The wars in France, the men and women he had met—Ned, Pietro Claveggio, Irene, Septilos in all his different shapes and forms, Guido Alessi, Matteleone, Renaldi and finally Maria—all these had been his teachers. Now he knew that life was neither plain nor simple. At the same time he now realized that he no longer even knew what it was he wanted, except that it was not what he had started out wanting.

And it had been his recognition of that realization that had made him turn away from Maria and the way home, in order to board a vessel, filled with people whose language he did not speak, and sailing to some purpose he did not know.

A feeling of sadness filled him as he sat on the cask, watching the shore recede—like the sadness he had felt on leaving home, but without the anger that had accompanied it then. The sort of sadness that went with a saying of a farewell forever to something once held dear.

Strangely, the words of Johannes Septilos, the Oxford doctor—or at least he who had appeared first in the guise of Septilos—came back to him, in all their pompous and fruity tones.

". . . not *things*, young man! Things—empires, kingdoms, castles and wealth—these are nothing. Mere forms of more enduring entities. Such things are here today and gone, or in the hands of another, only a few years hence. But knowledge, ideas, truths, these are the real materials out of which life is made and measured. The great science of philosophy, from which are derived all the lesser sciences, including that even of magic, which is of the realm of ideas and knowledge—"

"Doctor," he had interrupted, "what good are all these ideas of yours if I take my sword right now and cut your head off? Where are your ideas, then?"

"Young man," Septilos had said with a strange smile, "why don't you try just that and find out? Well? Come, come, what stops you?"

"You know very well what stops me," Jamie had growled. "Master Shipman here and his merrymen would string me up by the neck if I slew you without reason."

"Ah, and why?" said Septilos. "Would they not do so because it is a belief of theirs that you should have a reason to kill another man? And what is such a belief but an idea, and what is an idea but part of a philosophy—for they, like all others, think they live by wind and wave and blade, but actually they live each by a personal philosophy that dictates how he must act and react to what you just suggested, and all other things. . . ."

Jamie sat watching the shore diminish to a gray line in the distance, and wondered—as someone might wonder whether it would rain tomorrow—where this ship was taking him.